Lisa's Refuge

MICHAEL ALLEN GEORGE

Published in the United States of America

Brilliant Books Literary
137 Forest Park Lane Thomasville
North Carolina 27360 USA

ISBN:
Paperback: 979-8-88945-142-6
E-book: 979-8-88945-143-3

Books by Michael George

The Refuge Mystery Series

Why A Refuge	Book One
Bridge to no good	Book Two
Grass Was Greener	Book Three
To Save The Refuge	Book Four
Without Refuge	Book Five
Refuge Of Another Kind	Book Six

Written as Michael Allen George

Places Of Refuge	Book Seven
Refuge Life And Home	Book Eight
Refuge Rescuers	Book Nine
Walking The Refuge	Book Ten
Lisa's Refuge	Book Eleven

Books Written as Michael George

Horses Lemons And Pretty Girls
More Horses And Pretty Girls
Finding Peri Gray
Of Rain Barrels And Bridges

**Books Written With Bud George
And David George**

Stories From Three Brothers
More Stories From Three Brothers

For the one
I miss the most
My Wife **Marilynn**
We had 55 years
I could have used
A whole lot more

PROLOGUE

Lisa Anderson barely noticed the town's activity as she sat in the cab of the old Pickup. She was sixteen years old and impatient with this kind of waiting. So she was anxious for the bus to come. Her attention was focused out the truck's rear window, on the north end of main street. She watched for the bus to appear around the curve in the road. Several times she was sure she saw it in the heavy evening traffic. She got out of the truck, only to see that it was a semi or camper coming.

"Settle down," her mother, Margaret, complained. "The bus will wait for you when it gets here."

"I know it will, Mom," Lisa answered. "I'm just tired of waiting. It wouldn't be so bad if we weren't at the feed store so long."

"I needed to stop there, and there wasn't any sense in making two trips to town today."

"I'm still tired of waiting."

"And excited about spending the next few days with your cousin, Nancy."

"Kind of. I haven't been there for a long time."

When the bus finally arrived, Lisa nearly missed it. She was staring at two men, parked across the street. She knew them and that they were dangerous. They stared back at her.

"Lisa," Margaret said, not noticing the car, "the bus is here."

"Oh. Don't leave until I get on. Okay?"

"Of course not. Why are you worried about it? You know I wouldn't."

"Nate Bear and his friend are parked across the street."

"Oh," Margaret said, hiding the fear she felt inside, "don't worry about them. I'll wait until the bus leaves."

"Call the deputy sheriff, Mack Thomas, when you get home. Tell him we saw them. He might want to arrest them."

"Okay. But now get on the bus."

Margaret walked her to the bus. She watched Nate Bear drive away after Lisa boarded. The car turned at the first intersection. It appeared again behind Lis's bus as it left town. Margaret watched both until they were out of sight. She shivered at the thought of Nate anywhere near Lisa. Yet, she was secure in the thought that Lisa's uncle would meet her at the bus station in Minneapolis.

By the time she got home, Margaret had her mind on other things, so she never thought to call Mack Thomas. Lisa too, quickly forgot about Nate and his friend. As soon as she put her suitcase in the rack above her, she sat down and took out a book. She hoped it would take her mind off the long bus ride, with its many stops.

The book proved to be too deep for her to concentrate on, so she put it away. She decided to find something else to read when the bus made the right stop. With only a few minutes to spend at the stop, she followed the driver out of the bus, and hurried to a nearby drugstore. The Reader's Digest was on a rack near the door, so she bought a copy. She left the store immediately.

Nate Bear was waiting for her outside. He grabbed her arm. She smelled whiskey on his breath, even before she saw his face.

"I've got a gun in my pocket," he warned, "so unless you want me to use it, you will come with me."

Her terror was instant. It took such control over her that Nate needed to hold her up as they walked to his car. He pushed her in the front seat between the two of them. Before she gathered her wits enough to scream, she noticed a scar on the other man's neck. She screamed then, and Nate hit her on the mouth.

They were on the highway when the bus driver returned to the bus. Numbed by what was happening, the ride in the speeding car was blur to Lisa. Her senses were overwhelmed by the stench of whiskey and the men's unwashed bodies.

She didn't know where she was when they left he highway. Soon, the car was stopped and Nate pulled Lisa out of the front seat and pushed her into the back.

He ripped her clothes off. She struggled to stop him, so he knocked her senseless. He mounted her and she screamed in pain. She felt the flow blood between her legs. Nate quickly moaned with satisfaction and got off her.

The big man took more time with her. To Lisa, it seemed endless. He was rougher with her. He slapped her and twisted her nipples hard. She didn't feel most of it. Mostly she felt a deep searing pain between her legs. When he was done, they threw her back into the front seat of the car. They took her to a place that was a pure hell for her. A place where the constant pain and terror went beyond anything she could have ever imagined.

For some days, she was repeatedly raped by a long line of men. Men who's faces would be forever etched into her brain. Men that she would forever hate. Men who, in years to come, would wish they'd never done to her what they did.

CHAPTER 1

It was spring and the wild flowers were blooming. The fall rain and winter snow fell in the perfect amount. Enough to moisten the soil without saturating it and causing flooding. Plants throughout the refuge loved it, and they celebrated the weather with spectacular flowers.

Everywhere they looked, Mack and Lisa Thomas saw an array of color that was almost unbelievable. They were barely into their Sunday morning hike, and were astonished at the changes that occurred since their hike the previous Sunday.

"Not too bad a view," Mack said, "for a place that wouldn't be able to grow anything for a hundred years."

Lisa groaned. "Yeah, the Republicans and their asinine predictions. I remember them after the refuge burned. Getting on every news or talk show they could. Radio or television, it didn't matter. They just had to tell the world about what a huge disaster the fire was."

"Yeah, they were, as usual, a bunch of ignorant creeps. As far as they were concerned, we absolutely had to get rid of the refuge. Since it could no longer support life of any kind, it only made sense to turn it into some kind of commercial project or another."

"That's right. This land wasn't making money for someone rich, so it was a total waste as far as they were concerned."

"The hell of it is, Lisa, for them, it still is. Even if any of them bothered to come and see what it is now, they'd still hate it. All this beautiful color is for them a total waste. The only color they care about is the green paper lining some rich man's pockets."

"You're right. But enough of them. They're all too ignorant, too stupid, to waste our time even thinking about, let alone talking about."

She took his hand and they continued down the trail they were hiking. The time since the fire was enough so the poplar trees, along with an occasional birch, were now tall enough to feel like a normal woods as the trail took them through it.

They enjoyed the walk through the woods, and the various critters they saw. They often stopped to watch during their walk. But now, with the flowers in full bloom, the open ground was the most spectacular. They decided because of that, not to stop at the normal place for this trail when they were about halfway into the hike. Instead, they rested at the top of a grassy knoll.

As soon as they sat down, Lisa put her arms around Mack and kissed him. She put all that she could into it, and held it for a long time.

Mack was smiling when they parted. "Now, what was that all about, Lisa? I'm not at all complaining. As always, I loved it. Even so, was there a reason for it? Or are you just in the mood?"

"With you, Mack, I'm most of the time in the mood. It's not why I kissed you though. I just wanted to say I'm sorry. I think Kathy and I got too carried away last night."

Kathy was married to Dale Magee, the sheriff of Clayborne County, where they lived and where the refuge was located. The four of them were best friends. They'd spent the previous evening together.

"Well," Mack said, "the two of you did get awful flirty. But not so bad that you owe me an apology."

"I don't know. I sat in Dale's lap for a long time. Too long. I thought you might be upset by it."

"Did I seen upset after we finally got to bed last night?"

"No, but maybe Kathy had something to do with the mood you were in."

Mack realized then, that Lisa wasn't just feeling guilty, she was a bit jealous too. Something that, as far as he was concerned, was a good thing. There was a lot of genuine affection between him and Kathy. But there was every bit as much between her and Dale. None of those feelings, however, had ever gone beyond holding hands and an occasional overly friendly kiss.

Because they agreed that their feelings were open and honest, they also agreed that regardless of how they felt, touching was to be off limits. Holding hands or kissing, okay. Hands where they didn't belong, not okay.

"I admit, Lisa, that I didn't do anything to get rid of Kathy when she sat on my lap. Having her there was definitely not a burden. At the same time, you didn't seem to be in any hurry to leave Dale's lap."

"I know. I wasn't. That's why I apologized. I really shouldn't have done that."

"Why do you say that?" Were you doing something with him I couldn't see?"

"No. But I was kind of thinking about it. That's what I was doing wrong. We aren't ever supposed to think that way about anyone but the one we're married to, are we?"

"That's something that's probably impossible to do. Feeling the way you do about Dale, how could you not have those thoughts sometimes? The only thing I wonder about you, is how do you feel about anything like that. After what happened to you when Nate Bear and his friend kidnapped you, do you still have those kind of feelings? Other than with me, that is?"

"Yes, but it's only sometimes with Dale. Only, the feelings toward him are different from anything I have with you. I love you in ways I couldn't possibly love anyone else. With Dale, it's more like I feel that I should be able to share more with him. Why would it be a bad thing if he touched me. It seems like we should be able to be as close to each other as we could get. At the same time, I don't love him the way I love you. I could never feel anything like that, the way I feel it with you. I don't want to make love with him. I can only do that with you. So I keep telling myself, that if I ever did share with Dale the way it sometimes seems like I should be able to do, it would be wrong. But I still keep asking myself why. Why would it be so wrong?"

"I can't answer that question for you Lisa. That is something you'll have to work out for yourself. I love you too much to tell you what you can and cannot do. I don't own you. Only you can own and control you. But maybe Kathy can help. Have you talked to her about it?"

"Yes. A lot, actually. The trouble is, she has the same problem that I do. Except for her, it's worse. She has the question. Why would it be so wrong if you touched her. For her though, it goes way beyond touching. For her, it's what would be wrong with you making love to her. It's not only sharing something. She's in love with you, Mack. She truly loves Dale too. And she doesn't ever want to do something to lose him. He's her rock. He's what keeps her steady. But you…you do special things to her. She said that you give her wings that allow her to fly to places where she can breath free. That you can steal away all the cares and drudgery of everyday life. When she holds your hand you fill her with a joy she's never had before. And when you kiss her, she sometimes just wants to die in your arms."

"I hope you just made that up."

"No, Mack, I didn't. Not one word. And I think you already knew how she feels. She's told you all that, hasn't she?"

"She's tried. And I've tried to not hear her."

"Why? Why haven't you listened to her? You should. Not listening to the people we most care about? That's a big part of what's wrong with the world, isn't it?"

"It sure is. And that's what makes all this so damn hard. If I listen the way I really should, I risk the chance of hurting you. And hurting you in any way, is on the top of my list of the things I never, ever want to do. And then there's Dale. If anything like that happened between Kathy and me, I doubt very much that he could deal with it. He could handle it okay if it was you and him, especially if I didn't know about it. But Kathy and me, never."

"I wish I could tell you that you're wrong, Mack, but I can't. Dale's really a good man. That's why I feel about him the way I do. But he does have that one glaring flaw. He does his best to give Kathy all the space she needs. But when it comes to what Kathy not only wants, but really needs, he'll never be able to truly fulfill her needs. The physical ones, yes. But the emotional ones, no."

"At the same time, Lisa, it's probably not a bad thing that it is hard for any of those things to happen.. If we followed our hearts, our desires, it could all get real complicated."

"But with you and me, we don't have any of those complications. So how would it be with you, if you hold my hand and walk me in the direction of home."

"I can do that. What are you plans when we get there?"

"Well, you know all that touching and other stuff we've been talking about?"

"The stuff we can't do? Yes, I know about it. Do you want to go home and talk about it some more?"

"No, I don't think so." Her face filled with a broad grin. "I want to go home and for the next few hours, I want to practice doing all the kissing and touching and other stuff until we get really good at it."

"But we are already are really good at it."

"Okay. Then we'll practice until we're perfect at doing all of it."

They didn't quite make perfect, but they did their best to get there.

CHAPTER 2

Titus Trump struggled up from his over-sized chair and moved to the head of the group. He looked them over, and felt a sense of pride in them. In somewhat less than a year, since he became their Supreme Commander, he'd managed to increase the membership by nearly fifty. The MAGA Fellows were now up to seventy-five members. That meant they were ready to start the work needed to turn the county around. For too long now, the do-gooder liberals were getting more than what they deserved. He was certain that he and his group of loyal MAGAs could make a good start on the job of giving them what they really deserved.

As he stood at the dais, one that he himself had chosen, he let his stare tell the group to settle down and listen. He had important things to tell them. For some unfathomable reason, the group watched his face, especially his eyes, rather than his huge stomach hanging out both sides of his oversized dais. His deep, resounding voice tended to mesmerize them.

"As we all know," he began, enunciating slowly, wanting every word out of his mouth to sink in, "the election was stolen by the Democrats. It was the most flagrant abuse of power this country has ever seen. It means that it is time for us to act. We can no longer sit by and let them get away with any more abuse of power."

He paused in his speech, letting conversations start up among the men. And that's who was sitting there listening. Men, and only men. Men who knew what God intended. That all women, no matter their supposed status in society, were inferior. Their purpose was to serve men and make babies. They should never be involved in anything other than keeping a proper house, taking care of the children, and satisfying their man. At the top of the list of what they should never be allowed to do was vote. They were a good part of the reasons for the skewed election.

When the conversations reached the proper volume, Titus again took charge. "Now that you've had a few moments to talk and think about what I just told you, I want to tell you what I have in mind." He paused for only a moment this time. Just enough so that all eyes in the crowd were focused on him.

"We haven't grown enough yet, to take on some of the bigger projects I'd like to tackle. But there are any number of smaller one's we can handle. We all know that there are large numbers of liberals in Kingsburg, Way too many. They all use that damn super market that's owned by the employees. That alone is a commie thing. Add to that, There's a goddamned woman running the place. If anyone's ever gone against God's will, those people have. So for our first project, I propose that we bomb it, that we blow it all to hell."

That left a stunned silence. Nearly half the men in the meeting had wives who shopped in that store. It was the most popular food store in Clayborne County. Titus again let the conversations reach a certain level before he again attempted to take control of the meeting.

This time, however, he was immediately interrupted. A young man, Sandy Dennis, who was relatively new to the group and the only one there not wearing a red MAGA hat, asked Titus, "What will it prove if we do bomb the store? All I can see it do is make it harder for a lot of us to shop. We aren't all as rich as you, so losing that store would hurt. They not only have the best food, they have the best prices."

"What it will do," Titus tried to explain, "is make a statement. It will be a good way of telling all the hippy liberals who voted for that evil Democrat that we are no longer going to put up with their brand of intolerance and stupidity. We are going to take control, and make this country great again."

"But bombing that store will hurt a lot more people than just the liberals. I'm a conservative. I vote Republican. I always have. My whole family does. My folk's taught me right from wrong while I was still a kid. That's why I vote the way I do. But if you blow up the store, you will hurt my whole family. They all shop there."

"I understand that," Titus answered, with less confidence in his voice. "And that means bombing it would make an even bigger statement."

Someone else stood to make a comment this time. "I think," he said, "that getting rid of the super market would, in fact, hurt too many of us. Why don't we destroy the library. It's full of books. Books that go against God's will. They are all just propaganda machines. Let's get rid of them."

A third person stood. "Most of you might not know it, but kids nowadays do a lot of school work using computers. So does my daughter, but I can't afford the kind she needs, so she uses one at the library. What the hell is she supposed to do if you blow it up?"

Titus knew that he was losing control of the meeting. Ir was the worst thing that could happen to him. So he raised his hands and his voice. "Okay," he nearly yelled. "You've made it clear that there are some hardships you aren't ready to take on. But that doesn't change the fact that we need to retaliate the theft of the election some way."

The next suggestion was much more to everyone's liking. "Let's take out the courthouse. Do it during the day, when it's full of lawyers and judges and tax collectors.'

That idea brought on cheers from nearly all the men there. One man who didn't cheer was Sandy Dennis, who had objected to blowing up the super market. His wife worked as a clerk in the property tax department. He didn't want her killed in a bombing. In spite of the fact, that according to this group he shouldn't do it, he loved her and actually tried to share his life with her. He realized then, that the membership in this group was one he didn't need. He stood up one last time.

"My wife works in the courthouse. I'd prefer to keep her around for a while."

He was answered with a nearly total silence as he looked around the group. Most faces he saw were less than friendly. It was enough. It was obvious that for the men in the group, their grocery bill was far more important to them than his wife's life was. So he walked out of the meeting.

Titus shook his head as he watched Sandy leave. "That man simply does not have the right priorities. So we will disregard him. He certainly isn't one of us."

He paused a moment again, and turned to his second in command in the group, Jelly Norton, and lifted his eyebrows. Jelly quickly moved to the door and followed Sandy. Two men leaning against the wall inside, followed him out.

They caught Sandy before he reached his car. The two men grabbed his arms from behind and turned him around to face Jelly. "I don't know who you think you are?" he asked. "And I damn well don't care. You don't walk out on one of our meetings just because you don't like what we say about your wife. She's a woman, so she simply does not matter."

"He said we should kill her."

"That shouldn't be relevant to you. Put insurance n her. After, find another. There's plenty out there. But that's not why I'm here." He hit Sandy with a vicious blow to the stomach. "What I'm here to do is tell you, warn you, that if you ever talk to anyone about what was discussed in this meeting." He hit sandy again. "My next warning will be a bullet in your head." He landed another blow. "Do you understand me?"

Choking for breath, Sandy managed a feeble, "Yes, I understand."

"Good. Now just make damn sure you never forget it."

The three men left him, still choking to get a full breath. As soon as he recovered enough, he sat down in his car. When his breathing returned to a near normal, he started to search his cell phone. He looked for the name and number of a place he'd seen a couple of articles about. From what he remembered, it was a common kind of company that did business a lot different than others did.

It frustrated him as he struggle to remember the name. As he tried to concentrate on that, he suddenly remembered the name of the wife of a couple who worked there. It was Lisa. Then he remembered the husbands name. He googled them together. That led him to the name of the detective agency. Refuge Rescuers.

He called the phone number listed. As expected the place was closed, but he got a message. It was different because it offered a way to make an appointment if that was what the caller wanted. He opted to make one, and was then walked through a simple procedure to complete the task.

That done, he drove home, thinking about his wife, Michelle, all the way. She greeted him with a smile when he got there. "How was the meeting?" she asked.

He looked at her before he answered, and quickly realized that he'd forgotten how beautiful she was. "It wasn't what I expected," he said. He took her in his arms and kissed her. "I have to tell you," he said. "I Love you. I really really love you." He kissed her again.

His behavior startled her. He wan't normally that affectionate. She pulled away from him. looked him in the eye an asked, "Have you been drinking."

He wanted to laugh at her question, but wasn't able to. It told him who he was and how he'd behaved, especially toward her, for far too long. He again thought of losing her to a bomb, and vowed to do his best to change. She was, when all was said and done, the most important thing in his life.

"No," he said, coming close to a smile, "it's just that I realized that I haven't told you that for a long time. It's something I should do everyday. Because I do love you. More than life itself. And I need you even more than that." He took her in his arms again and kissed her.

She pulled her head back to look at him. When their eyes met and she saw the tears in his, she returned his kiss. Then they moved to their living room, sat together on their couch, and started to talk. He told her about the meeting. She listened to every word. She knew, as she did, that their life was now changed. Given what the world had been turned into by the radical, nutcase Trump and his Republican followers, nothing would be simple or safe again.

CHAPTER 3

Sandy Dennis made his nine o'clock meeting on time. Refuge Rescuers receptionist greeted him as he entered their office. Julie offered him a cup of coffee, which he accepted, and she took him to the meeting room where Mack and Lisa Thomas waited for him.

After their introductions, Mack asked him, "What is it that we can help you with today?"

"To start with," Sandy answered, "I'll be surprised if there's anything you can do about my problem. More than some advice anyway. I think my problem is too big for you or anyone to actually do anything about."

"That might be true, but we won't know for sure until you tell us what the problem is."

Sandy was hesitant to tell them what his problem was, but knew that if he didn't, there was no point in his being there. "Before I start," he said, "I have to ask. Will what I say be kept completely confidential?"

"If that's what you want, yes, of course it will."

Still hesitant, he studied their faces. There was something there, something about them that gave him confidence. He also found it reassuring that they hadn't as yet mentioned money. That was the first he expected them to do. "I was at a meeting last night," he began slowly, then told them everything that was talked about while he was there. He finished with, "They followed me outside. Two of them held me while the other one, I think his name was Jelly Norton, hit me in the gut a few times."

Lisa jolted upright at the table with the mention of Jelly Norton's name. "I've heard that name before," she said. "I don't remember where, but I remember there was no good connected to it."

"As far as I'm concerned," Sandy told her, "there is no good connected with him. He threatened to kill me if I told anyone about him or the meeting. He said he'd put a bullet in my head."

"That doesn't surprise me any," Mack said. "Those MEGA Fellows sound like a bunch of rightwing, mindless wonders. Something this whole country has way too many of now. My question for you is simple. Why the hell were you in that meeting in the first place?"

"When I was invited to go by a guy I know, he said they were a group who wanted to solve the kind of problems we're having in this country. I just want what's best for my wife and me. For the kids we want to have in the near future. I didn't know that they thought they could solve the problems by bombing a grocery store."

"I know it's none of my business. But I am real curious. How do you vote?"

Sandy stared at Mack for a moment, surprised by the question. "How is that relevant to anything we're talking about? How I vote is personal, and I don't see why you would ask me something like that."

"I know it's personal. But it also says a lot about a person. Especially now, with everything as screwed up as it is. If you vote Republican, and I suspect you do, you are voting in favor of everything that's wrong with this country. It means that you don't now and never have paid much attention to who does what in the government. There's not one person connected with Refuge Rescuers who isn't a liberal. I, and I'm sure everyone else here, understands your problem. But if we are going to work together to solve the biggest problem you've ever had, you are going to have to understand what we are up against. And it *is not* a liberal conspiracy."

"But they did steal the election."

"If you really believe that piece of total bullshit, I suggest you go back to your meeting, apologize for doubting your fearless leader, and go ahead and bomb your wife."

"Trump said he had proof."

"There's only one truth about Trump. And that is, he *never* tells it. And given your mindset, Sandy, I doubt that we will be able to do anything to help you."

"I don't see why not? I just vote my conscience."

"I don't doubt that you do. You were probably raised to do that. The thing is, it would be a very good thing if you would add using you brain to that."

"I guess I made a mistake coming here then."

"Not if you actually do some thinking after you leave here."

"What is it that I'm supposed to be thinking about?"

Mack sighed. This was the type of conversation that rarely ended positive. Sandy seemed like a decent person, but like so many Americans, he was so brainwashed by rightwing religion, politics, and media, that he didn't have many rational thoughts left. So he gave Sandy a short answer. "Right and wrong and who does what. Something you haven't been doing."

Sandy left them then, but only got as far as his car. He started it, sat staring at nothing, then shut it off. He leaned his head back and let his mind wander. He thought about the previous nights meeting, then let his memory deliver to him many of the speeches he'd heard Republicans make over the past several years. Too many of them sounded similar to what he'd heard the night before. They, the same as Titus Trump, didn't care if his wife lived or died. If he lived or died. It was all about money and power, and bombing anything they didn't like. He went back inside and found Mack and Lisa. He looked at her.

"I'm sorry," he said, not able to look her in the eye. "I've been wrong. You do matter. My wife matters. He didn't want to bomb the grocery store to make a point. He wanted to do it to kill her. She's a woman and she's the manager of the store. He hates women. You guys are right. I will try to do better. I know right from wrong. I've just been putting that knowing in the wrong places. I really want your help, if you will give it to me."

Mack smiled now. He knew that he had a long way to go with Sandy. But they'd made a start. And that was all Mack needed to move forward. Lisa was happy with the situation as it was now too. But something else kept running through her head. That name? Jelly Norton. Who was he?

They put together a contract then. One that shocked Sandy when he went to sign it. His fee was zero. They were going to handle his case pro bono.

"How can you do that?" he asked. "You can't stay in business doing things that way. Besides, why would you do that for me?"

"To start with," Mack explained, "we have a trust fund that helps cover things like this. I know that you make a reasonably decent living, but your income is no where near what this will end up costing. More than that though, we know how important it is to stay in front of groups like MAGA Fellows. So when we take on cases like yours, our concerns go beyond only you and your wife. We will probably do doing things not directly related to you. We sure as hell can't be charging you for any of that. Does that answer your question?"

"It does, but it brings up another one. Given that I'm not paying you to do anything, will you work as hard for me as you would if I was paying you?"

"Due to the nature of this case, we'll be working every bit as hard on it as any we've ever dealt with. And with this one, we'll be using more resources than we would on most jobs."

Sandy was satisfied with his answer. He went from there to work and finished out the day. His wife, Michelle, got home shortly after he did, and found it impossible to hide her fear and worry from him.

He did his best to sooth her feelings as he told her about Refuge Rescuers, and how anxious they were to help. She calmed a lot after he did. "And they're not charging you?" She asked.

"Not a dime."

He knew then that she'd had a hard enough day, and took her out for supper. They decided that if they were going out, they should eat something they like, but rarely ate at at home. So they went to a bar. They ate bacon cheeseburgers with fries, and shared a pitcher of beer. It was a very pleasant evening for both of them. Until it was time to leave the bar.

Jelly Newton and three of his friends came in then. He smiled when he saw them. It was an evil smile. He lifted his hand, shaped it like a gun and pointed it at them. Then he twitched it twice.

He terrified Michelle, and it took her breath away. Sandy was then filled with hate. It was one thing to threaten him. It was something else altogether to threaten Michelle. He was glad now that he'd gone to Refuge Rescuers for help. It was help, he knew, that he'd need in the future.

CHAPTER 4

As soon as Sandy Dennis left, Mack and Lisa took all the information they got from him into Sue Sartor's office. She was Refuge Rescuers technical wizard. There was almost nothing she couldn't do with, or accomplish with, a computer or other related devices like smart phones and tablets.

She was exceptional at doing anything and everything on the internet, but her specialty was doing research on people. As soon as they gave her the names of the two leaders of the MAGA Fellows, she began her search. She started with Titus Trump.

There wasn't much about him that wasn't part of the public record somewhere. He was arrested five different times. The first when he was fifteen for stealing a car to go joyriding in. The second was for firing a gun in a residential neighborhood. He was shooting out streetlights. The third was for inappropriately touching a minor who was sitting next to him during a church service. The evangelical preacher of the church talked the parents out of filing charges against him. The fourth was for killing his neighbors dog, who was barking too much. The fifth was for the statutory rape of a seventeen year old girl. It was a crime he was out on bail for. The court date had not yet been determined.

He was also a rabid fan of Donald Trump. Titus agreed with everything Donald had to say, no matter what the subject was. They had the same last name, even though Titus was bitterly disappointed that he wasn't related to Donald. He tried his best to emulate Donald's hair style, but found it difficult to duplicate its weirdness. He even used the same suntanning lotion Donald did.

With the same result. It gave him a burnt orange glow strong enough to cover his emaciated skin. Most of all, like Donald, he was a constant, consistent, continuous, calloused liar.

Along with his driver's license photo, Sue brought up several other pictures of him. All the way from his high school yearbook to his arrest reports. They illustrated that like Donald, he was an ugly child and hadn't improved any over the years.

Jelly Norton's history was worse. His criminal record ran from torturing small animals to raping little girls. He was a native of Minnesota, but until recently had lived in several other states. His arrest record showed that he was wanted in three other states, along with Minnesota.

Unlike Titus Trump, he didn't care one way or the other about Donald Trump. He simply didn't care about anything, other than doing whatever it was he felt like doing at any given moment. He liked being part of the MAGA Fellows though. They had proved to be a good group to hide out in.

He blended in good enough, so cops tended to miss the fact that his face was a good match for the one on his wanted poster. Lisa, however, didn't miss him when Sue brought up the poster. In fact, she gasped when she saw it. She then slammed the side of her fist onto the top of the table.

"Goddamn it all to hell," she said, a quiver in hr voice, as his picture filled the computer screen. "He's one of them. He's the one who tore up my insides. Jail is too good for him."

Mack put his arm around her. "Who is he, Lisa?"

"He is one of the men who raped me. He was just about the worst of all of them. I don't know what I'll do when I see him. It will be awful hard to keep from killing him."

"You can't just go after a man like that alone. He's obviously very dangerous."

"Mack, of all the people who know me, you should understand what I feel toward that man. You should know I don't have to win in order to win. All I have to do is hurt him. Not to mention, I have damn few doubts about being able to beat him."

"I have no doubt that you would have a good chance against him, but is he worth it. Even if you do beat him, he could hurt you. He could hurt you bad."

"I know, Mack. We'll just have to wait and see. But you have to understand how I feel, after what he and those other men did to me. For me, none of them are human, or anything close to human. Nor are they animals. There's not so much as one animal on our planet that doesn't have far more value the any of them. And I don't think you can know what my seeing that he's alive and around here is doing to me inside."

"I won't, I can't, argue with you about that. But as much as you hate them, as much as this is bothering you, I still don't want you to get hurt anymore than you already have been."

"I have a right to hate them, Mack. And no rules, no laws, can ever tell me different. Nor will anything stop me from getting my hands on him."

"As far as I'm concerned you do have every right to hate them. I hate them too. Even so, I want you to be careful. You'll find no satisfaction from dealing with that man, if he puts you in the hospital. So you are going to have to be damn careful on how you get your hands on him."

"I know. So let's make sure everyone is at breakfast tomorrow, so we can figure out the best way to deal with that bunch of useless creeps. Including Jelly Norton."

Mack had some paper work to do then, so Lisa decided to drive into town to work with Dale at the sheriff's office. He was an excellent sheriff. Few in the same office could match him. But when it came to keeping all the paperwork involved in running a sheriff's office, he left a lot to be desired.

Lisa though, was extremely good at it. So she volunteered her services when she had the free time. Other people probably could have done the same work for him, but they both enjoyed working together, and just plain enjoyed their time together. It was also obvious to Mack, and Dale's wife, Kathy, that was the reason Lisa did the volunteering. And as long as it was a friendship thing, and just two people enjoying each other's company, no one objected to what they were doing. It also would have been difficult for Mack or Kathy to object. Whenever it was possible for them to do it, Mack and Kathy spent Saturdays together exploring the wildlife refuge. And there were more places in the refuge for two people to get into mischief, then there were anywhere Lisa and Dale spent together.

On this afternoon, their time together was mostly frustrating. The office was particularly busy, and Dale was plagued by constant interruptions. It didn't slow down until it was near quitting time for Dale.

"It sure wasn't any kind of fun day," Dale said when the constant interruptions stopped.

Lisa shrugged. "It's okay. You're the sheriff and sometimes everyone needs you. It's just part of the job."

"It is, but I still like it better when we at least get to have some time to talk. I like talking to you."

"I feel the same way, Dale. I especially wanted to talk to you today."

"Is there something specific you wanted to talk about?"

"Yes. Other than Mack, I think you're the only man I could ever talk to about it."

"It sounds like something really personal. If it is, I'm not sure why it's me you want to talk with about it."

"That's easy, Dale. You're my friend. My special friend, actually. I know I can trust you. It's about my past being brought into the present, and you're the sheriff, so you might be able to help me with my legal rights."

"Now you've really got me curious. Is it going to take you long to tell me what it is you want to talk about?"

"Long enough to put it off for another day. We both have someone at home, waiting for us."

"We do have that, Lisa. But you really have me curious. I think I should call Kathy and you should call Mack, so we can tell them we'll be a little bit late tonight. Then we should go somewhere and have a drink. You can tell me whatever it is you want to talk about."

Lisa was sure that Mack would understand, so she agreed to Dale's suggestion. When she explained to him that she wanted to talk to Dale about discovering Jelly Norton, and wanted his advice on how to deal with the situation, Mack thought it was a good idea. Dale was a lot more conservative about fights, especially women getting into them, then Lisa or he was. So he hoped Dale would be able to talk her out of doing anything rash.

They went to a cafe/bar not too far out of town called the Mystic Curve Inn. Dale picked out a booth near the back of the place, which was fairly private. It wasn't until the waitress brought Lisa a second glass of wine and Dale a second beer, that Lisa started to tell him about Jelly Norton, and Lisa's strong desire for some payback.

Dale put his hand over hers as she talked. When he first did it, she felt like she she pull her hand away. But finding that she like the way it felt, she did nothing to stop his touch.

Mack ended up in a similar situation. After Lisa called, he decided to take a walk in the meadow located behind their house. He didn't get too far on his walk before he met Dale's wife, Kathy. Just the fall before, they'd built a house on the other side of the meadow from Mack and Lisa. Mack and Kathy had walked the meadow together before, so it wasn't any big surprise to see her.

Without a word, she gave him a broad smile, took his hand, and walked with him in the direction he was heading. After about two steps, she gave his hand a tight squeeze, then leaned against him. He squeezed her hand back.

They walked a little farther, with her seeming to get closer to him with each step. They didn't get far before she heaved a heavy sigh. She turned toward him, and pulling him down to her, she kissed him mightily on the lips. He wasn't expecting it, but he did answer her with one of his own.

He then pulled back away from her. "What brought that on?" he asked.

"Nothing special, Mack. Just the sight of you. The touch of your hand. And the fact that I love you."

"You can't love me," Mack said, afraid of what she said. He had strong feelings for her too, but he managed to override them with his feelings for Lisa. She was the love of his life, and that was something he had absolutely no desire to change. "I love Lisa and you love Dale. We can't, and we shouldn't, ever change that."

"I'm just as aware of that as you are. But I still love you, and I don't believe there's a damn thing on earth that's ever going to change that fact. It's not only possible for us to love more than one person in our life, it's highly unlikely that we will only love just one person. So I love you."

"Doesn't it sometimes worry you that the fact you do might screw up the lives of all four of us?"

"No. Not if we keep it in perspective. I don't expect that you and I will ever take our love any further that what we just did, so it shouldn't cause anyone any harm. But damnit, I sure do like kissing you. And I get a thrill from just holding your hand. I think making love to you would be almost worth dying for. But I won't hurt Dale again. So I guess it won't happen. And as long as it doesn't, we should be okay."

Instead of answering her, Mack told her something in another way. He kissed her. Then he said, "I like kissing you too."

She got a small laugh from that, and held tightly onto his hand for the rest of their walk. They kissed each other when they stopped at her house, just before she went inside. That left him wondering if they might be getting too liberal with their kisses and hand holding.

Lisa wondered the same thing when she held Dale's hand as they left the bar. Especially when she squeezed his, and he returned it with one of his own. That question grew stronger when he dropped her off at the sheriff's office to get her pickup.

He took her in his arms and kissed her before she got out of his car. She strongly responded, so they exchanged kisses for several minutes before she escaped his strong arms.

She thought about their relationship all the way home. It seemed strange to her that she could feel about him the way she did. She loved Mack with everything she had, with everything she was, and knew that hurting him would be the worst, most stupid thing she could ever do. Yet, there was that part of her that wondered if there should be more. But more that that, she wondered if she would ever be able to allow more.

She tried her best to rid herself of those thoughts before she went inside the house, where Mack waited for her. He smiled broadly when she came in, and he took her in his arms and kissed her.

She laughed when he let her go. "Now that was quite the greeting, Mack," she said. "I'm not that damn late."

"I know, but I've missed you anyway. The thing I most look forward to everyday, is coming home and being alone with you. So, did you and Dale have a good talk?"

"We did. It was mostly about Jelly Norton and what he did to me. He told me the same things you did. He wants me to be careful. He can't stand the idea of me being hurt. I think he's even more worried than you. But then, he doesn't know me as well as you do."

"I should hope not. I wouldn't want anyone to know you as well as I do."

"I feel the same way about you? Did you see Kathy tonight?"

"I did. Not on purpose, but yes, I did see her. I met her out in the meadow. I guess she decided to do the same thing as me, when she found out Dale was going to be late coming home."

"I have no doubt that you met her by accident. But I know damn well it was no accident that she met you. It was on purpose. Did she kiss you when you met."

"Yes, and held my hand too. Dose that upset you?"

"It should, I guess. But Dale kissed me, and I held his hand. It seems like now, that whenever we see them, there's some kissing going on."

"It does. Do you think we should put a stop to it? I really care about Kathy, but I don't want to do anything that will ever get between you and me. As I've told you many times, Lisa, you are the most important thing in my life. Nothing or no-one means as much to me as you do."

Lisa moved close and gave Mack a hug. "That goes both ways, Mack. But for now, I don't think a little extra kissing will hurt us any. There's something about that kind of sharing that seems special. Lately too, it seems that after finding out about Jelly Norton, that extra stuff means even more. And Kathy and Dale are extra special friends after all. I just need to know that no matter what, you will never stop loving me. If you did, it would be awful hard to ever again find something that mattered."

CHAPTER 5

Mack wanted to be sure he had it together in the morning, so his presentation of their latest case made sense to everyone at the breakfast meeting. Apparently it did, because everyone sitting at Ben and Theresa's huge dining table listened with rapt attention as he gave it. It was so quiet that it worried him some that it was a total failure. Roy was the first to dispel that worry.

"I think, Mack," he said, "you've put us in a serious position. Not one I'm at all objecting to, just one that's serious. And probably somewhat dangerous. All those militia groups are made up of brain parts missing psychopaths, who like nothing more than an excuse to hurt or kill someone. So if we're going to do this, we have to be damn sure we don't take on but one group at a time."

Detective Paul Danielson gave his opinion next. "I agree with Roy. I'm all for taking on this case, but we damn sure need to be extra careful on this one. But I also think that we have to figure out a way to help Lisa follow through with that Jelly Norton character."

Ben surprised everyone when he spoke up. "Mack," he said, his tone of voice as serious as he ever used, "it was me and Roy who found Lisa that night, after she escaped those creatures. I'll never know the kind of hell she went through with them. But I know it was horrible. I want to be part of this case. I want it enough so don't bother arguing with me. Most of all, I want to be there the first time she sees that Jelly Norton. I want to see him destroyed. Audrey Nelson, the manager of the super market, is a good friend of mine. In the past I sold her a lot of vegetables. She was great to work with. She's the best kind of people. I damn sure don't ever want her to be hurt in any way, bombing or otherwise. So we domn well need to stop those guys."

Wanda was the one who brought up the one thing on everyone's mind. "I think we all agree that taking on this case is a good idea. We don't need any nutcase bunch of simple minded, toy soldiers bombing anything where we live. So we all have the same question. What are we going to do to let them know that they are being watched, and that if they blow something up, we will be coming after them?"

This was when Mack decided to tell them about the idea he had on how to deal with the MAGA Fellows. It was radical, so at first he was hesitant about suggesting it. "If we were still connected to the sheriff's office," he began, "there's no way we could consider what I'm going to propose. So don't hesitate when I finish, to speak up. Either way. Negative or positive."

He paused, looking each one of them in the eyes before he continued. "I think we should hit one of their meetings. All of of us who want to be there. We should be fully armed. Rifles, shotguns, and handguns. We should warn them that they are being watched. That if they attempt to do anything to harm anything or anyone, we will come after them. Finally, doing this will be fully voluntary. Anyone, who for any reason doesn't want to be part of it, is more than welcome to stay out of it."

It was Sue Sartor's turn. "You couldn't keep me out of this. I'm a hundred percent with you, Mack."

Theresa was the biggest surprise. "I'm in too. As long as I can carry my thirty thirty lever action. I don't like hand guns and I don't want a rifle that's too big for me."

"Having your support, Theresa," Mack told her, "is such a boost for all of us so that if all you carried was a BB gun, it would be okay. And before I forget, we will all be wearing body armor. No exceptions."

Mack was followed by someone none of them expected to here from. Julie's voice was soft, and she was obviously nervous when she spoke up. "I want to go along too," she said. "I know I'm young, and I know you all won't want me along. But that man who's there. The one who hurt Lisa. I want to tell him, if he ever hurts anyone else, I will probably have to kill him. And you all know I've been training, so I'm a good enough shot to do it with either a handgun or a rifle. I won't even have to get up close."

Mack was too shocked by her request to answer her right away. So Lisa did. "I appreciate how you feel, Julie. If I were you, I'd want the same thing you do. But if I let you go with us to do something like this, I think dad might kill me."

Lisa and Julie were sisters, and Lisa was sure that their father, Bob Anderson, would be extremely unhappy if Julie were allowed to go along on such a potentially dangerous venture.

"Lisa's right," Mack finally said. "Your dad would be extremely unhappy if we brought you along when we visit the MAGA Fellows."

"You're probably right. But what if he's says it's okay? Will you let me go along then?"

"If your dad says it's okay, you still will have to get it past Lisa. She might consider you far more important than anything we might do to the Fascist MAGA Fellows."

Julie turned to her sister. "Well, Lisa, if dad says it's okay, will you let me go?"

Lisa didn't know how to answer Julie, because she wasn't sure what the right answer was. So she fudged it. "I don't know, Julie. So we'll just have to wait and see. I'll tell you if and when the time comes."

And that time came quicker than they expected. When Mack explained the situation to Bob, he quickly asked one question.

"So one of the men, the second in command of that bunch, is definitely one of the men who raped Lisa?"

"He is. Lisa's a hundred percent sure of it."

"Okay, then this is my decision. Julie has my permission and my blessing, to go with you guys when you raid those bastards. With one condition. That I get to go along too."

"You might have a problem making it, Bob. Most likely, we'll be hitting them right about milking time. I know you never neglect your cows, and I can't change the timing of it any. We have to hit them when we have to hit them."

"That's okay. I can get backup help for Beth that night. She'll do fine. She can handle it every bit as good as I can."

"Okay, Bob, then you're more than welcome to be with us. As far as Julie goes now, Lisa will make the final decision. She has some really mixed feelings about letting Julie come along."

"So do I, but if it gives us a chance to at least see one of the men who did it to Lisa, it'll all be worth it. Because once we see him, we'll be able to find him again."

Mack and Lisa, along with Paul Danielson, watched from under cover, the next two meetings the MAGA Fellows held. They counted the number of men who went into the meeting, and paid close attention to what kind of men they were. The first, most outstanding feature of all of them, was the hat they wore. It was Trump's red, 'Make America Great Again' (MAGA) hat. That alone was proof positive they were a group of semi-retarded idiots.

They decided then that if push came to shove, their own group would be able to handle them. It didn't matter that they were outnumbered three or four to one. Almost all of the MAGA Fellows appeared to be grossly out of condition. All of the Fellows thought they looked strong and dangerous, dressed as they were in their military equipment and clothing. But nothing could have been further from the truth. They looked ridiculous.

There were only about six of them who seemed like they could handle themselves in a fight. Jelly Norton was one of them, and he looked as if he was the most fit of all of them.

That fact didn't affect Lisa at all. The few times she actually saw him, she tensed up and her deep set hatred and anger rose to the surface. It was all she could do to stay in place, and not give up the fact to the men in the meeting that they were being watched. She wanted him, and she badly wanted to beat him.

Watching him wasn't all detrimental for her though. What she did see of him, gave her the chance to study the way he moved and acted. He went beyond confident. He was cocky. The fact that he considered himself to be *the man*, was obvious. It was something, that given the chance to go after him, Lisa could use to her advantage.

She could also tell, from his heavily muscled body, that he would be less agile than her, and slightly stiff in his movements. He was strong and relatively fast, she was sure. But she could turn some of that strength against him, and knew her moves would be lightening quick compared to his. What she needed the most was the chance to get her hands on him. She wanted it one on one. Convincing everyone to let her do it was the problem as far as she was concerned. Not fighting him.

Mack was beginning to see the same thing. It was changing his feelings about the whole issue. It wasn't her getting hurt that worried him the most. It was her taking her anger too far. He didn't think she could do anything to the man he didn't deserve. And just dying was way too good for him. What concerned Mack now, was Lisa going to jail. He knew he would need to watch her closely.

He asked her about her feelings when they ended their surveillance. "How do you feel about this case now?" he asked her.

"Like it's going to be a long one. I don't think we'll actually solve it, even if all those ridiculous MAGA Fellows end up in jail."

"I wonder," Mack asked, "is jail where you really want them to end up? Or do you have other things in mind for at least some of them?"

"If you're referring to Jelly Norton, yes, I do have something else in mind for him. But killing him isn't it. Even hurting him bad isn't the final solution I want. Although, I have to admit, I will be hurting him. No! What I want most is to totally humiliate him in front of his toy soldier friends. I want to push him to the point he never again can look directly into another man's eyes."

"You're full of a lot of hate, aren't you Lisa?"

"Do you honestly expect me to be otherwise? Because if you do, then you certainly are not the man I thought you were."

"No, I definitely do not expect anything else from you. As far as I'm concerned, there would be something lacking in you if you didn't hate him. However, I am worried that you might let it control you to the point you take things too far. The truth is, my concerns are selfish as much as anything. If you go to jail, my life will be more than just empty. Compared to what it is now, life wouldn't make much sense."

"Don't worry, Mack. I won't take it that far, unless it's a situation where I'm forced to defend myself."

"But you still want to fight him?"

"Not really. I still want to beat the crap out of him. I have no desire to face him and fight him while following any kind of rules. Do you think I want to get myself killed?"

Mack couldn't help himself. He laughed. "Okay, Lisa, I understand what you're saying. But I still want you to be careful. It's better for all of us if you don't beat him to death."

"I won't. If I did, he wouldn't feel the humiliation I want him to feel. And not only him, but the whole bunch of them. It's going to say a lot to the whole bunch of them when a woman my size dose to him what I will do to him. He's the toughest one of them. How do you think they will feel when they're forced to look down at him, lying unconscious in pool of blood? And I'm the one who put him there?"

Paul, who had politely kept silent while they talked, finally added his opinion. "They're going to feel mostly shocked," he said. "And I, like Mack, do think you can take him. But you do have to be damn careful. And never forget, you won't be having a fair fight. You'll be in a war. It'll be one you want to keep relatively short. No getting cute. Just take the son of a bitch out as quick as you can. When he goes down, you keep him down. You give him a chance at all, and it'll be you in the pool of blood."

Lisa turned to him. The instant she caught the look in his eyes, she knew he was right. Nothing cute with Jelly. Just as fast and nasty as she could make it.

CHAPTER 6

Wanda and Roy were in the Kingsburg Natural Food Market, leisurely shopping for staples like coffee, milk, and butter. The two of them enjoying a rare, weekday afternoon off.

They were in the dairy department, looking through the selection of cheese made in neighboring Wisconsin. Wanda then saw a man she had decided a long time ago that she never wanted to see again. She caught her breath at the sight of him. Her body stiffened as she suddenly stood up perfectly straight.

Roy noticed the change in her as it happened. He put his hand on her arm and looked at her face. "What is it, Wanda? What's wrong?"

She pointed to a big man, staring at her from the end of the aisle. The first thing Roy noticed was his red, MAGA hat, sitting backwards on his rather blocky head. He stood an easy six foot six, in spite of his rather short legs. His arms were filled with a lot of muscle mass, but they looked like they were turning to fat as much as anything. His gut hung over his belt far enough so that the tee shirt he was wearing didn't quite cover it.

"The big asshole at the end of the aisle. It's Lance North, my ex-husband. I haven't seen him in years. I was hoping I never would."

"He's the one who put you in the hospital?"

"He is. But it was a long time ago, so let's just get out of here. I don't want to have anything to do with him."

"Are you still afraid of him?"

"No, Roy. I just don't want to have anything to do with him. He isn't worth the effort it would take to knock him on his ass. Something I have no doubt you can do."

"Oh, I don't know, Wanda. The main problem with men like him is the fact that they don't get the shit kicked out of them near often enough."

"The trouble is, Roy, he's too stupid to learn. And as much as I would enjoy seeing him get his ass kicked, I'd like it even better if we can just walk away. Fighting with him just isn't worth it."

"Okay. I'll let it go this time if that's what you want. But he has to do the same. You know that I can't, in any way, put up with any bullshit from him. I already hate the asshole."

Roy picked out a couple of blocks of cheese, and then pushed their cart to the checkout. He didn't notice Lance in the same checkout line until he had the grocery cart emptied. Even then, he ignored the man.

They finished checking out and had their groceries loaded in Roy's pickup. He was backing out of his parking space, when Lance stepped in his way. He held up his hand for Roy to stop.

"So much for avoiding the asshole," Roy said.

"I should have known he'd pull a stunt like this," Wanda complained. "Watch him, Roy. He likes to sucker punch. If you have to fight him, don't quit until you knock him out. Then, for me, kick him in the balls. Hard!"

They got out of the truck. Roy walked up close to Lance. He glared into his eyes and said, "You want something?"

"I want to talk to her," Lance growled. "So get your sorry little ass back in the truck. What I got to say to her is between me and her."

"It's like this. You don't have anything to say to her that she wants to hear. So you move *your sorry ass* the hell out of my way, before I'm forced to kick it."

Lance tried to slam the palm of his hand into Roy's shoulder to move him. Roy was faster. He dodged to one side and grabbed Lance's hand as it flew by him. He gave his wrist a sharp twist as he pulled Lance's arm around behind him. He twisted it upward until Lance screamed in pain, then pushed him away. As Lance tried to regain his balance, Roy grabbed his shoulder and spun him around until they were facing each other.

At this point Roy decided that he'd already had enough of the man. He hit him, knocking him down. "It's up to you now," Roy told him. "You can stay down, or you can get up and get hurt."

"You had no reason to do that," Lance whined. "I just wanted to talk to my wife. Something I have every right to do."

"You've got no rights with her. She hasn't been your wife for many years. She's my wife now, so you'd better treat her the respect she deserves."

"When she made her vows with me before God, she became my wife forever."

"I think that you've got a lot to learn," Roy told him. "And you'd best learn it before I'm forced to teach you. Because if I'm forced to, I will. With lessons you will have to live with for a very long time."

"You can't threaten me. Not about her. You don't have a right to her. I do. In the eyes of God, she's still my wife."

That was all Wanda was willing to listen to. "It's like this, you lowlife piece of shit. I am not married to you. I learned, from the day I married you, I wasn't going to be married to you for very long. I'm married to Roy now, and I have been for several years. He's a real man. He knows how to love a woman. All you can do is beat on one with your fists. Beyond that, you are a total incompetent in bed, the same as you are with everything in your worthless life. You never did manage to have me. Certainly not the way Roy does. Every night. And will continue to do so, every moment. Day or night."

Wanda knew her words were both insulting and hurtful. But they weren't near as hurtful as his fists in her face had been during the short time they were married. He also took away her dignity and nearly all the confidence she had in herself. She went into a downhill spin that seemed as if it would never stop. Then came that fateful night she drank too much beer with Mack Thomas. After that, no matter what his life circumstances were, Mack always treated her with kindness. More than that, with respect. She loved him for that. Roy was her man, and the love of her life. But Mack would always have a special place in her heart.

Lance North though, the man now standing in front of her, would never get anything from her beyond a deep, undying contempt. Among his other faults, he was a slow learner and an even worse listener.

"Like it or not," he claimed, "you are still my wife. You can't go beyond the word of God, and his word says you are. So you will be coming home with me. Where you belong. Where you should have been all these years."

Wanda laughed at him. It was a harsh laugh, and she followed it with a sudden, sharp slap across his face. "If you don't back off from me now," she threatened him, "I'm going to knock you on your ass. Then I'm going to kick you in the nuts so hard you have trouble walking for the next several weeks."

"Don't be silly. Neither one of you can possibly take me on. I'm much bigger and stronger that either one of you."

"You've got until the count of five to back off. One, two..."

A short siren went off as a sheriff's car pulled into the store's parking lot. It drove up to them. Dale Magee got out of the car. He approached Roy. "Do we have a problem here?" he asked.

"Nothing too serious, Dale. Just this total moron here hassling my wife."

Dale looked at Lance. "Ah, yes," he said, a bit of a grin on his face. "Lance North. I remember you from way back. Still trying to throw your weight around?"

"No. I'm only following God's will, and claiming what's mine."

"And what might that be?"

"Her. Wanda. In the eyes of God, she's still my wife."

"Now that sure is too damn bad," Dale said. "Because in the eyes of the law, she damn sure isn't. So if you are trying to claim her, to take her with you, it's called attempted kidnapping. That leaves me no choice. I have to take you in."

Dale cuffed Lance and loaded him in the back of his car. "When you get the chance," he said, "you guys can stop by and fill out the papers. In the meantime, I'll keep him safe and secure for you." With that, he gave them a wink, then drove back to the sheriff's office. He had no real intention of putting Lance under official arrest. He was only getting him out of there to diffuse the situation with Wanda and Roy. He would only go through the motions. So he planned to keep Lance locked up for a couple of days. It would be a good lesson for him.

Satisfied with what Dale did, Roy and Wanda went home. Tomorrow, they figured, would be soon enough to do the paperwork on Lance North.

But it was paperwork that wasn't going to happen. Dale let Lance make his one allowed phone call. Before he got the chance to start any paperwork, he got a visit from the FBI. They wanted Lance. So they used their power and took him with them. He was one of their informants.

As soon as they had him out of the sheriff's office, he demanded that the agents help him get his wife back from the man who took her. Since they knew little to nothing about their informant, they believed what he told them. They took him directly to Roy and Wanda's home.

"You want what?" Roy asked them when they demanded that Roy turn Wanda over to them.

"We need you to turn that woman over to her lawful husband," the lead agent said. "And we need you to do it right now."

"You can stick that up your ass," Roy answered. "She's my wife. She divorced that asshole years ago. So, obviously, you aren't taking her anywhere."

"We can't just accept what you say. You are going to have to provide some proof that she's your wife. And proof she actually divorced him."

"You two are damn lucky I'm in a decent mood right now," Roy said, an evil grin now filling his face. "Otherwise, FBI agents or not, I'd be kicking your asses just for saying something like that."

Wanda, who had been standing behind Roy when the agents made their first demands, went and got all the documents they requested. She pushed them into the agents hands. He took them, then grabbed her.

"We'll have to have these authenticated before we can accept them as real. So she will be coming with us, and going home with her husband where she belongs."

"Not hardly." Roy slammed the side of his fist down on the agents wrist, breaking Wanda free. Before the agent could react, Roy spun him around and held him in a choke hold. He pulled the agent's handgun from its shoulder holster and pushed him away. He pointed the gun at the second agent. "Now yours," he said. He gave Roy his gun. "Call, Dale," he told Wanda. "Then Mack."

Mack was working with Lisa and Paul, so all three of them joined Roy. Paul was surprised to see Roy holding a gun on the two agents. Agents he'd worked with while he was a detective on the Minneapolis police force.

"What's going on, Roy?" he asked. "Why are you holding a gun on these guys? They're FBI agents."

"That doesn't matter a damn to me. They came here to kidnap Wanda, and give her to a man who will try to beat the living hell out of her as soon as he gets her alone. They claim she's married to him. He grabbed the papers out the agents hand. "This all the proof we need to show that Wanda divorced that big asshole standing there. Our wedding license is there too. These two stupid asses wouldn't accept them as proof."

"Well," Paul asked. "Why are you still trying to take this woman with you. You've got all the proof you need to know what the real truth is?"

"Look," the agent said, a bit of a whine in his voice. "We're just doing our jobs the best way we can. This guy here is one of our informants. The kind of information he gives is far more important than any domestic dispute. Married to him or not, it's not really going to hurt her any to spend some time with our informant. Not to mention, it's his word against her's."

"Not anymore. It's his word against five of us. So I suggest you guys back the fuck off. And think twice before you pull a stunt like this again."

"Well, I guess we can take your word for it." He turned to the second agent. "Let's get the hell out of here."

"Now you just wait a minute," Lance wailed. "It don't matter what them people or them paper's say. She's still my wife. She said those vows with me. That makes her forever my wife."

"Okay," said the senior agent, realizing that he'd made a big mistake trying to take Wanda. "We are out of here."

"No, you are not going anywhere," Roy growled. He wiggled the hand holding the agents gun. "You are staying here until the sheriff gets here. Then I'm going to swear out a warrant for your arrest. Kidnapping is still a crime."

The agent quickly turned a bright red. "You can't arrest a FBI agent for doing his duty. Any damn fool knows that."

"Save the damn fool descriptions for yourself," Roy said, his voice still filled with anger.

"I demand that you do something," Lance again whined. "In the eyes of God, she is my wife. And you all know that what God wants is far more important than what's on papers or what these people say."

Wanda, who was mostly quiet throughout the whole ordeal, finally spoke up. "I have listened to you long enough, Lance. So shut the hell up."

"I will not. And there's nothing you can do to stop me."

"I can kick your ass."

"You couldn't kick a brand-new babies ass. There ain't nothing to you. I remember how weak you were. It never took no effort at all to teach you how to behave. One or two good smacks across the face, and you were done."

The look on the faces of the two agents was far different now than it was when they got there. The look on Wanda's face didn't change. It was still filled with the same contempt she had when the whole incident started. She walked up to Lance, stopping only when she was just inches from him.

"How about now, Lance?" She spit out the words, hard enough to cover much of his face with her saliva. "You think you can smack me? Come on, you chickenshit twit. You ain't nothing but a half man who can't it get up any better than a wet noodle. A small one at that. You couldn't satisfy a plastic doll. Even they would reject you, inept as you are. I bet your own hands won't to go near you."

That's when Wanda accomplished her goal. Her goading of Lance set him off the way she wanted him set off. He took a hard swing at her. As his fist flew by her head, she palmed him in the face. Just as she planned, his nose made a loud crunch. He screamed when he saw the blood flow. He did his best to grab her. He left his oversized gut open when he did. She managed to land four or five blows to it before he realized that she hit him. He wilted when he felt the delayed pain. She joined her hands and slammed them down on the back of his head before the three men hoping to stop her could get to her. Roy and Mack were not part of the three men.

Lance was sprawled on the ground, his face in the dirt, when the two agents finally got a hold on her.

"Let her go," Roy told them. "Now!"

"She just assaulted a representative of the United States Government," the agent complained. "I have to arrest her."

"The trouble with that idea," Roy said, "is the fact that you can't arrest anyone. You are the one under arrest."

Lisa told them something they didn't like then. "What Wanda just did," she told the agents, "was self defense. And I was wearing my body cam, so I recorded the whole thing."

"That's evidence," claimed the agent, "so you'll have to turn it over to us right now."

"No, I don't. And I already downloaded it. So even if I did give it to you, you can't get rid of it. It's probably in a hundred places by now. You hand any of us anymore shit, and it will be all over the internet. Lance's face included. He won't be much an informant after that, now will he?""

"You people sure don't have any respect for the law, do you?"

"I guess that depends on how you look at it," Lisa said. "It's people like you that we mostly disrespect. You made a big mistake when you decided to come here to throw your weight around."

Dale pulled into the yard then. He shook his head when he saw who was there. He then had to suppress a smile when he saw Lance sitting on the ground, bleeding from his nose.

"Anyone call an ambulance for the person on the ground?" he asked.

"Not yet," The agent answered. "I'm not sure he needs one. All he's got is a nose bleed."

Roy spoke up then. "I don't care much if you call one, Dale. But whether you do or don't, I want him and these two guys arrested. They came here to illegally take Wanda somewhere so Lance there could beat and rape her."

"How do you mean, take her illegally?"

"I mean they tried to take her away by using threats. They said they could do it only because they are FBI agents."

"That true?" Dale asked them.

"Not exactly. We were told that she was Lance's wife. All we were trying to do is help get her home where she belongs."

"They did it, Dale, even after I showed them all the paperwork proving she divorced him and married me. They would have taken her no matter what if I would have let them. So they are the criminals and I want them arrested. If you won't do it, then I'll call the state police."

"I'll take them in," Dale agreed. "But you know as well as I do, the FBI will have them out in a matter of hours."

"I know. But it won't hurt to let the media in on it. It'll make a good story for all the morning shows on TV. They might like the part about how he tried to beat Wanda up, and got a bloody nose for it."

"I've got it on tape too, Dale," Lisa explained. "It's downloaded already, and I texted Sue to tell her what to do with it if the

FBI doesn't do something with all three of these ridiculous toy boy scouts. We all want a written apology from them."

"Do you guys really want to push them that hard? They'll be damn good and pissed off if you do."

Make stepped in. "I don't care. Enough is enough. No matter what, they don't have the right to come to a man's home and try to take his wife. Not when there's no reason."

"Well, I guess I'll do what you want then. But one of you will have to meet me at the office, to sign some of the initial papers."

Lisa immediately volunteered. "I can do it," she said. She looked at Mack. "I won't be long. If I go, it will give you and Paul a chance to finish up what we were working on. And Wanda and Roy will want to unwind after the ordeal they just went through."

Mack just nodded his head, and waited around until it was time for Lisa to leave for town. Her kiss before she went was telling.

CHAPTER 7

Mack was out on the back deck, nursing a beer when Lisa got home. She took one look at him and knew that something was wrong. She sat in the chair across from him.

"I'm sorry I'm late," she said, "it's just that it…"

"Don't lie, Lisa. That's not who we are. Not what we're supposed to be anyway. Just tell me how it was with you and Dale. How far past the only holding hands and kissing rule did you go this time? Did you manage to go all the way?"

"Mack! Why are you asking me questions like that?"

"Only because I want you to tell me the answers." Mack knew that something was wrong, that Lisa was troubled about something, and that even if she didn't realize it, they needed to talk about it. She was shutting him out of part of her life recently. So he decided to push her until she willingly talked to him about what was troubling her. Something she obviously didn't want to do.

"I don't own you, Lisa. I don't want to own you. So I'm not going to tell you what you can or cannot do with your body. That's not what this is about. I just need to have some answers about why you're doing what you're doing. You are my wife, so since you are having an affair with Dale, I want to know about it. I need to know how serious it is. It is starting to have a bad affect on us, on our marriage."

"I'm not having an affair with Dale. So I don't know what the bad affect you're talking about is."

"What do you call it then. What is it you and Dale were doing for those extra hours you've been with him today, if it isn't having an affair? You were having sex with him. What you were doing is written all over your face."

"We're just friends. We like each other's company. So we just forgot about the time while we were talking."

"I understand that. What I want to know, is far how did you go with him while you were talking."

"God, Mack, don't make me talk about it. We didn't do that much. So please, don't do this."

"Okay, Lisa. I won't. But since you won't talk to me about it, it has got to be awful serious. Enough so, that I can assume you're in love with him. That means you've most likely lost a lot of your feelings for me. I love you, Lisa, but since you're in love with someone else, it looks like it could be over between us. To start how this works, I was in this house first, and all my family is around me here. I'm going to stay in the house when we split. You can sleep on the couch tonight. But tomorrow I want you to pack what you need for a while and leave. When you get settled, I'll ship everything that's yours to you. And I'll have the lawyers start the divorce papers tomorrow. Don't worry. Half of what we are worth will go to you. I don't give a damn about the money. And last, if you want to keep Refuge Rescuers going, find somewhere else for the office. I'm out of it now. It's time for me to move on. I'll need to be doing something away from you. I love you too much to be able to stay close to you after we've split up. If you don't want to keep Rescuers going, I'm sure Dale will hire you back as a deputy."

Lisa didn't answer because she couldn't. She was in shock. It had never occurred to her that what she was doing with Dale was in any way bothering Mack. He did say, more than once, that it wasn't up to him to tell her what she could do with her body. What she didn't yet realize was that Mack was more concerned about the way she was doing it, then what she was doing. She'd also forgotten who he was. What kind of man he was. He was ready to let her go, if Dale was what she wanted. He didn't believe it was right to stand in the way of what she wanted. It was her right to choose how to live her life.

When she managed to get control of her tears enough, she asked, "Why, Mack? Why this sudden change? You always said that my body was mine. Why are you suddenly angry about what I do with it."

"I'm not angry. Disappointed about the way you're doing what you're doing... but not angry. What's wrong is that you're lying to me. You are trying to pretend that what you were doing, you weren't doing. You want to make it a secret. That's what's wrong. What you are doing with Dale is too important for you to be hiding it from me. If you're hiding that, what else are you hiding. Other than the fact you must not care much about me anymore."

"I'm not trying to hide anything from you. You knew where I was tonight. It's no secret."

"Maybe. But since you refuse to talk about it, you could have been anywhere and doing anything with Dale. As long as you insist on having your affair with him, and refuse to acknowledge the fact and won't talk about it, it proves that it is far more important to you than I am. Or what we used to be to each other. So it seems to me that because of your feelings now, the life we had must be done. You want something new. I love you too much to stop you from having what you want."

"But I'm not having an affair. It's not like that."

"Then what is it like? Tell me. Talk to me. Tell me what you do. What you were doing tonight. If you can't do that, then it can't possibly work between you and I. You can't expect me to stay with you when you're living a separate life and lying about it."

"What do you want to know, Mack? This is really hard, but I'll try to tell you. You have to know though, I'm not living a separate life. I just shared a few moments with Dale."

"To start with, and just to start with, I want to know exactly what it is that you and Dale shared tonight." He didn't really want to hear the gory details, but felt that if she couldn't share them, it was because she was already in too deep for the two of them to recover what, up until recently, they had together. "I don't want to hear you try to skirt around any of it. I want the details. For example, which one of you unbuttoned and opened your blouse? But start with the kissing."

Lisa started talking, but was frequently interrupted by Mack, asking for more detail. He thought it was important for her to realize how much she'd been keeping from him. She ended with, "I stopped it when he pushed his hand between my legs."

"Was that inside or outside?"

"God, Mack, what's the difference?"

"Number one, the truth. But as much, can you be honest enough to tell me how intimate you got."

"It was inside, but I pushed him away right away. I wasn't ready for him to go that far."

"You weren't ready for him yet. But you did plan on it for sometime in the future."

She tipped her head. "Yes," she answered, her voice barely above a whisper.

"Okay. Now how do you feel about having to answer my questions and describing everything to me that way?'"

"It bothers me. I didn't like having to do it. I don't think that it's fair that you made me do it."

"Do you want a divorce? If talking to me is something you don't like to do, and you think isn't fair, we might as well get one."

"Absolutely not, Mack. I haven't stopped loving you at all. You're always almost perfect. I know I could never love anyone the way I love you. I think that's why it's so hard for me to understand what you just made me do."

"I didn't make you do it, Lisa. You say you didn't like it, so you could have kept quiet. This isn't only about you. It's mostly about us. That's why I asked you to talk about it. The trouble now is the fact that you think it's only about you. That when it comes to what you do, as far as you're concerned, I don't matter."

"You said I could have kept quiet. What if I did? Then what?"

"We'd be getting a divorce. Right now, it sure seems like we might as well. There are things you have to know about, that are going to happen because of your affair with Dale. Any of them might cause us to get a divorce. Refusing to talk to me about what's going on and what you've been doing, is at the top of the list. It's not what you're doing, it's how you feel about it. The way you do it."

"I still don't think I'm having an affair. I just care about Dale a lot. He's been such a good friend. It's just that sometimes, I feel like I want to share more of who I am with him, than what most people might do. He's the only one I'd ever do that with."

"I understand that. It's called having an affair. It's called being turned on and wanting to have sex with someone. If you continue having an affair with him, an affair that I know about, and we stay married, that means that we will be having what's called an open marriage. Part of that open marriage will have to be you and I sharing things about the affairs we have. For me, an open marriage will have to be completely open, or I won't be able to handle it."

Lisa's eyes widened when Mack commented about the *affairs* they would have. "What are you talking about? What affairs? I don't consider what I do with Dale an affair. So what's this about other affairs. Do you plan on having one."

"I sure do. If you and Dale are going to be making love on a regular basis from now on, I won't be sitting home and waiting for you. The nights you go out, I go out."

"Who do you plan on having an affair with?"

'That's a silly question. Kathy, of course. To start with anyway. There probably will be more. I expect that you will be busy enough with Dale, so that you'll pretty much forget about me and what I do."

"What about Dale. That'll hurt him bad if Kathy cheats on him."

"He'll be fucking you, so he won't be in any position to complain. And since he's playing so loose and friendly with my wife, I frankly don't give a damn what it does to him or how it will affect him when I have sex with Kathy."

"When do you plan to start your affair with her?"

"Tonight, if she's ready after I explain to her about the affair you and Dale are having. And that way, you can spend the night with Dale. That's what you want, isn't it?"

"What if I don't want you to do that. I don't think I'll like it much if you do what you say you're going to do. And I don't want to spend the night with Dale."

"I didn't tell you that you couldn't. I haven't had any desire for other women since we've been together, but since you're pretty much tossing me aside for Dale, I'm beginning to think different. If I'm not supposed to care what you and he do, why should you care about what I do? At least I'm being honest about it. You aren't being honest with me about what you're doing or why you're doing it."

"I know you didn't tell me I couldn't spend the night with him. But you want me to tell you all about it. Right down to details that are embarrassing. You call doing that being honest. I wouldn't ask you to do that. And I care about what you do because I love you."

"The thing is, it doesn't seem like you do right now. Part of how this affair business is going to work, I will tell you every detail of what I do with Kathy." Mack paused, letting his sarcastic tone settle in. He wanted her to be uncomfortable with what he was saying. At the moment, it seemed like the best way to get the idea that they needed to be open with each other across to her. An affair with Dale was one thing. Trying to keep any part of it hidden was much worse. "In fact," Mack continued, trying to be as sarcastic as possible, "I think it'll be fun telling you every single detail. Every time we go out on out dates, we can come home and tell each other what we did. That might even get erotic enough that sometimes we might get so turned on that we want to do it with each other." As he hoped it would, his last statement shocked her.

Lisa was crying again. Mack wanted to hold her, but knew it was too soon. He had to wait until she understood what it was that she was doing, and how it was having even more serious negative affects on their marriage. The fooling around was one thing, but she'd reached the stage where she didn't want Mack to know exactly what she was doing. That was dishonest, and honesty was one of the main things they needed to continue to have between them. It was also an indication of how serious it was between her and Dale. If, that is, they were going to stay together through this change in their lives that she wanted. He knew that no matter what, if sneaking around was part of it, it would never work. It had to be open and honest.

It took a while, but Lisa finally managed to choke back her tears. "Did you mean that, Mack? You don't want me anymore? Why? I'm still the person I've always been."

"No, Lisa, I didn't mean I don't want you. But you definitely are not the same person you were. Now you are the young woman who is married to one man and has the hots for another man. What's bothering me so much is the fact that you decided that you have to sneak around about it. That you can no longer trust me enough to be honest with me. I won't tell you what to do. If you want to have your affair with Dale, I won't do a damn thing to stop you. That's something only you can do. But you can't have it without it affecting our lives. And not just the sex part. It will be part of everything we do. If it's something as simple as you and I on a walk in the refuge, I'll always be wondering if you wouldn't rather be holding his hand than mine. Things like that."

"If I still do things with Dale, what do I have to do to make it okay with you? I don't ever want to hurt you Mack. When I'm with Dale, I just feel like I'm only sharing a small part of who I am with him. When I'm with you, I feel so much more. I'm not just sharing myself with you. When I'm with you, I give you my soul. I totally lose myself in you."

"You can never make it what I'd call okay. Not the way you've been doing it. But we might be able to make it work if you will be willing to be totally honest with me. That means that if you plan on doing anything with Dale, you tell me ahead of time. If you don't plan it, but it happens anyway, you tell me about it after. When you and Dale are doing it, I want you to think about where your soul is at that very moment. Is it still with me or the man you are having sex with? Then when you come home, if you come home, I'm going to ask you about where your soul's been. Will you be able to tell me?"

"I don't know. I don't think I will like it much. It will feel like you've put me in a cage. I think you're asking too much."

"That's okay, Lisa. We all make choices. Some are hard, some are easy. Apparently this one was easy for you. You have no interest in sharing your feelings with me. As long as trusting me, being honest with me, is putting you in a cage, it's not going to work between us. I will want you to leave in the morning. The quicker we end this, the better it will be for all four of us. For me, there's already too much pain from what we've just lost. Stretching out the pain any further doesn't make any sense at all."

"What do you mean, end it now? I don't want to end it, Mack. We can't quit on each other, just because some things are hard for me to talk about."

"Yes, you do want to end it. If what you do with Dale is so important that you can't be open about it, then it's more important than you and I. It's more important than us. You won't like it if you have to be honest about it. That's okay, then you don't have to. But it does mean that it's over between us. I hate more than anything to lose you, Lisa, but I don't want to spend any part of my life making you do things you don't want to do. So it does look like I'm losing you."

"You're not being fair, Mack. I've never done anything on purpose to hurt you. But now you want a divorce for something you think I might do."

"No, not for that. The best thing we've always had since we've been married, is the way we've been able to talk to each other. You want to change that. You want to keep secrets. I don't want you to have an affair with Dale. But I love you enough to let you have what you want. But an affair isn't enough for you. You want to change who we were. I don't. If I have to do that, then I'm going to let you go. We do it your way, and we'll end up hating each other. I hope you have a good life. I sure wouldn't want anything bad for you. But I'm not going to live a life of lies and half truths. Living that way would be nothing but a life of misery."

"Jesus, Mack," she cried, "it sounds like you're trying to force me into doing something I just can't do. Why can't we just move on, and forget what happened tonight?"

"I'm not forcing you into anything. You want to have an affair, you're going to have an affair. You don't want to talk about it, you don't have to. I'm not asking anything more than trust, honesty, and openness from you. You can't give it. That's okay. For you anyway. But it does mean that our lives are changed more than you realize. We can't just move on because you've made this a big part of our lives now. So big a part, that it appears to have destroyed the life we once shared."

He stopped talking and watched her. She looked lost and confused, yet still determined to stand her ground. She still wanted to avoid talking about what was bothering her. It was more than Dale, that much was obvious. He now had the distinct feeing of having lost. It shocked him at how close the feeling was to the feeling he had the night his fiancé, Mandy died.

When he first started this conversation, he thought they could talk their way through their problems. Instead he realized now, they had failed. He hadn't managed to solve anything. He lost, and now getting through losing another woman he loved was going to be beyond difficult. He knew he would have to make some drastic changes in his own life.

So he told her, "And now that I've thought about it. You can stay in the house. There'll be too many memories of you in it for me to stay here. I've only got two things to do now. Have a talk with our newest neighbors, Dale and Kathy, tonight. Then the lawyers tomorrow. I think I'll buy me a small RV and whatever equipment I need to travel with it. Probably some kind of small car to tow behind it too. I'm going to take a nice long trip. Even though I spent a lot of time there while I was riding rodeo, there's still a lot of the west I haven't seen yet. There's a lot I'd like to see again too. I prefer to try to mend my heart, which you are breaking, no, shattering, somewhere alone. Trying to do that is something I expect to be doing for a very long time. Losing you, Lisa, is the *last loss* I want to go through. It's the hardest. When the other loses happened, it was too late for me to do anything. With you, it's because you want it. I thought we could talk our way through it, but you will have none of that. That makes it double hard, knowing our breaking up didn't have to happen. That I wasn't good enough to stop it, to fix it. So for me, starting very soon, I'll be somewhere far away from here, where maybe I won't think about you so much. Where I can maybe fill part of the empty that I already am. You can tell everyone at breakfast that I said goodbye. Then maybe you can explain to them why you threw me away."

Lisa looked him in the eyes. All she saw there was lost hope. There was no doubt in her mind. Mack was about to leave. And she knew then that if she let him go, it would be the end of him in her life. She might never see him again. With him gone, she was sure in her heart, her life would never compare to what it was with him. A life which was better than she would have ever expected.

She also knew that if he wanted to, he'd not have any problem finding someone else. Hell, he might even take someone from right here with him. From this awesome place surrounded by his family on one side and many wild things on the other. There were two woman here that likely would go with him if he asked. Kathy or Sue. Not to mention that most women found him more than just attractive. They all felt that he would make a great soulmate. Exactly what he was for her. So what was she thinking. How could she consider a life without Mack. Where the hell had her brains gone. She was about to lose him because she had the stupid idea she couldn't talk to him. That telling him the truth of all of it was too hard?

Mack felt nothing but empty. It didn't seem as though he was getting through to her at all. Maybe she did care about Dale too much to talk about him, or the gap she'd created between them. He stared at her, wondering what she was thinking. He'd made some threats to her, hoping she would realize how serious he considered the problem they were having was. It didn't seem to be working. It was all but certain now, that he would actually have to follow through with them. As long as she couldn't communicate with him about their lives, he knew he couldn't stay with her. It would only be a life of constant conflict between them. And if he didn't stay with her, a life of wandering would be the best way to get over her. Or at least be able to deal with the fact that he'd lost her. He knew it would be close to impossible to manage the loss of her if he stayed anywhere close to her.

His mind then started to drift back in time. He'd lost others. His first wife, murdered because someone was worried he might interfere somehow, with the sale of the refuge to the corporation that bought it. The accident that killed her was intended for him, but she was the one who died. He could feel the same kind of pain now that he felt that lonely day in the desert when they lowered her into the ground.

He remembered coming home, and falling in love again, then losing Mandy. She too was murdered. By someone else involved with the sale of the refuge. He thought then, that he would never heal. But thanks to Wanda, and his Uncle Roy, he made it through. He remembered leaving home shortly after she was killed. He thought he would go alone, but thanks to Roy who convinced her to do it, he left with Wanda. If she wasn't so happily married to Roy now, he might ask her to come with him on a long trip exploring the west. She would be good company, and knew him well enough to be able to help him through this crisis in his life.

Just as Lisa was now starting to have an affair with Dale, he too had an affair. He wasn't married when he had it, but he didn't try to hide it the way Lisa was doing now. Even Lisa knew about it at the time. Linda was Kathy's mother. And like the other two, she was also murdered. That affair had somehow given him and Kathy some kind of special connection. But again, a connection that was out in the open. Now though, it was a connection he might take advantage of. And if not now, sometime in the future. He had no doubt she would be available in the future. After Dale finished destroying his marriage to her by his affair with Lisa.

Neither Kathy nor Dale would be willing to compromise the way he was. She gave up a large part of her singing career for him. That was reason enough to not tolerate his having an affair.

An affair with Dale is what Lisa was thinking about. All along she'd expected Mack to mostly just ignore her and Dale. She was sure their marriage and love for each other was so strong that he would understand her frustration with the way she sometimes felt about herself. Of how she sometimes felt lacking in everyday life. And to a large extent he did ignore them. But now that what she and Dale were doing was growing more serious, he needed to have more involvement in it. At first it surprised her. Then it made her angry. And now, because of her fear of his leaving her, she was beginning to understand why he felt the way he did. She hadn't been honest with him about it. She hid it so she wouldn't have to share it with him. Given who she and Mack were, it was far worse thing to do than being open about it. So Mack did have the right to be upset, especially since it wasn't what she was doing that upset him. It was the way she was doing it. A way there was no real excuse for.

She had thought about and talked about how what she was doing was only sharing. But she was only partially sharing. And that was just with Dale. It finally registered inside her brain that she'd been wrong. She'd only been filled with what she wanted and thought she needed. She felt that all that was happening needed to be what she wanted, the way she wanted it. Mack at least wanted to share it in some way with her. She now knew though, that the kind of sharing that really mattered could only be her and Mack. They needed to get back the trust she now realized she'd gone a long way toward destroying. She loved him with everything she had, with everything she was, and to do anything that would cause her to lose him, would be so far beyond stupid that there was no way to explain it. And understanding that, she finally fully realized that Mack was right. She wasn't just sharing an extra part of herself with Dale. She had become involved too deeply with him. She was close to creating another life for herself, separate from Mack. Ever since the first sight of Jelly Norton, and all the horrible memories that came flooding back, she'd felt lost and alone. Like she needed a place to hide from what was. She had thought Dale was that place. She thought that he would somehow help her get rid of those memories she was sure she should have been rid of years ago. She forgot that the only person who had really been able to help her since it happened was Mack. He was the one she needed to get through this crisis of memories. Not Dale. Only Mack could make the memories fade, simply by holding her and whispering in her ear that it would all be okay.

It was something she'd decided to forget though. She hadn't spent time with Dale on this day because they liked to talk. She did it to feel his touch. She wanted to do something to erase the memories. She wanted him to make her feel something she wasn't normally able to feel unless it was with Mack. But because she didn't want Mack to know that, she was wrong in what she was doing, and wrong in the way she refused to talk to him. She tried to escape from what was, into some kind of refuge from the terrors the memories brought with them. Worst of all the things she'd done, she'd forgotten who and what Mack was. She'd forgotten that he was more of what she needed than most people ever get, and she'd turned her back on it. Dale's touch was nice, but he still couldn't make her feel any part of what Mack did. She was feeling somewhat desperate now, to fix with Mack the mess she'd created.

She finally took his hand and tried to smile. It was a feeble one and did nothing to ease the tension between them. "I'm sorry," she said, her tears flowing again. "I should be able to tell you anything you want to know. Anytime you want to know it. I always thought I could before. But this is…no, was different in a way that I still don't think I can share it with you the way you want me to. The way I know I should. I just don't have the right words to tell you what it is. But if I have another idea for a way to solve that problem, is there a chance you would accept it."

He was beyond trying to convince her that she at least needed to trust him enough to be totally honest with him, so the disgust he felt showed in his voice. "A damn slim one. I think

I'm done accepting anything more from you about this. You're going to end up with everything you really want. And I'm going to be long gone out of your way for the rest of your life. So it just doesn't matter much, now does it?"

"Yes, it does matter. Our life together is everything to me. All the rest are only things and stuff and happenings I can live without. For me, Mack Thomas, the love I have for you is all of it. If I don't have you, then what do I have? Nothing that matters. My problem is this. I can't tell you about it because I don't know how to do it. I was wrong when I thought how I felt right now shouldn't matter to you. It's true that I have feelings and urges and that I am awful curious about, and memories I should be rid of. I keep wondering whether I could ever make love with anyone other than you. But none of that matters at all if it means I will lose you." She paused and took a deep breath, trying to gather her thoughts.

"So there is only one way around that. No affair. No more letting things go a little farther this time. No more it's just sharing. If I share anymore, I share with you. Only you. Would that idea work for you? I was being stupid to do what I did the way I did it. Will you forgive me and can we just forget this fight and get on with our lives? You forgave Kathy right away when she made her huge mistake. Can you do that for me?"

"If you actually mean it, of course I forgive you. But the trust and honesty thing still goes. Anything, and I mean anything that happens between you and Dale, beyond holding hands or sharing an occasional kiss, and you tell me. That kind of thing starts and you don't tell me, when I find out about it, we will be done. If an accident happens between you two, we might be able to work through it. But only if you trust me enough to be up front about it. Hiding or lying about it will never work."

"Right now, Mack, at this moment, doing anything with anyone but you turns me totally off. Even with Dale. The thought of losing you is the worst nightmare I could ever have. You are all there is for me. So how about we go inside and you take full advantage of me. I really need you to hold me right now. I want you to hold me and love me until I'm so worn out I can't move."

He kissed her, then said, "I would do it right now, but before we do, I think it's time that we paid our neighbors a visit."

"Why? What do you want to say to them now?"

"The truth, Lisa. Let's get all this shit out in the open. If they want to hate us after, so be it. But I don't want anymore games. I pretty much hate games. This is probably something we'll have to do periodically, and the time to start doing it is now."

It was well into the evening when Mack and Lisa knocked on their door. Dale was surprised to see them when he answered it. "What's up?" he asked when he saw the serious look on Mack's face. The intensely serious look on Lisa's face bothered him even more.

"We brought the wine," Mack answered. "I assume you've got some cold beer on hand."

"We do."

"Good. Go inside, get the beer, glasses for the wine, and Kathy. We need to talk."

Dale knew better than to ask any questions right away. He was also sure that the conversation they were about to have was about the time he'd spent with Lisa earlier that day. He quietly went inside. When he and Kathy came out, they sat in separate chairs. Mack and Lisa shared a love seat, each against an arm of it. They weren't touching. Mack was the one to start talking. When no one interrupted him with any questions, he continued with his story. It was mostly about the long fight he and Lisa had just gotten over.

When he finished, Kathy got up and sat on his lap. She put her arms around his neck, then with a broad grin on her face, looked at Dale. "Is that what you want? Do you want to have an affair with Lisa? Because if you do, you can damn well bet that Mack and I will have one. And likely as not, I won't do much to hide that fact from anyone."

Dale knew from the looks he was getting that there was no sense in trying to lie. "Yes and no. I admit that the attraction I have for Lisa is incredibly strong, but at the same time, I do love you, Kathy. I couldn't love anyone more. So yes, the thought of an affair is in some ways very attractive. But I now realize how it could mess up all our lives. So it has stopped being such a good idea."

"How about you, Lisa?" Kathy asked her. She then wiggled in Mack's lap. Intentionally making it look like she was doing something to him that she shouldn't be doing. Something she actually was doing to him. She was also enjoying it, and wanted Dale and Lisa to know she was enjoying it. Sometimes a little revenge is sweet.

"Up until just a short while ago, I thought I wanted one. I'm very much attracted to Dale. But when I realized I was about to lose Mack because of it, that desire evaporated in a real short amount of time. Like not even a minute. Now, when I think about it, I wonder what the hell it was that I was thinking. Pretty much about the same way I would guess you were thinking about Dale after you left him and realized your mistake."

"Now stop," Mack said to Kathy when she made another move on his lap. "Behave yourself." In spite of the seriousness of the situation, he had a small smile on his face. There was no way he could not like what she was doing.

"Okay," Kathy said to Lisa. "So are you and Dale going to continue with your affair?"

"No," Lisa explained. "That's the main reason we came over here tonight. To clear the air, and to make sure we can all be friends without any of us thinking anymore about affairs."

"Is that how you feel, Mack. You don't want to have an affair with me?" Kathy wiggled again, then chuckled."Because, you know, I kind of think I might really enjoy having one with you." She turned to Dale. "See, Honey, this affair thing can easy be a two way street." She emphasized her comment by the way she moved on Mack's lap again. She didn't care much if Dale and Lisa had something going. Her life, and her attitude about it, was radically changed while she was going through her separation from Dale.

"I'm no different from Lisa and Dale," Mack said, to answer Kathy's question. "Sure I would. But if any of us does that, life can and will get awful complicated. So I think it's best we don't. Maybe sometime, in the distant future, we'll be able to. Not now. That said, however, we decided a while back that holding hands and occasional kissing would be okay. I think it still should be. I just think we should all be a lot more careful that we don't push it beyond that, the way those two have."

"Good answer," Kathy said. She gave herself another serious wiggle on Mack's lap, then kissed him in a way that said she had special feelings for him that went beyond a simple attraction. "Now I'm going to tell all of you something. To start with, yes, I do love Dale. I love him dearly. I want to keep him my husband forever. But something inside me changed after I did that stupid, terrible thing when I asked him for a divorce. I realized that I needed him as much as I do. But when I came home, there was only one person who didn't judge me at all. Mack just accepted that I'd made a serious mistake, and that I was sick over it. Those first few days, he was nothing but kind. I didn't know him very well when I called him in the middle of the night before I came back. Yet he took the time to talk to me with no judgements. Since then, I've gotten to know him infinitely better, and I've fallen in love with him. Don't worry, Lisa. I couldn't steal him from you even if I wanted to, which I don't. Not yet anyway. But you and Dale better let me be his friend, without you two thinking you need to have an affair because we are friends. Because if you do, be warned. If he leaves you because you want a secret affair with Dale, I damn sure will go with him. No more lies, Guys. Let's all keep it honest. And the honest truth about Mack and me now is the fact that we will continue to walk the refuge together when we can. I will hold his hand. I love holding Mack's hand. Sometimes, when I need to, I will kiss him. But because he is who he is, it will always stop there."

She stood up, then pulled Mack up. She kissed him again. She winked at Lisa, who had a very anxious look about her. "I think," Kathy said, laughing now, "that you two best go home now." She kissed Mack one more time. One that had all the feelings she had for him in it. "Yes, it is time for you guys to go.

Mack has gotten me so horny, it's going to take Dale all night to get me over it."

No one knew what to say at that point. It wasn't that long ago that Kathy would never even have considered saying or doing what she'd just said and done. Dale just stood there with his mouth open, until Kathy took his hand and practically dragged him into the house.

Mack held Lisa's hand as they walked through the meadow on their way home. The full moon gave them more than enough light to follow the path. About halfway, they stopped under a huge old maple, and Mack took her in his arms.

"I won't ever do that with Dale again," she promised. "Not anyway, without talking to you first. I want you to know, I need you so bad, Mack. I'm sorry I was being so stupid."

"It'll be okay now, Lisa. I think we've all learned better, how to live with our feelings." He took her hand again and started walking.

"When I said I needed you so bad, Mack, I wasn't talking about the future. I was talking about right now." Before she finished talking, her jeans were down past her knees. "Don't wait, damnit, don't wait."

He didn't. And he found her nearly perfect young body delightful in the moonlight. They didn't dress again for the rest of their walk home. In bed, they held each other, and breathing heavy, savored the closeness of their bodies. Again, as it was before this night, there was no doubt about their love for each other. Just a lingering curiosity about what the future might have waiting for them.

Along with that, there was still an unanswered question on Lisa's mind. A question she knew she'd need to find an answer for.

CHAPTER 8

Lisa quietly left the bed. Mack was still sleeping, so she was careful to not wake him. She used the bathroom, then took a long hot shower. She needed it. It had been a long night for her, with only a few moments of restless sleep. Most of it was spent remembering the previous evening, and her argument with Mack.

He wanted honest answers from her. Why had she done with Dale the way she did it with him? They'd settled their differences. At least, Mack had. She had managed a compromise, but it still wasn't the real truth. She'd told Mack a lot. More than she wanted to tell him. Yet, when it came to the truth, she didn't actually get close enough to it. The truth was something she'd never told anyone. The truth was, she thought she was turned into some kind of freak by the men who raped her. The refreshed memories of being raped repeatedly the way she was, which were brought on by seeing Jelly Newton, were still having a profound affect on her. Those memories were a huge problem. She was sure she should have gotten past them a long time ago. She felt guilty that she wasn't able to rid herself of them.It was her confused emotions that had driven her too Dale to be comforted. She thought that if she could give herself to him, it would make the memories go away.

Her failure to do it was giving her a feeling she hated. She knew she should share the demons it was creating inside her with someone. After all her talk about sharing her body. All her saying she thought she should be able to do that. She'd never told anyone what she really meant when she said it.

She was scared now. She was going to force herself to tell Mack about it this morning. He might be repelled by her after she did. But she knew now, after last night, that if there was any person who would understand, it would be him. She had to trust him. She knew that talking to Mack wouldn't cure her problem, but it was the hope for the start she needed. The rest would have to somehow work itself out on its own. If it could be worked out. Either way, she knew that Mack would stick by her. All she needed to do was be honest with him. She knew, after all that happened yesterday, that he would understand her better if she finally told him everything.

She crawled back in bed, waking him. She kissed him. "Now, go use the bathroom for what you do in the morning, then take a long hot shower. When you come back, I'm going to be honest with you. The kind of honest you want me to be."

"I thought you were last night."

"Last night was good. Last night I told you a lot of honest things. But I haven't told you the truth yet. I've never told anyone the truth yet. You might not like me so much when I'm done, Mack. But I will finally have been totally honest with you, and I will have told you the truth. More than that. I will have trusted you more than I have ever trusted anyone else."

Mack did what she asked, but wasn't able to make his shower a long one. What she'd told him so far left him too filled with anxiety to wait that long for whatever it was she wanted to tell him.

When he came out of the bathroom, she patted the bed next to where she was sitting up. He joined her on it. She kissed him with all the passion she had in her. She took a couple of very deep breaths. Mack could easily see that what she was about to say, to talk about, was having a strong affect on her. She seemed scared of what she was going to say.

"You don't have to do this, Lisa," he said. "I'm okay with what we talked about last night."

"I'm not though. I was awake most of the night, trying to figure out how to tell you what I really need to tell you."

"Well, whatever it is, I promise you that I won't judge you for it."

"I know that. The closest I ever saw you do that to anyone was also last night, when I was having trouble telling you what went on with me and Dale. And I know now, that was because you were deeply hurt that I was cutting you out of part of my life. I was wrong for doing that. But there's a reason for how I reacted. Right or wrong, I want to tell the reason. A reason that you already sort of know about, but do not yet understand fully."

"I'm sorry, Lisa. I'm sure I don't always understand everything about you. Especially how things that have happened to you have affected you."

"It would be impossible for you to do that. That's why I'm talking to you now." After a couple more deep breaths, she continued. "I'll be surprised if you haven't already guessed that this is all because I was raped the way I was. It's the cause of everything that I've done, that I've been doing, that I shouldn't. At least, not the way I did them. Ever since it happened, the very thought of any man, other than you, trying to have sex with me is a total turn-off. With most men, the thought can literally make sick."

She looked at Mack and lightly touched his cheek. She kissed him, also lightly. She tried to smile, but couldn't quite manage one. "Two other men have managed to get me to the point that I thought I could do it with them. You know how much I loved Dave Sanders. He had Linda's blessing to do with me whatever I would allow him to do. And when we came close to doing it, it was me, and only me who stopped it before we did it. I didn't tell you the truth because I thought I was a freak for not being able to let him."

This time she was surprised by Mack. There was a no look of disgust about him. Only love and compassion. And a couple of lonely tears in his eyes. She dropped her head down, fervently hoping that look would be there when she finished.

"As you know, the other man is Dale. We pretty much followed the holding hands, kissing rule with only occasionally light touching. Until the day I saw Jelly Newton. Everything came back to me. The terror, the hate, and most of all, the feeling that all those filthy men made me into some kind of freak. It felt horrible. I didn't want to be like that. I wanted to be normal. To feel normal. So I started to get more and more aggressive with Dale. Each time I saw him, I would encourage him to go just a little further with me. To touch me more. I just had to know. Could I do it with someone, with anyone other than you. I thought I was some kind of crazy for not being able to. When it came to sex with you, everything was so good. Great, in fact. It never seemed as though I could ever get enough of you, let alone too much. When I'm with you, when we make love, the horror goes away. I know my reactions to you are because of how much I love you. The fact that I find you to be the sexiest man alive doesn't hurt any either. I also know deep in my heart that no matter what I might ever do, there's no way you would ever hurt me. At the same time though, I hated the fact that I felt about all other men the way I feel. It takes so little for you to turn me on. It takes less for most men to turn me off."

This time when she paused, she managed a smile. It was a small smile, but it was there. Mack's look of compassion was still there too, along with his love for her. Something else good for this conversation was happening. She could see that she had his full attention. He definitely wanted to hear everything she had to say.

"Anyway, all that led up to yesterday. You were right. I volunteered to take care of those papers so I could have time with Dale. It was my full intention to have sex with him. By then, I was almost desperate to prove to myself that I was whole. That I wasn't a freak. That I could be a real woman with someone other than you. And it was working. Damn, I was so ready for it. His hands were everywhere and I loved it. I was finally becoming a woman on my own. I was wanting to do it without your loving arms around me. It was the first time since the rape that I felt that way. I was the one who opened my pants and moved them down below my knees. I took his hand, and pushed it between my legs. It felt so good there. Then he moved his fingers and I lost it. I screamed and pushed him away. All of the sudden it was over. I couldn't do it. It was different this time though. It wasn't just because I didn't want him to do it because of the rape. So now the trouble is, I still don't know if I'm a freak or not. If it wasn't just the feeling that I was cheating on you that I suddenly got from him that made me stop, it was still probably the freak thing too. I hate it that I am one. I just want to be normal. It seems like I should have gotten over all this a long time ago. As bad as it might seem, it probably would have been better if I would have finished it with Dale. I think that's most of the reason I couldn't talk to you about it last night."

"So you still want to do it with Dale?"

"Yes. I'm sorry. I know I shouldn't. What happened yesterday between you and me tells me I shouldn't. But I want to know. Who the hell am I. I know I'm normal when I'm with you, but why can't I get past the rape thing? I've wanted to know that for so long now. When I say things like, 'why can't I let him touch me?', it hasn't been what you think. It's never been about what society expects. It's always been about me and the rape and what it did to me."

Mack was seeing her in a different light now. As much as anyone could, he understood her frustration and her confusion. Her life was confusing. The way she consistently responded to him. The fact that she so much enjoyed it. And she did it in ways she couldn't fake. Yet she was tortured from wondering why he was the only one she could do that with. It wasn't that she needed to do it. It was because she wanted to know if she ever could. He wanted to fix her, to make it better. To make her feel whole again. How could that be done? But he knew was a dumb question. She had to have the chance to prove to herself that she wasn't a freak.

"If you could do anything, Lisa, to prove to yourself that you actually are a whole woman, what would you do?"

"I don't know, Mack. I thought I did yesterday, but I proved to myself I can't do it that way."

"What if you got the chance to do it again, but didn't have to feel guilty about it? Would you like to try it?"

"What is this now, Mack? Are you giving me some kind of test?

"No I'm not. It's a real, legitimate question. Do you want to try again?"

"Okay, I'm not sure I like where this is going, but yes. I would very much like to try again if I could do it without the guilt. Without knowing how much I would hurt you if I did. Right now, I just want to be able to look in a mirror and know that I've gotten somewhere beyond what those men did to me. Just once, Mack. That's all I'd need to know that I'm at least on my way to knowing who I am. They hurt me in a lot of ways. Making me feel like freak instead of a real woman was close to the worst of them."

"You mean that you want to be able to do it, just to do it?"

"No. I could never do that. Whoever it was, I would have to have a lot of feelings for them. I'll never have the kind of love for anyone else that I have for you. But it would have to be someone who mattered."

"And that's why you picked Dale."

"Well sure. Like I've told you so many times. He's always been a good friend. To both of us. And if I did it with him, it would just be a thing of him and me sharing something special. There sure wouldn't be a macho male competition about it. But we already settled that last night. It's not to be."

"That was last night. That was before you finally decided that you could talk to me. That was before I could understand what your real problem was. But now that I do, I want you to get it fixed."

"How and when am I supposed to do that?"

"This morning, actually. It's still early enough for everyone to still be home. So I think this is the time. Do you want to take care of it today?"

"Jesus, Mack, I don't understand what you want. How the hell can I fix a problem I've had for years, just because you want me to."

Mack chuckled softly. "By putting on that white blouse of yours. The one that's kind of translucent. No bra. And that full skirt. The one that's too short. Some kind of slip on shoes. As soon as we're dressed, we'll walk over there."

"Are you telling me that you want me to do it with Dale right now? How is that going to work? What about Kathy. Won't she have something to say about it?"

"Probably not. That's a price we'll both have to pay. While you are fixing yourself with Dale, odds are, I will at least be doing some serious fooling around with Kathy. That's the compromise I'm pretty sure she'll want us to make, to let this happen."

"It sounds like you've done it with her before."

"No, I haven't. But she's all but said that she's willing if I am. So I think she'll want at least some serious fooling around. Otherwise, she might object to you and Dale taking care of your problem, even if she doesn't really care what you and Dale do."

"I don't know, Mack. This is an awful big step to take. I don't want this to push us back to where we were when I came home last night."

"For me, what you might do with Dale today isn't the same as what you were doing yesterday. Today makes sense. If it works and you are no longer kept awake by those feelings, that alone makes it worth it. It also is, for now anyway, only a one time thing. When it's over and you come back home to me, it can be like it never have happened, if that's what you want. We can talk about it or not, but that choice is all yours. As far as how it affects the future, we'll have to wait and see how it plays out. Most of all, it won't be a goddamn secret. And it was the secret thing that was bothering me. That, and being pushed out of your life. Today will be both of us. I love you now, and I'll still love you when you come home later."

"Okay, Mack. We can try. Just don't be upset if I fail. Especially don't be upset if it works."

"I'll love you as much either way."

Mack dressed at his normal speed. Lisa dawdled, and he noticed that she watched herself in the mirror as she did. She did her best to take as much time as she could, but she wasn't putting on enough clothes to be able to slow down the process much.

They held hands again as they crossed the meadow. Lisa kept her eyes on the ground. She couldn't look at Mack. More than anything else now, she was embarrassed about what she was doing. She kept her head down when a surprised Kathy answered their door.

"So what brings you guys here a this hour?" she asked. She looked at Lisa, and her eyes widened when she realized how minimally she was dressed. "Is there something special going on, Lisa?"

Mack answered. "Actually, there is. Lisa finally told me what her real problem is. She has some really serious issues, resulting from when she was raped, to be resolved. Lisa needs Dale's help to get past them. When we talked about it this morning, we decided that the sooner she does it, the better."

"Well, he's getting ready to go to work right now."

"That's okay. Would you ask him to come here. We'd sure appreciate it."

Kathy nodded her head yes and went for Dale. He was only dressed as far as his pants when he came to the door. Lisa looked at his bare chest, and in spite of the embarrassment she felt about why she was there, she kind of liked what she saw. It was a good sign. She was starting to anticipate what might happen this day.

Mack knew there was no easy way to say what he had to say, so he just started talking. "This includes all of us," he started. "And it isn't easy for me to come here and talk about it. But I'm going to try. Lisa has a serious problem, stemming from when she was raped. As you learned yesterday, Dale, it does affect what she feels and how she reacts. She desperately needs to prove to herself that she's normal. That she can react positively to a man other than me. She wants you to be that man, Dale. Are you willing?"

"What the hell are you asking me? You sound weird, Mack."

"No, Dale. It's not weird. It'll just be you and Lisa. I don't think I need to explain anything further than that."

"Wait a minute," Kathy said. "What about me? What am I supposed to be doing while they're doing whatever?"

"You'll be with me. We'll be doing our whatever."

"Don't I have anything to say about that?" Dale asked.

"Sure you do," Mack told him. "The same amount that I had to say about what you and Lisa were doing yesterday." He waited until he caught Dale's eye. "It's only for one day. You can live with that, same as I can."

Dale just nodded yes. He stepped outside, and walked up to Lisa. He took her hands. "Is this your idea too?"

"It's Mack's idea, but I like it. Somehow, sometime, I have to get past this. I'll explain it if you want me to. But yes, I do want to do this."

"What about Mack and Kathy. How do you feel about the chance they'll be doing the same thing?"

Lisa giggled. "What I feel most about it is probably terrible. Because the one thing I'd like to do about it is watch them. They're so damn cute together. I bet it won't be that much different than them holding hands. It'll just be like they somehow belong together. Whatever they do, it won't hurt either one of us a damn bit. So are you going to take me inside, or should Mack and I turn around and go home."

Kathy answered the question. She took Mack's hand. "I think it's time we got the hell out of their way, don't you, Mack?"

He squeezed her hand and then held it as they walked across the meadow. She softly hummed a beautiful love song as they walked. It had sold better for her than anything else she ever recorded.

"That song I was humming, Mack," she said as they went in the house, "every time I sing it now, I will always think of you."

"And every time I hear you sing it, I will remember today."

"Good. So now are we going to play the usual games, or are we going to go ahead and do what we both want?"

"What do you think it is that we both want, Kathy?"

She started opening the buttons on her blouse. "The bed. Sex. I want to make love to you Mack Thomas. I want to in the worst way. Since this might be our only legitimate chance, I want to take full advantage of it."

Mack found her to be much the same in bed as she was when she was the woman who loved walking the refuge with him. It was a fun, joyful thing. Full of love and giving and taking. It was playful, and they were able to repeat it.

Hours later, when they thought it was time to return her home and reclaim Lisa, they knew that if they didn't have the partners they had, they could easily join together for a lifetime. So their walk through the meadow was happy for what they shared, but sad for what was ending. Even so, they knew they'd experienced a new beginning. It hadn't taken anything away from any of them. It had only added a new dimension to their lives.

Dale and Lisa were waiting for them when they got there. They were both quiet, but seemed to be contented with the day they had. Not much was said when Dale took Kathy in his arms and kissed her. Mack did the same to Lisa and they quietly left. They were silent as they held hands while walking through the meadow.

"I'm going to tell you about it, Mack," she said when they got home. "And even if you don't want me too, let me."

"Okay, Lisa. Whatever you want."

"It worked, Mack. I don't feel so much like a freak now. Dale made me feel all those things I didn't think I could. But something happened that I never expected to happen. Do you want to know what it was?"

"It depends. If you've fallen in love with Dale and want to leave me, no, I don't want to hear it."

"I didn't, so I guess I'll tell you. We did everything the way I guess everyone else does. It surprised me when it happened. We weren't even undressed all the way. All of the sudden he brought me to the point that I did it. I had an orgasm. Since I was raped, the only time I've been able to do it has been with you. No other way. He looked at me when it happened, shook his head, and stopped what he was doing. I was still turned-on, still ready for him to keep going. I would have liked it if he did. But when he stopped like that, I was, in a way, glad that he did. We didn't do anything more. What Dale said to me then was…"

"It looks like we've accomplished what we were supposed to. You now know you can do what you thought you couldn't do. You learned what you needed to know. Going any further when we don't need to prove anything more, isn't right for us. Not today it isn't. You and I are friends. Really good friends. But we aren't lovers. So for this time, we should stop now. Our first time shouldn't be so calculated. We'll finish when the timing is better."

She gave Mack a big smile. "So we stopped what we were doing."

"That must have been awful rough on him, leaving him hanging like that."

"Well, it could have been." She couldn't keep herself from having a soft chuckle. Then in a sheepish voice she said, "But I couldn't do that to him, so I helped him with my hand. He watched my eyes while I did it for him." She chuckled again. "But still, the main thing is, we didn't go all the way. I'm still, technically anyway, all yours. And that's what I'm going to stay. The only thing that will change that, is if I find out I have to finish it with him. When, like Dale said, the timing is better. If that happens, I will tell you before I do it, and I really do expect you to understand."

Now Mack felt truly guilty. And it showed. "I'm sorry, Lisa. I wasn't so well behaved. I'm afraid Kathy and I did do it. It was something we both wanted. There was no way then that I would have believed you wouldn't. Most of all though, it seemed like the right thing for us to do. You've talked a lot about sharing. This time, Kathy and I shared."

"That's okay, Mack. Both Dale and I figured you would. He said to tell you that he knows it's different for you and Kathy. He and I are really just good friends. You and Kathy are in love. I think it's even more than that. She isn't just someone for you to love. She brings something of Linda back into your life. And somehow, in some way, you do the same for her. Plus, Linda is still an influence on both of you. And in Linda's world, what you and Kathy did is what normal should be. So it's okay. He even said that it was probably a good thing for Kathy. He said they'd both been way too uptight for too long. It would be good for her to finally let loose. He wasn't at all upset. He knows that their life has changed since she asked him for a divorce. That when he didn't respond to her right away when she went back to him, it changed her."

"But don't you feel kind of cheated?" Mack asked. "I did it and you didn't."

"No. It's me with you now. You're mine again. You are what I need, Mack. You always have been. When I was with Dale, I realized that what you and I have is better than normal. And it wasn't just what those evil men did to me that made it seem impossible to respond to men. It was also partly you. You did something to the way I felt about that part of life the first time I ever saw you. Now you fulfill me to the point that nothing else seems right. Maybe the day will come when I want or need more, but that day isn't here now. You and Kathy share that beautiful refuge you love so much. But you are *my refuge*. No one shares with you the way I do."

CHAPTER 9

Mack, Lisa, Paul, Roy, and Wanda were getting ready to leave the sheriff's office when Dale got the call. "I'm on my way," he said just moments after he answered it. "Something real weird is going on at the high school," he said to them. "You know I wouldn't normally do this, but why don't you guys meet me there? If it's what I think it is, I might need you to provide me with some backup."

They were surprised by his request. They'd just finished up with the reports for the FBI, relating to their attempting to turn Wanda over to her ex-husband, and were planning on going home. And it was very unusual for Dale to ask for a civilian's help with an official matter. Not to mention against someone's rule somewhere.

Given that it was Dale asking, they didn't hesitate. Rules or no rules. There was no question about whether they would assist him. They'd driven to the office in three vehicles, and they did the same on the drive to the high school.

It was in total chaos when they got there. A half dozen town cops were there, along with four sheriff's deputies. They weren't the problem. The problem was the men in the red hats. Trump MAGA hats. They were all heavily armed, and trying mightily to herd students who were outside the building into groups. What kind of groups it was impossible to tell. But into groups, nonetheless.

Dale looked around at the confusion, trying to see if he could pick out a leader. His eyes finally landed on Jelly Norton.

Titus Trump, who was too big to move well enough to take part in their game, wasn't there. At the same time Dale picked Jelly Norton out, so did Lisa. She knew that it was the MAGA Fellows with the red hats who were the problem. Dale approached Jelly. So did Lisa. Mack wasn't far behind.

"What in the hell is going on here?" Dale demanded. "What do you people think you're doing?"

"We are only doing our constitutional duty. There have been reports that some of these students are being taught about abortion. As you know, abortion is now illegal in this country. The supreme court has declared it so. That means teaching children how to have one is a crime. We are attempting to arrest the guilty parties."

"So who the hell do you think are the guilty parties?"

"The teachers teaching that abomination called abortion. And the sinful students wanting to learn about such an evil thing."

Lisa was close enough to them to hear the conversation. That meant she was close enough to Jelly Norton to see the smirk on his face. At any time it probably would have been something she could tolerate. But after all that she'd been through in the past twenty-four hours, with Mack especially, but Dale and Kathy too, his smirk was more than she could handle. All that had happened between her and them was a direct result of her being raped years ago. Jelly was one of the rapists. Under any circumstances, she could do nothing but hate him. With him here, raising hell at the high school, she now had an excuse. She wasn't about to wait for some other opportune time. She could, and decided that she definitely would, take him out. Fight him fair? Hell no. Simply take him out. He deserved nothing better.

Everyone she was with, along with Dale, were aware of how close she was to Jelly, but none of them was ready to try to control her yet. If they didn't want her to do what she was going to do, they should have. But because of the chaos going on, no one was much concerned about what Lisa might do to Jelly Norton.

She walked up to him until she was inches from him. "Teaching abortion ain't illegal, you fucking asshole," she snarled, making sure she spit in his face as she did. "So I'm giving you exactly one minute to get yourself and your herd of toy-boy clowns to pack it up and get the living hell out of here."

He laughed. "So what is a tiny little girl like you going to do about it if I don't?"

"I'm going to beat the shit out of you," she snarled some more, spitting again. "I'm going to hurt you so you can never commit another rape for the rest of the short life you have left. Then, when you get out of the hospital, I'm going to kill you."

He laughed some more, then moved to grab her. It was exactly what she expected him to do. She slammed the palm of her hand into his nose with all the force she could put into it. She knew it was possible to kill him, hitting him that hard, but at that moment didn't care if she did.

Blood erupted from his face and he staggered back, unable to defend himself. She went after the obvious target. The one she most wanted to damage. She kicked him in the testicles as hard as she could kick. She was wearing her pointed toe western boots, so the kick did the maximum damage. It also doubled him over.

Dale grabbed her then, trying to stop her attack. She turned on him. "I've waited years for this. He's one of them. So back the fuck off. There's no way I can really do to him what he's got coming." Dale let her go and backed off. Whatever happened now, he was in her corner. If he was one of the rapists, she was right. She couldn't hurt him enough. Besides, he was actually enjoying watching her beat the living hell out of Jelly. He was well aware of all the insanity going on in America, and Jelly Norton was a perfect example of that insanity. Including the fact that people like him and Donald Trump raped little girls.

Lisa turned back to Jelly. he was now sitting on the ground, both hands hanging on between his legs, even though blood was still pouring from his face. She filled her right hand with his hair and snapped his head back hard.

"You don't remember me, do you, you useless slime bag." He looked at her, too stunned to answer. She held his head back and slapped him hard across the face a couple of times. "You raped me, and now you are going to pay for it. I said I would hurt you, and now I'm going to."

She stepped back and kicked him in the chest. He flew over backward so hard that his hands flew into the air. That left him open again, and she again slammed her boot between his legs. He screamed. She was tempted to stomp down on his hands so he couldn't hold himself, but the horrible anger that filled her when she started had abated.

"He's yours now, Dale. But I want him arrested for rape of a minor. And don't give me any crap about it being too long since the crime and too late to prosecute. If you can't, I want him in custody, under guard, until he gets out of the hospital. If I have to, I will see to it that he is punished for what he did to me then."

"He hasn't been punished enough already?"

"Absolutely not, Dale. For me, that was just a small start. And I will want to talk to him, when he can talk. He might know where I can find some of the other men who were part of it."

"What if he does? What will you do to them?"

"Hurt them. You know me well enough now to know why. Especially after what you and I have just been through."

"Yes, Lisa, I do. Now how about we try to round up all of these jerks with the red hats. They are disrupting the school day here."

Lisa looked at Mack then. "Thank you," was all she said. then she went with him through the school, telling the Fellows they'd better leave in a hurry if they didn't want to be arrested. Only about five of them demanded the right to find the abortion teachers. Dale arrested them.

The rest of them returned to their meeting place and their leader, Titus Trump. He was less than happy with them. He became furious when he learned the fate of Jelly Norton.

"How could all of you people stand by while he was being beaten? How could you let a gang of men attack him and not defend him? I don't understand."

No one answered him. So he screamed, "How in heavens name could you do it. Please tell me? He was your leader."

Finally, a small man near the back of the room answered him. "He wasn't beaten by a bunch of men. A woman did it."

"What the hell do you mean, a woman did it?"

"Just that. A woman. She all of the sudden lit into him. It seemed like it was over before anyone could even take a deep breath, he was on his ass and she was looking at him like she was near ready to kill him."

"A woman? How could a mere woman whip Jelly Norton. He was the best, the toughest among us. There's got to be something wrong with what you're saying. I can't believe there's a woman alive who could do that."

"There was," Lance North told him. He started by talking about Lisa, but he was thinking more about Wanda. Being a FBI informant didn't stop him from using these guy to help him get his revenge on Wanda and her relatives. "I know about her. Her name is Lisa Thomas. She used to be a deputy sheriff. She's married to a man named Mack Thomas. He used to be a deputy sheriff. There was a second woman there too. Her name is Wanda Thomas. Married to Roy Thomas. They are all bad people. They work at a detective agency called Refuge Rescuers. You want to do something to make this country a better place? The kind of place Donald Trump wants it to be? I say that we should bomb their office. If we do it some morning, we might get lucky and kill them all. The more dead, the better life will be."

"Well, we are past due making a significant statement backing our belief in a truly free America. So bombing them might be a good start. Our abortion protest certainly isn't going to do much."

"I wasn't there for it," Lance said, "but you are right, it didn't do much. One other thing though. A thing I think it might say even more. If we capture those women from that detective agency instead of killing them right away. That Lisa person should be first, of course. Then that Wanda one. I heard she was really pushy when they were rounding up our guys at the school. Like all of them liberal women are. Damn fools think they should have the same rights as a man. It won't hurt either, if we can do it without too much trouble, to grab the other two women who work in the agency. One of them is real young. We could maybe teach her what a real man is about, then let her go to tell them goddamn liberals what is really what in this world."

"You know," Titus agreed, the thought of raping a young girl starting to arouse him, "I think you might have hit on a good idea. First thing tomorrow, we should start checking out all those people. We can first use all their woman to teach them what real men are. Then we will bomb them all to hell."

CHAPTER 10

When the five MAGA Fellows went before a judge for a bail hearing, they got lucky and drew a Trump judge. Since he was following the party line, he was against abortion. Which was actually only part of his belief on that subject. He was against all and any form of birth control. He believed that if a man and a woman had sex, they should attempt to have a child each time. Nothing they did should deviate from that mission. And he included everyone on earth in that opinion. Everyone other than he and his mistress.

He also considered all of the paramilitary groups filling various niches around the county, to be America's best patriots. So he set bail for each of the men at only fifty dollars each. He also demanded that Dale immediately release Jelly Norton from jail.

"I can't do that," Dale told him.

"You have to. I'm a judge and I just ordered you to."

"Orders or not," Dale smiled. He was enjoying the fact that he was aggravating the judge. "It's impossible for me to release Jelly Norton from jail right now."

"I insist that you do what I tell you to do, if you don't want to be found in contempt of court, and thrown in jail."

"Even if you do that, *Judge*, he won't be released from jail."

"I've just about had enough of you," the judge barked. "I want that man released."

"Again, I can't release him from jail. It's physically impossible to do it."

"How can that be? What's wrong with your jail?"

"It's not my jail. It belongs to the county."

"It doesn't matter. He needs to be set free."

"That I can do, *Judge*. As soon as the doctors treating him are willing to release him. And, of course, he has his bail hearing."

"What's this about doctors? What have doctors got to do with this case?"

"He's in the hospital. He was seriously beaten up."

"Well, I certainly hope you arrested those people who did it."

"No, I haven't. And there was only one."

"Why the hell haven't you arrested him?" The judges voice was getting shaky now. He had put more effort into questioning Dale than he'd put into anything for quite awhile. Other than bedding his mistress.

"I didn't arrest him, because he is a she. And she swore out a warrant for his arrest. He raped her several years ago. So she was a little rough when she put him into the condition that made it safer for me to arrest him."

"If he's in the hospital, how rough is a little rough?"

"Other than his thoroughly broken nose, both of his testicles might need to be removed. The doctors aren't sure yet whether they can save them."

"That sounds horrible. She should be in jail for what she did to him."

"After what he did to her, I don't think so. She was completely justified in doing what she did to him."

"But she may have destroyed his ability to be a whole man." the judge rolled his eyes up in his head to illustrate what a horrible thing it was that Lisa did. "That's far worse than just raping someone. I'm ordering you to arrest her."

"Number one, Judge, you don't have the authority to order me to do that. Two, if he never regains his manhood, it's a good thing. He won't breed any children."

The judge stood up from his throne. "I should find you in contempt for your insolence alone. But I'm going to be generous today, and let you walk out of here." he grimaced and bit his lower lip. "But you keep it in mind. If you continue to try to punish

Jelly Norton for what is probably a false accusation, it could cause some serious repercussions in the future."

The judge then left the courtroom. It was all Dale could do to keep from lifting his middle finger as he watched him go. The assistant DA next to him finally smiled after the Judge was gone.

"It takes a lot of guts to aggravate a judge the way you just did. But the odds are, he's going to get even somewhere along the line. Do you really think it was worth it?"

"Who the hell knows. But given the way our justice system is going to hell with all the newly appointed conservative judges, I have to wonder if anything is much worth it anymore."

"I agree that it sure can be frustrating," the DA agreed. "The liberal judges we used to have, tended to grab onto technicalities a little too quickly. But these assholes. They don't seem to give a rat's ass about the law at all when they make their decisions. And as far as the constitution goes, they not only don't know diddly about ours, I don't think most of them even know what one is. And even if they do know something, they don't care a damn about what it says. It's the party line that matters to them. Not what's right."

"Yeah, and in the meantime, I think you and I better keep at it. We need to do what we can to stop them. We don't, and before we know it, there won't be much of anything left."

When Dale finally got outside, the dirty, exhaust filled air felt good. Nearly anything would have beaten the corrupt air of the courtroom he'd just escaped from.

He thought about what he'd just done to the judge. He knew that he'd pushed against the stupidity of him harder than he he should have, if playing it safe was what he wanted. It wasn't though. He was done with the idea that it was almost always best to stay within the guidelines. No matter what the circumstances were or what the guidelines for that particular time were.

His whole life was changed now, and so was he. His personal life had taken so many twists and turns recently, that it was difficult for him to keep track of them. The biggest change was his relationship with his wife, Kathy. In some ways, they were closer than ever. In others, they'd lost some of the sharing things with each other they once had.

The main change that felt strange was in bed. She was always somewhat reserved for most of their married life. It wasn't so much that she ever said no, as it was that she always seemed reluctant to show much in the way of enthusiasm. She was the opposite now, and was actually starting to wear him down. So much so, that he was beginning to doubt that he was going to be able to keep up with her much longer.

Other things, like her calling him after one of her concerts, were not the same. Now when she called to tell him about it, it felt to him that she no longer cared much if it mattered to him or not. Often he got the feeling from her, that the concerts themselves had lost much of their importance to her. There were many other day to day things that felt the same way. The thing holding them together though, was the fact that mixed in with those feelings was the way she so often tried to simply show him that she loved him as much as she ever did. And that she needed him even more.

There was a third thing though, that kept him thinking and wondering more than anything else. Their relationship with Mack and Lisa. Because of a problem Lisa had stemming from the time she was kidnapped and raped, they'd taken their relationship as far as it was possible to take it.   They'd solved Lisa's problem, but they'd also changed their relationship.

He wasn't surprised that Mack had dealt with what Lisa did with patience, love, and understanding. That was who and what Mack was. Aways considering the other person ahead of himself.

What surprised Dale the most was his own reaction. In the past, he was very jealous when it came to Kathy. So much so that when she wanted his forgiveness for her mistake when she asked for a divorce, when she desperately needed that forgiveness and wanted so much to be welcomed back in his arms, he'd hesitated too long. So long that he almost lost her. This time, when she actually did go all the way with Mack, while he and Lisa were solving her problem, she didn't ask for anything from him because of it. She expected him to accept it. He did, and in doing so he discovered that he wasn't at all jealous. Not even about the fact that she and Mack were, in their own strange way, in love with each other. He also knew that because none of them planned on a repeat of what happened that day, it was easier to accept.

His job was also different for him now. More than ever, he wanted to be the absolute best sheriff anyone could be. But he was done playing any kind of games to keep the job. From now on, he intended to what he believed to be the right thing, rather than what some parts of the voting public, or the county commissioners might expect. If that meant he could lose an election, so be it. He knew he could always go to work for Refuge Rescuers. He still considered Mack to be his best friend, and was sure Mack felt the same way about him.

Overall, he was satisfied with his own personality changes. And with the changes in his life. He even planned to make more of them. He'd always known and respected the boundaries the sheriff's department was given. He believed that he and everyone who was part of it should basically follow the letter the law. Even when it might cost them.

Not anymore though. The political climate had reached the point, that it was becoming close to impossible to maintain the peace and safety of the community if he and his department continued to be as ridged as they were in the past. There were what seemed like endless problems created by Trump and his imbecilic followers. One of the worst of them was the untold numbers of paramilitary militias being formed across the country.

The MAGA Fellows that he'd just had to deal with in court were the most prominent of them in Clayborne County at the moment. Dale had recently learned that Refuge Rescuers were planning on interrupting one of their meetings in the near future.

Dale was now planning to join them in their effort. When he first considered doing it, he thought he'd go along in civilian clothes and participate as an ordinary citizen. But after the results in court today, he changed his mind. He was going to go dressed in full sheriff's uniform and make it an official visit. He also decided to offer the option to go to about a half dozen of his most loyal deputies.

So he called Mack and asked him to meet at Katies Kafe for a late afternoon cup of coffee. Mack was more than happy to meet him. It would be the first time the two of them got together alone for a very long time, and Mack figured it would be a good time to talk about relationships, along with whatever it was that Dale wanted to talk about.

When they first met, they shook hands, but didn't seem to know what to say to each other. It was almost as if there was some kind of physical barrier between. Normally, in this kind of situation, Mack would have been the one to break the ice and start the conversation. This time, to the surprise to both of them, it was Dale.

He leaned back in his chair, smiled at Mack, and said, "the hell with it. I know this is a hard thing for either one of us to say, but all that happened, well damnit, it happened. There's no changing it. The thing is, I don't yet understand why, but I'm okay with it. I know you and Kathy have something special between you. I know it's something, at least for right now, that you can't share all of with Lisa and I. As long as you two don't try to take the wrong kind of advantage of it, I'm okay with it. As far as what happened between Lisa and I early on, before we all knew what was going on with her, I apologize for it. I was out of line."

"I wasn't upset so much with what you are doing," Mack said. "Life is what it is and things happen. What upset me is the way you two were trying to hide it. But it's all out in the open now, so as far as I'm concerned, all that's left to do is get on with our lives. You and Lisa have a strong friendship which should continue. It's good for both of you. Kathy and I have what we have. I'm not exactly sure what it is, but whatever it is, we want to keep it. And yes, in the future, we'll behave properly."

Dale laughed at Mack's last line. "Properly, Mack? Okay, but if there's ever any kind of truth to be told, don't forget how important honesty can be."

"That's something I'm not likely to forget. Not as much as I value it in others. But now that we've got that settled, you called me to talk. I'm assuming it was about something other than our wives."

"It most definitely is. I've heard that you, along with the rest of Refuge Rescuers, are planing to pay those MAGA Fellows a visit during one of their meetings in the near future."

"Where did you hear that?"

That was one question Dale didn't want to answer. For the moment, it would compromise someone he wanted to keep anonymous. "If you don't mind too much, Mack, I prefer to not say. At least not yet. But because of our relationship, I want to assure you that it wasn't Lisa."

"Okay, I can let that slide. For now anyway. As long as you don't plan on trying to stop us."

"No, I sure don't. I think it's a good idea. So good in fact, that I want to come along."

"I assume that if you do that, Dale, it will be without your uniform. I can't imagine you wanting to get your department involved with something like that."

Dale shrugged at Mack's comment. "The truth is, that's exactly what I do want to do. I want to go along on your raid as the sheriff of Clayborne County. I also plan on bringing anywhere from four to six deputies with me."

"Won't that put you in a bit of a compromised position. It could get you fired. Or you might piss off the public enough so that you don't get reelected."

Dale shrugged again. "If that happens, so be it. I'll go to work for you. A lot has changed for me, Mack, since Kathy asked me for a divorce. All I want out of life now is the chance to do the right thing. And doing the right thing includes going after creeps like those MAGA Fellows. No matter who does or doesn't like it. I no longer believe that I need to tow the line. No matter who expects me to. So I'm not going to be near so rigid about things. Not on the job and not in my personal life. You and I have been friends for a long time. You know me pretty well. So you know that it wasn't that long ago that I'd have gone near nuts if what's happened to the four of us now happened then. I still know right from wrong. But the world has tilted just enough for me, that the lines between them have blurred some."

"And you know me well enough, Dale, to know that there's no one I'd rather have along than you. I just don't want you to jeopardize your career to help us. What you do as sheriff is important. Even more for the community than for you personally. So I should tell you no. But as totally fucked up as these kind of things are, I'll be very happy to have you part of it. If we are ever going to bring some common sense back to this abortion of a society created by that useless Trump and his zombie followers, we are going to have to seriously deal with all the MAGA Fellow types out there."

Dale finally smiled. "Good, I'll be looking forward to our visit to the MAGA Fellows meeting."

When they got up to leave, Dale did something he'd never done before. Instead of shaking Mack's hand, he gave him a quick hug. Mack knew then, that even with all that had happened, they were still the best of friends.

CHAPTER 11

Simply because he enjoyed doing it, Mack watched Lisa dress. It didn't matter whether she was dressing or undressing, watching her perfect body aroused him every time. This time, she surprised him when she put on a bra. Normally, she only wore one when she was working out.

She knew he was watching her, and that he would be curious about it. "I know, Mack," she said, "that you're wondering about it. It's a sports bra. It holds everything in place when I'm really active. Like when I'm working out. I might need that tonight."

"Why? We're only going to visit the creeps. You already put Jelly Norton in the hospital, so there won't be any need to start any fights tonight."

"Maybe not. But then, it doesn't hurt to be ready for whatever might come."

"You wouldn't be planning to start something tonight, would you?"

"Now, Mack, would I do something like that?"

"You sure would."

Lisa shook her head no, but her eyes said that she was hoping to do exactly that. "I guess we'll just have to wait and see."

Mack knew that it would be a wasted effort to try to convince her to not start something. Jelly Norton was the second in command of the MAGA Fellows militia. Even so, he was still a rapist. All the members of the militia were his associates, so as far as she was concerned, they were, likely as not, rapists too. Even if she wasn't one of their victims, it still meant that she wouldn't at all mind kicking the shit out of at least a few of them. So she wore the bra to hold everything in place while she did the kicking.

"You know, Lisa," Mack told her, "that when I have the privilege of watching you dress, it always makes me want to undress you. Which is exactly what I'd be trying to do right now, if we didn't have all those people waiting for us."

She responded to his comment with a broad smile. "When we get home tonight, I promise I'll let you do that. All by yourself, with no help at all from me."

Mack took her in his arms, kissed her, and then took her hand to lead her outside to his truck. Their mood quickly changed as they got in the truck and started toward their destination. Dale was already there when they arrived, organizing people as they joined their group. Mack was more than pleased to see him doing it. His uniform lent him the authority he needed to get the disorganized, untrained group that was there organized. His skill at putting everyone in the right place was superior to anyone else's.

Once they were all gathered together in some kind of controllable fashion, he started them walking the block they needed to get to the MAGA meeting. All their vehicles were in an empty parking lot, close enough to be noticed by normal people. But this was a meeting of MAGAs, so they weren't aware enough of their surroundings to notice the dozen or so vehicles in the lot. They were too busy admiring each other, dressed up in their playtime soldier clothes, to pay any attention to anything going on around them.

The main door to the MAGA Fellow's meeting hall was open, and there were no guards there, so Dale led the procession following him inside. Once there, they moved in a circle until they surrounded the seventy-five or so men sitting in rapt attention, listening to their leader, Titus Trump.

As expected, Titus did not like or appreciated the intrusion. "What do you people think you are doing? This is a private meeting. You have no business here."

"That's your opinion, not mine," Dale said, moving to the dais, and pushing Titus to the side. It was no easy feat, given that he weighed near three hundred fifty pounds. Dale glared at the MAGAs for a moment before he started talking. They were already restless, but weren't trying to do anything to stop Dale from speaking. They were aware this time, of the large number of guns pointed at them. All of their rifles and shotguns were piled in a small room next to the one they were in.

"We are here," Dale began, "to warn you about pulling any more crap like you did at the high school. We will not be tolerating any of that kind of nonsense from you again. There are a lot of ways for us to retaliate against traitors and dip twits like the bunch of you. And that is exactly what we will do if you pull anymore of your terrorist bullshit."

Dale paused and waved too Lisa, just as they'd previously agreed to do. She joined him, then lifted her middle finger to the group. Dale spoke again. "To give you and idea of our true strength, I want you to take a good look at this young lady. You can see her size. I'm sure that there isn't a single one of you who doesn't think you could do whatever it is you want to do to her, whenever you want to do it. You are wrong if you are foolish enough, if you are stupid enough, to think that way. She's the one who put your mindless, idiot leader into the hospital. She did it with her bare hands and a little help from her feet." He motioned for her to go back where she was standing next to Mack.

"It should be obvious to all of you, that given her size, she isn't the toughest among us. Yet, if I turned her loose, there isn't a one of you boy-toy soldiers whose ass she couldn't kick."

He was quickly interrupted by a chorus of, "Let me at her. Ain't no way she can kick my ass. She's just a fucking bitch. I can take her." and finally, "You assholes are full of shit. You wouldn't dare let her take on one of us. You dan't want that pretty face all fucked up."

That was enough for Lisa. They were requesting it, so as far as she was concerned, what she was about to do was completely legitimate. She again stood next to Dale.

"What I want to know, before I take on the first of you pissant jokes claiming to be men, is who of you is the best friend of Jelly Norton?" Three men raised their hands. She gave them a grim smile. "Okay, who wants to be first?" She stepped away from Dale.

All three of the men were shocked by her response to them. So shocked that they are hesitant to make a move. They were all told that Norton was put in the hospital by a woman, but they'd all assumed that she would have been some kind of Amazon to do it. Now they were faced with Lisa, who they'd been sure just moments ago was a fake. But her confidence was unmistakeable.

Lisa could see from their faces that they were all losing their supreme confidence in their own abilities to fight. She was sure now, that those abilities were only a piece of typical macho ignorance. It was highly unlikely that any of them had any training. So she decided to teach them, along with the rest of the rather feeble Fellows, a lesson.

She walked to the three men, sitting at one side of the group. Without hesitation, she slammed both hands on the shoulders of the man closest hard enough to tip his chair over. As soon as he landed on his back, she reached down and tweaked his nose as hard as she could. He screamed and the blood flow immediately started. Before anyone could react, she grabbed the second man by the hair, snapped his head back, and slammed the palm of her right hand under his chin, then kicked him his the chest hard enough to also tip his chair over.

The third good friend of Jelly Norton was now leaving his chair, trying desperately to get away from Lisa. She laughed at him as he did. Then she pointed at him and said to the mighty Fellows, "He's peed his pants. Probably shit them too." She looked around the room. "So now, which one of you macho assholes is next?" None of them responded. "That's about what I thought. Ain't a one of you with anything that comes near having any balls. You and your boy-toy soldier outfits. Each and everyone of you are nothing more than a real small time, chickenshit joke." She rejoined Mack.

Dale spoke up again. "What you just witnessed is only a small example of the kind of retribution you will be facing if any of you get out of line. You'll all have a better life if you remember that. And if any of you ever go after any of the women here tonight, I can promise I will come after you and I will catch you. When I do, don't count on me arresting you."

He was about to walk away when he noticed a man at the back of the group. He was slouched down in his chair and had his MAGA hat pulled down low over his his face. It was Lance North. Dale wasn't sure what to do about him. For a few moments, he considered ignoring him. But Dale found that impossible to do. After what he put Roy and Wanda through, he couldn't let him off.

He looked around until he found where she was. When their eyes met, he said, "Wanda," then pointed at Lance.

Her eyes lit up the instant she saw him. She considered telling the MAGA Fellows who and what he was, but decided to keep the FBI out of what they are doing on this night. It would have to be enough for her to do to him, what Lisa did to the first two macho men. Lance really didn't think Wanda had either the skill or the courage to do anything to him when she approached him. He was too much bigger than she was. So he sat there with his arms crossed as she approached him. His face registered total shock when his chair went over backward. It registered mostly pain when she finished with him.

She then leaned over, close to his face and said, "If you ever try to fuck with me or Roy again, the next time I'm going to beat you so bad I might kill you. And no, I won't go to jail for it. There are too many places to bury you. Places where they won't ever find the body."

She walked away from him them, and began to assist in the examining of the many guns they found on the MAGAs and in the room where they kept them during their meetings.

Dale asked his group what they wanted to do with the assault rifles. All the options were discussed, and they decided in the end to just disable them. So they did. To the point that the repair costs would come close to buying them new. Dale told the MAGAs that they could do either one, but that he would be back to disable them again.

They confiscated the hand guns that anyone had, but didn't have a permit to carry it. The ones they didn't take with them, they unloaded and took the bullets with them.

When they left the MAGA meeting, they did it in the opposite order from what they entered the place. When they got to the parking lot where all their vehicles were parked, Dale had them circle around him.

"I'd like to hear what you guys think about what we did tonight. Was it enough, too much, or would you all have liked to do more?"

Bob Anderson was the first to speak up. "I think what we did to them was enough for now. At least they're aware that there are a lot of people who aren't about to sit back and let them do whatever they want. That said, I think you let Lisa push too hard. They're going to hate her now, and that means they might go after her. That worries me."

Lisa had full respect for her father, but she couldn't let his comments stand without explaining why she did whaat she did. "I understand your concern, Dad, but it wasn't a matter of them letting me go too far. It was all me. I wanted an excuse to go after some of them. When the creeps gave me the opening, I took it. I'll do it again, every chance I get. For me, it's payback time. And there's no way I can pay them back as much as they so justly deserve."

Bob considered arguing with her more, but knew it would be fruitless in this time and place. Besides, part of him knew she was right.

"I like the fact," Paul said, "that it was Lisa and Wanda who did the ass kicking. According to those guys, women are useless for anything but taking care of their home and fulfilling their sexual gratification. Tonight should be a good lesson for them."

"All I can say about what we did tonight," Julie said, "is that I want more than ever to be like my sister. After what I watched her do tonight, I'm going to be working twice as hard in my training to be a cop. If women everywhere were more like Lisa, we damn sure wouldn't have so many men practicing their sexual harassment."

The next comment came from an unexpected source. Theresa said, "It was a good thing what we did, going there. Even if it means we set them off or made them more determined to do their evil, they know now that we, all of us being we men or women, will stand up to them."

"It was a good start," Mack said.

One block away the discussion was far more muted. The general feeling among the MAGA Fellows, was that they were embarrassed by the way they were so easily controlled. And by a group made up of a lot of women. It was true that they had people with authority with them. But four of the six sheriff's deputies were women. All of their fighting was done by women who soundly defeated their own men. One of them so bad he needed to go home to clean the shit out of his pants. And he wasn't even touched, let alone injured in anyway.

Titus Trump was so shocked by the ordeal he'd just been put through that he wasn't able to speak. It was Lance North who finally did all the talking.

"Okay, Guys," he practically yelled to get their attention. "The problem is simple. Those goddamned women. What we got to do now is get ahold of them, one by one, and use 'em until they bleed. Then we use 'em some more. When we get done with 'em, we cut their guts out and leave the bodies for that goddamn sheriff to find."

Only a few in the bunch of pseudo soldiers answered his brave proposal. They were comments like, "You bet, cause like they sure won't do nothin' about it." Or, "You bet. 'Cause we all know how good a fight you put up tonight."

When they broke up for the night, they were like a bunch of teenage boys who were just turned down by the pretty little girl they'd just asked to dance. Their heads were hanging low as they left for home.

There were, however, twelve men who felt differently. Three of them were men Lisa had taken on and beaten. They were all willing to follow Lance's lead now, and go after the women. They decided that it didn't matter who or what they were, there was no way any of those women could defend themselves against thirteen strong men. Not if they went after them one at a time.

CHAPTER 12

It was the Saturday morning they'd been looking forward to for a while. Kathy did concerts three weekends in a row, so she was constantly busy with them that whole time. Along with that, to keep promises she'd made to Dale she spent all her time the weekend before the concerts started and the weekend after they ended with him.

The concerts were a very gratifying experience for her. All three were filled with sellout crowds who made no secret of the fact that they loved her music and that she was as popular as ever. She also enjoyed and appreciated her time with Dale. They didn't do anything special, but they seemed as though they grew closer from the time they spent alone together. But she looked forward anyway, to this Saturday she would be spending with her extra special friend, Mack Thomas. Walking the refuge.

Mack felt the same way. He lived a full, busy life, filled with satisfying work. Even better was his time spent alone with Lisa. She was a fun, intelligent woman who with him, always seemed to want to give more than she got. And even though she was a still somewhat troubled from the kidnapping and multiple rapes she suffered when she was only sixteen, it all went away when she was alone with Mack. Other than the fact that she was deeply in love with him, even she didn't understand why there was such a radical difference in her relationship with him, compared to other men.

All four of them, Dale, Kathy, Lisa, and Mack were happy with their lives. All four of them often spent time together, and always enjoyed it. And since they only lived a few hundred yards apart, it was easy for them to do.

But great as all that was, Dale and Lisa occasionally enjoyed time together alone. Often, they worked in the sheriff's office, with Lisa assisting Dale with the task of keeping it organized. On rare occasions they'd go out to eat. They went to the movies a couple of times. But after the second time, they came close to breaking the rule they had about touching. They did some of what was allowed and kissed each other, but that led to Dale's hand landing in the wrong place. Lisa removed it, and after they decided that movies weren't such a good idea. For them that decision was relatively easy. They did have a definite physical attraction for each other, but their emotional attraction was more of a friendship than it was romantic.

For Kathy and Mack, they almost always did the same thing when they were alone together. They hiked the trails in the refuge. She didn't have the same deep feelings for the place he did, but when she was there with him, she loved it. She felt freer there than anyplace else. Almost as if she could fly to some far away land filled with peace and love. A place where she could be totally free with Mack, without hurting anyone by doing it.

She always held his hand while they walked, and only let go of it if they stopped to look at something up close. If it was an animal or bird or anything off in the distance, She squeezed his hand when they stopped, then leaned tight against him. She almost always kissed him when they were ready to start walking again.

On this warm, late spring day she was wearing her usual somewhat tight jeans and a light weight cotton blouse. They started their walk in the early hours that morning, and the air carried a chill. So she wore a sweater too. But now it had warmed enough to make the sweater uncomfortable. She took it off and used the arms of it to tie it around her waist. Mack wasn't paying much attention to what she was doing, until she took his hand again. She gave his a light squeeze, and he turned to her. He stepped back in surprise. The way her blouse covered her, instantly told him that she wasn't wearing a bra. It definitely wasn't the way she normally dressed. He liked what he saw, but it scared the hell out of him too.

She gave him a big grin. "Something wrong, Mack?" she asked.

"Wrong? No, not wrong. Just kind of surprising." He smiled back at her. "I kind of like it. It's way too tempting, but I like it."

"When I decided to leave the damn thing off this morning, I thought it might be. Then I thought about Dale and Lisa having their day together. She never wears one, so why the hell should I. Besides, we don't have any hard, fast rules about looking."

She pulled him hard to her, making him feel her breasts tight against him. She then kissed him, starting soft and slow. Soon though, her tongue was probing his mouth. He quickly did the same to her. They laid down on the soft grass and he moved his hand over her breast. She let out a low moan when he touched her. Rather than unbutton her blouse, she pulled it loose from her jeans and guided his hand under it.

That's when it hit him. He pulled his hand away. He looked at her, kissed her again with all that he had in him, then stood up. She followed him up. She didn't say anything, but looked deep into his eyes.

"Okay," she finally said. "I understand. We made promises, and you're too much of a straight arrow to break them. But I think you know. I'm not. Not like I used to be anyway. It's strange how things have worked out. I was the one who started all the problems we had, and I'm the one those problems changed the most. I've known you for a long time, Mack, and I never would, until I started all this, have dreamed I'd feel about you the way I do now."

"The same goes for me, Kathy. But other than how I feel about you, I haven't changed. So as bad as I want you right now, I still have to keep my promise."

"I know. And I would think the same way. But as much as I love Dale, as much as I need and want him, I still can't completely forgive him for the way he treated me when I came home and I admitted my guilt. If he would have been able to take me back the way you accepted me, I think I would be a different person now.

But he didn't. He waited way too long, and it changed how I feel about some things. How I feel about you too."

"He's forgiven you though. That means a lot."

"He does his best to make it seem as though he has. But every now and then, I can see the question in his eyes. Why did she do it. Why did she want to divorce me. I'd tell him, but I don't know myself. He's different about you and I and what we did. It doesn't seem to bother him at all. I think his relationship with Lisa has a lot to do with that."

"Do you think they are in love?"

"No, I don't. I think what they have is a lot stronger than a love affair. It's way different than you and I. What we have is different too, from what would normally be called a love affair. I know it's strange, but what you and I have is far more like what you and mom had. It would never work in this life as a permanent thing. But another place and time, and yes it would. You and I could have a love to end them all. I think then, the only singing I'd ever have to do is when you and I were in bed."

"I think you're right about a different time and place. But not about this life. There are only two things to stop it from happening in this life. Our partners. Lisa and Dale. As long as we have them, or could have them, we can't be more than friends. I love you, Kathy, but I'll never throw Lisa away. I love her dearly and she's my life now. All you can do for me now is to continue to make it better. Which is what I always try to do for you."

"I agree with you. All you can do is continue to make my life better. I truly do love these times we have together. But if we can ever take it further without any lies or sneaking around, and still not hurt anyone, I definitely want to share a lot more with you than I do now."

She finally got around to tucking her blouse back into her jeans again, then with another grin, she unbuttoned the three top buttons of her blouse. "Just a little bit of payback torture for you, Mack. Because again, we didn't make any rules about looking."

She took his hand, gave it a light squeeze, and they resumed their walk. They spent a relatively quiet day then, content to be together out in this still somewhat wild place.

They stayed on the far back trails, many that were not open to the public. Mack felt free to go there because he was one of the people who actually owned the refuge. He was also chairman of the board that managed it.

Back on those trails, they avoided people entirely, which made for a far more pleasant walk. They also saw more wildlife. And on this day as they were nearing the end of their hike, they got a rare treat. They also got told about what they should and shouldn't do.

They stopped to look over Rice Lake, and Kathy felt very mischievous. Mack had his arm around her, and she leaned hard against him. She finished unbuttoning her blouse and opened it, leaving her breasts exposed. She turned toward him, kissed him, and moved his hand to her breast. The instant he touched her, they heard a roar coming out of the brush behind them. They turned to see what it was.

A rather large black bear was less than a hundred feet from them. He slowly shook his head, then stood on his hind legs. His eyes seemed to concentrate on Kathy first. He then focused on Mack. He waved a paw at him as if to say he shouldn't be doing what he was doing. He then shook his head as if he was saying no. His face lost its severe frown. He dropped back down on all four legs, turned and sauntered away. It was obvious who, of the three of them, he considered to be the superior one.

Mack looked into Kathy's eyes, then at her breasts. shook his head and laughed. "I don't know about you," he told her, "but I think he was trying to tell us something."

With that, he slowly buttoned her up, but occasionally let his hand slip over her very stiff nipples. She shivered every time he did it. When he completed his task, she said, "That bear really didn't approve of what we were doing, did he?"

"I'm not so sure he was disapproving so much as he was warning us that we could be doing dangerous things."

"But were we?"

"You know we were."

"I do. But you make me want to do them, Mack Thomas."

"I know. And maybe in another time and another place, we will."

They looked at each other then, and both wondered how, when they had partners that they loved so dearly, they could have such tangled feelings about each other.

Without any kind of answer to the question, they held hands the rest of the way back to the beginning of the trail and the parking area. There, she kissed him for the last time that day.

CHAPTER 13

Lance and his twelve followers periodically watched the part of the four hundred acre farm/ranch where the homes of the Thomas's, Sue Sartor, and Dale and Kathy were. The Refuge Rescuers office was there too. Their spying on the property was intermittent because they were too restless and lazy to do it constantly. They were hoping to catch one or more of the women who lived and/or worked there leaving, so they could grab them. All of the MAGA Fellows swore an oath to take control of the country back from the liberals, but it took second place to the chance to kidnap and rape one or more of the women connected to Refuge Rescuers. Nothing could beat raping a beautiful woman.

Their master plan was to eventually capture all the woman. Rape and kill them. Then bomb everything else. They were confident that they'd escape blame for doing it, because they were going to attempt to leave clues that indicated that the MAGA Fellows were responsible. Lance would also feed the FBI false information, blaming it all on the MAGA Fellows. The thirteen considered them to be a good scapegoat, now that they had quit them and gone on their own.

Lance loved the new setup. For the first time in his life, he was the leader. He had big plans for his new group that they had named Steal Men. None of the thirteen could spell any better than Trump could, so they didn't realize what they were calling themselves. They also wouldn't have ever realized that the wrong name they used better suited them than the right name, Steel, would have. He was sure either way, that under his leadership, they would achieve great things. After they completely destroyed Refuge Rescuers and everyone in it, they would start on the government buildings. The sheriff's office would be the first to go. After that, they'd take them out in a random fashion.

For Lance though, his first desire was getting the women. With Wanda being his main focus. She wasn't the first one though, that they got the chance to grab. Lance wasn't part of the surveillance team when the opportunity came up. Three of the other Steal Men were.

Julie had dropped off her car for regular maintenance on he way to work that morning, and Sue picked her up. Now that they were at the end of their work day, Sue was going to drop her off there. As soon as they got on the county road, they realized that they were being followed.

Sue had programed all of the phones belonging to everyone who was a part of Refuge Rescuers, so they were equipped with a special alert button. When any of them pushed that button, it sent an emergency signal to every cell phone in their group. It also gave them all the GPS location of the person in trouble. Julie pushed that button.

A second car then forced Sue and Julie to stop. All three of the Steal Men got out of the car in back to grab the women when they were forced to stop by a second Steal Men vehicle. The two men in the second vehicle got out too. The men didn't know it, but they had their own problems. Sue and Julie were armed and not about to give themselves up to the men. They knew that if they did, their chances of long term survival were slim to none.

They crouched low against the side of Sue's car. "It would be a good idea for all of you to drop your weapons," Sue told them. "If you don't, and you get any closer to us, we will shoot you."

Of course, all five men laughed. They had no doubts that the two good looking broads they were after would neither have the guts to shoot, nor even know how to use a gun. Let alone actually shoot them. They were wrong.

Sue and Julie were both getting intensive law enforcement training. Part of that training was shooting. Both of them were already shooting close to the excellent range. Any of the five men was a far larger target than the paper ones they most often shot at.

From their spot next to her car, Sue could see parts of the two men from the car in front of them. She only debated with herself for a few moments on whether it would be best to wait for a better target, or shoot at them right away. She decided to shoot as soon as she had any kind of a shot. One of the two men got cocky and decided they two women alone had to be defenseless, and exposed himself as he made his move to grab them. The second she got a glimpse of him, Sue fired. The intensive training Mack gave her paid off.

Her shot was just a little low, so instead of hitting him in the head, she hit him in the neck. But she hit an artery, and he went down holding his throat, desperately trying to stop the flow of blood. He failed to do it.

Within a couple of minutes, Julie, who was watching the car behind them, saw one of the three men try to move up closer to them. Without questioning herself about what she was about to do, she fired at him. Her training also paid off. She aimed at his chest, as she was taught to do in this situation, and that's where she hit him. In the heart. He died quickly.

Only a couple of minutes had gone by since Julie pushed the special button on the phone, so it was too soon to expect help. Sue knew it was coming, but worried that it might not be soon enough. So she thought about their options. There were only a few. They could surrender, but she was sure that all they'd gain if they did was a very short time to live. And it would be a time in hell.

They could wait for the three men to make their move to attack, and hope to out-gun them. They could attack the one man in front, and gain some time with their better position. It might prove to be enough for someone from Refuge Rescuers to get there.

The last option was to do the totally unexpected. Attack the two men behind the car in back of them. Hoping the men wouldn't shoot her, Sue moved into a position where she could get at least a peek at the two men. They were staying under cover, but weren't paying any attention to anything on either side of them. After thinking about the position she and Julie were in, and the location and vigilance of the two men, she decided that the best option was to go after them.

Talking to Julie in a mere whisper, she explained to an amazingly calm Julie what she wanted to do. Julie slowly shook her head as she listened. When Sue finished her explanation, she vigorously nodded her head yes. As far as she was concerned, dying in a gun battle was better than enduring even a small part of what her sister, Lisa, had gone through so many years ago.

"On three," Sue said, then used her fingers to count. The instant she raised her third finger, they jumped away from Sue's car. As they agreed when the made the decision to go after the men, Julie took the one on the right and Sue took the one on the left. They both held semi-automatics with twelve round magazines.

Sue fired five times before her man even saw her. Four were on target. Julie fired four times. Only two were on target, but they were both kill shots.

The man in front of them now realized what happened and got into his car. He managed to get it started and in gear, but hadn't gotten but a few feet away when Sue and Julie fired at the car. They both aimed at the left side of the rear window. They then emptied the magazines in the handguns they fired. There were a lot of bullet holes in the car by then. Some of them even got all the way through the windshield. But four stoped in the body of the last of the five Steal Men.

Mack and Lisa got there about three minutes later. Sue and Julie were calmly sitting on the ground and leaning against Sue's car. There were no tears or shakes or fear written on their faces. Only a determined look that said, "We did what we had to do."

Looking at the carnage around them, Lisa was immediately concerned about Julie. she kneeled down by her and asked, "Are you okay after all this?"

Julie just shook her head yes, and gave Lisa a half smile.

Sue looked at Lisa. She gave her a full smile. "We are both okay, Lisa. I suppose we should feel bad about what we did, but we can't. If we wouldn't have done it, we'd be someplace we wouldn't want to be. And there'd be God only knows how many guys, standing in line to rape us. Like I've heard Roy say a time or two, making those five men dead only improved planet earth some. So neither one of us plans to feel one damn bit guilty."

Mack, who just finished looking around, said, "You two are really something. You were out numbered and way out-gunned. You did some real good thinking, to take all of them the way you did."

Nodding her head, Sue looked at him. "It was the training, Mack. It wasn't that long ago that Julie and I wouldn't have had a chance today. So I've got to thank you for it. I also want to remind you, that the training better continue."

Julie added to that. "Tomorrow. Tomorrow you and Lisa need to have the next training class. That's what saved our lives. Your training."

They heard the sirens then. The sheriff's department was arriving. The two deputies took a quick look around and called Dale. They figured it would be best to let him sort things out.

There were a lot of people involved in the sorting out process, and someone in that group decided to call the local radio station. Knowing that if there was any truth to what the caller told them, it could turn into a big story, they rushed two people to the scene.

They arrived only minutes before the five bodies were loaded up, to be hauled to the morgue. Most of the people working the scene tried to avoid their questions, but a few told them enough so they could piece together a story. It was broadcast from the scene within forty minutes of their arrival to it.

They did their best then, to interview Sue and Julie for a follow up story, but both of them declined to do one. The radio people did manage to get their names though, and of course used them in their second special news break about what they managed to do against five dangerous men.

As what all too frequently happens, the rest of the media in the Twin Cities area quickly picked up on the story. It didn't take them long to get reporters working on the story. Two of the local TV stations sent reporters to the scene via helicopter. They got to the scene shortly before the authorities there were going to finally let Sue and Julie leave it.

They would have already been gone if it would have been up to Dale, but as soon as word got out about the incident, representatives from all of the law enforcement agencies showed up. The two state police and the four FBI agents out ranked him, so they insisted Sue and Julie needed to stay around longer. Never mind how obvious it was, what actually happened. Two of the FBI agents even thought it might be a good idea to keep them in custody. They were having a hard time believing that two, what would normally be helpless, women could do what they did. The agents were sure they must have had help, or something.

Fortunately there were enough rational heads involved in the investigation, so that didn't happen. Everyone from Refuge Rescuers and Julie's family, all breathed a sigh of relief when they were told they could leave and go home. Everyone except Mack and Lisa.

They took Bob Anderson, and his wife, Beth, who was Julie's step mom, aside before they left.

"I hate to have to tell you this, Bob," Mack said, "but because of all the news coverage this is getting, I'm more than a little concerned for Julie. I know that you want to take her home with you tonight, but I'm not so sure it's a good idea. With the number of total nutcases out there nowadays, damn near anything could happen."

"I know that is a concern. But at the same time, after what she's just been through, not to mention what she's done, she probably needs family around her."

"Yes, she definitely does. But Lisa's family too. And they are close. More now since they've been working together, than ever before. I can only try to imagine how you feel about all this, and how bad you want your daughter home with you now. But I'm really concerned about her safety. Especially going and coming to work, which she told me she definitely wants to keep on doing."

Bob frowned. He didn't like the idea of her not coming home. But he and his family had been through enough to know that a lot of things could go wrong. And he knew that Mack and Lisa were better equipped to deal with those things than he was.

"Okay, Mack. She can stay with you for a while. At least until we can be sure she's reasonably safe." He took deep breath, as if he was trying to pull the conflicts going on in his head together. "You know, Mack, there are a lot of days I wish that neither of my kids were involved in any of this law enforcement or private detective stuff. But then I remember what happened to Lisa. If she would have had half the defense skills she has now, it might never have happened to her. So even if they're involved in things that are dangerous, because of all they've learned, they're in a lot of ways safer than they would be if they never would have gotten involved. I want you to know, I appreciate that."

When they left for home, Lisa rode with Sue and Julie with Mack. Later, when Mack and Lisa were in bed, she asked him how he thought what had happened would effect Sue and Julie. "What they did is a pretty big deal. Killing someone isn't an easy thing to accept."

"No, it sure isn't. But they know, without a doubt, what would have happened to them if those men would have accomplished what they wanted to do. And they've both been around long enough, and have seen enough, to know that the idea that all human life is sacred just plain isn't true. So, hopefully, they know that something like accidentally hitting a dog with your car, is much worse than what they did today."

"I hope you're right, Mack. But I guess we'll just have to wait and see."

CHAPTER 14

Lance North was devastated. Five of his men were dead. Killed by two women who, as far as he was concerned, held no value to anyone. Let alone the Steal Men. And now he had to explain to the seven men he had left in his new militia, what happened.

It was going to be difficult to justify going after the women from Refuge Rescuers, after two of them beat five of their guys in a gun fight. Especially given the fact that they were a mere receptionist and a techie. As bad as that, they were only armed with rather lightweight hand guns. The handguns their five guys carried were among the most powerful ever made.

Added to the disaster was the fact that their guys should never let it go so far. They should have had the women long before the shooting started. Because they hadn't managed to do that, Lance was now convinced that trying to capture any of those women by stopping them on the road, probably wasn't the best method of capturing them. Especially not Wanda.

Lance learned years ago, during the short time he was married to her, how good she was with a gun. So he knew it would be prudent to avoid any chance of a gun fight with her. But he did decide to go after her next. And to do it himself. After he figured out how.

First though, he needed to meet with his men, before they talked themselves into rejoining the MAGA Fellows. He started the meeting by attempting to sound strong and on top of the problem of losing so many men so quickly.

"I know," he claimed, "that it seems like the shootout our guys had was a disaster. But it wasn't near so bed as it seems. It taught us a lot. We now know that they are well prepared to defend themselves against that type of attack. We also know now that they all must have at least some training on the gun range. When we go after them in the future, we will need to take a different approach."

One of the seven Steal Men interrupted him. "I'm no longer convinced that there is a good approach. Those people are really tough. It's going to take a hell of a lot more than eight of us to beat them."

"It sounds to me," Lance argued, "like you're afraid of them."

"In a lot of ways I am. They came to a MAGA Fellows meeting and raise royal hell with us. None of us made a move to stop them, even if it was mostly women who did it. Then when five of us Steal Men tried to make a simple grab on two of their women, women who aren't supposed to be even able to defend themselves, them women mange to kill all five of our guys. So yeah, given that I ain't in no hurry to die, I am just a little nervous."

"The thing is," Lance said loudly, hoping the extra noise would help him maintain control, "we need to plan better. We need to prepare better."

"That might be true. But we need a lot more men too." The man arguing with Lance dropped his head, and slumped his shoulders. He continued to stare at the floor, even as he talked. "I for one, don't think I will stick around if we don't get more men to join us." He looked up at Lance. "And you need to get us much more ammo. All of us need to practice more if we are going to, in any way, take on those Refuge Rescuers. Those people for damn sure know how to shoot."

Lance continued to try to convince all of his men to stay with him. All through the debate, he followed Donald Trumps edict about never apologizing, or admitting the he'd made any kind of mistake. Given his men were as addle brained as they were, he convinced them to stay with him for a least another week.

Knowing now that they wouldn't quit him, not right away, anyway, he set to work on a plan to capture Wanda. He was obsessed by her now. He hadn't thought much about her for years, until he saw her in the grocery store. When he did see her after all that time, it set off something inside of him. She was always a pretty woman, but in the years since he last saw her, she'd turned herself into beautiful woman.

That alone might have set him off. But the confident look on her face and the way she carried herself was more than he could walk away from. He had to have her again. She needed to be controlled, to be frequently used, and to be totally dominated. And he was the only man on earth who should be allowed to do it.

After going through all of the options he could think of, which meant his options were limited, he came up with an idea he liked. It would involve the FBI. He was what they considered to be their number one informant they used against the various missions in the area. So he was sure he could talk them into helping him set things up so he could capture Wanda.

He sat down and wrote up a report for them detailing all activity of the MAGA Fellows. It covered everything they did since his last report to the FBI. It was of course, total fiction, but he believed it read well.

With that done, he sat back and thought about all the things he would do to her, once he had Wanda in his clutches. A feeling of satisfaction washed over him as he realized that he'd come up with a plan that Wanda and her soon to be helpless husband couldn't win. Not only was he smarter than them, he also had God on his side.

CHAPTER 15

Lisa, Sue, and Julie were the only ones in the office when the woman walked in. Julie gave her the normal greeting, then asked how they could help her.

"I need help with my husband," she said. "He's ruining my life."

"I'm sorry," Julie told her. "We don't do cases dealing with spousal problems. There are a lot of agencies that do though. I'll be glad to help you find one of those if you want the help."

"I don't want to hire you to make dirty pictures of him or anything like that. I want to see someone who can help me stop him from doing to me what he's doing."

"If he's abusing you, there are organizations who can help you. I can help you get in touch with one of them too."

"All I want to do is talk to someone. I've read about this place online. I found all kinds of things when I Googled you. One of things that I read was that you help people. I don't expect you to be able to really fix things, but I do need some advice on how to help myself. I'll pay for someone's time, if you let me talk to them."

"Lisa is the only agent in the office right now. I'll ask her if she has time to talk."

Julie found Lisa in Sue's office. They were out on the web researching the men who were part of the MAGA Fellows. They were working on a man whose last name started with an 'M', so they hadn't got to Lance North yet.

Julie explained about the woman, and asked Lisa if she wanted to talk to her. Lisa was hesitant, but because she was ready for a break anyway, she decided to talk to the woman. The woman was surprised though, when Julie brought Lisa out to her.

Before Julie could introduce them, the woman said, "I hope you're not the agent I'm supposed to talk to. You're way too young to be of any help to me."

"Well," Lisa said, "I'm sorry then. I'm the only agent here right now, so I guess we won't be able to do anything for you. Do you want Julie to help you find a different agency?"

"She already asked me that. I don't think so. Why are you the only agent here? From what I read about you, I thought there'd be a lot of agents here."

"We are a relatively small agency, with no plans to get any bigger. From what Julie told me about your case, we probably wouldn't want to take it on. We are always busy, so we can avoid your type of case."

"Really now? How can someone so young as you understand anything about my kind of case. You probably haven't had a steady boyfriend yet."

Lisa couldn't help herself. She laughed at the woman. "You talk about not being able to read people. I've been married for several years now. Long enough to have a good idea about what kind of problems married people might have."

"So you think you already know about my problem?"

"No ma'am, I don't. That's what I came out here to discuss with you. It was you who decided that you didn't want to talk to me. Not the other way around. So if you want to try talking to someone else at this agency,, Julie can make an appointment for you."

"Will I be able to talk to a woman? "

"That I can't tell you. Wanda, the only other female agent, has been incredibly busy lately. So it will probably a fair amount of time before she can see you. But again, there are other agencies who can probably help you right away."

The woman gave Lisa a hard look. "If I talk to you, can you guaranty that what I tell you will be held in confidence?"

"That's just a part of our normal procedure. The only way I would ever talk to anyone about what you tell me is if another one of our agents needs to be involved in your case. Or if it somehow ends up in court, and I'm forced to under oath."

"Well, I guess that's all I can expect. So how much are you going to charge me to ask to you?"

"Nothing. We don't charge for the first consultation. Charges don't go into effect until after we accept the case and begin working it."

"You don't even charge clients like me who can afford to pay?"

"That's right. We only charge for our services when you are using them. So have you decided. Do you want to talk to me, wait for Wanda, or go somewhere else?"

"I have one more question. You don't seem to be very concerned about whether you get me for a client or not. My question is this, why aren't you. Most places, it would be possible to be fired for losing a paying client. Especially when you don't seem to be trying very hard to keep me as one."

"It's not that I don't want you as one, so much as I think you're going to be difficult to deal with. I'm also not at all convinced you're the type of client we want. And I'm not worried about what my boss might like or not like because I am my own boss. I'm a full partner in the agency. And last, we are not at all hurting for business. Most of the time, we are too busy. The hours can get awful long."

"You're not making that up are you? The part about being a partner?"

"No, I'm not. I also have a fair amount of experience in law enforcement. I was a deputy sheriff for a few years."

The woman stood up and pushed her hand out for Lisa to shake. "I'm Donna Slater. Sorry to have given you so much trouble. But my problem with my husband is serious enough so that I really do need help with it. You see, he's turned me into a prostitute."

"How exactly. What is he actually doing?"

"He forces me to have sex with other men. Sometimes more than one at a time. Last time it was six. It's something I have no desire to do. I want to stop it, but I don't know how to do it on my own. That's why I came here. I have to do something."

"The best thing to do in situations like that," Lisa explained, "is to leave him. Go to court and get a restraining order against him. Find a safe place to live, or stay with a friend or your family."

"I've tried that. He always finds me. When he does, he beats the hell out of me."

"I don't see any sign of that on you."

"You won't either, unless I undress for you. He always stays away from my face, or anywhere someone could see the bruises."

"Have you gone to the police?"

"I have, but they haven't been much help. They try, but they are limited to what they can do. My husband, Charles, is an executive with an insurance company, and has a lot of influence. He's wealthy, and can buy his way out of anything I can do to him."

"Well, I think that to start with, we have to get you the hell out of your house and someplace safe. Then we need to go after your husband. If we get you to a safe place, the worst thing we can do, in my opinion, is to wait to see what your husband does."

"How can you go after him? He has everything on his side. Money, influence, and power."

"The truth is, Donna, none of that means a damn thing to me. He doesn't have what I have. A deep down permanent hatred for rapists. And that's what he is. A pimp and a rapist. That's about as lowlife as a human can get. So if you want us take your case and try to help you, you have to totally agree with our going after him with every means and method humanly possible. I won't take this case unless I can make his life miserable. Maybe even destroy it."

"Those are some pretty strong words, Lisa. It's obvious that you already hate my husband. I can't say anything against that. I hate him too. But you have to tell me. Why are you feelings against him so strong?"

Lisa leaned beck in her chair and looked at the ceiling. Staring at it, she debated with herself about telling Donna her own story. Would it mean anything to her. Finally, she decided that telling it would be the only way she could explain why she felt the way she did.

"When I was sixteen," she began, "I was kidnapped and raped by a lot of men." Lisa went on to tell the whole story. She finished with, "So the sooner we stop what's happening to you, the better chance you have to heal completely. I know that you are older than I was when it happened to me, and can probably handle it better than what I've been able to do. But it probably will have some negative effect on you anyway. So again, the sooner we get you out of your situation, the better."

"I have to agree with you about getting me out of there," Donna said. "But I don't want to go back there for anything. I'm afraid of him. If I go into that house to get my personal things, he might try to kill me."

"He won't. I will be with you. So will my husband. We'll also get a court order allowing us to chaperone you while you are there. And if your husband tries to do anything to you while we are there, I will personally kick his sorry ass."

Donna's mouth dropped open and her eyes went wide. "That's an awful strong threat coming from someone your size. My husband his well over six feet all and strong as an ox. I truly doubt that you can even begin to defend yourself against him. Kick his ass? I don't think so."

"Okay, Donna. If you want to believe that, it's fine by me. You can plan on my husband, Mack, to keep you safe."

"Come on now, Lisa. You don't really think you could even start to fight with someone like my husband, do you?"

"Donna, I'm not going to try to convince you of anything. But you do have to make me one promise. And that is that you will not be one of those abused wives who get angry with me when you see him laying on the floor in a pool of blood, after I put him there."

"Has anything like that actually happened to you."

"Too many times, Donna. Too Goddamn many times."

CHAPTER 16

Lance North was surprised, but extremely pleased with the FBIs willingness to fulfill his request. They didn't mind at all helping him out. His last report to them, covering the activities of the MAGA Fellows, was outstanding as far as they were concerned.

They had an even bigger reason for helping him out. He wanted them to arrest Roy and hold him for at least several days, or even a week if possible. They hated Roy for taking control away from them when they tried to grab Wanda and give her to Lance, so this was also a good chance to get even. As much as anything though, they enjoyed the sense of power they got when they arrested people. The idea of guilt or innocence had nothing to do with it.

They went to work right away. Using GPS and Wanda's cell phone, they tracked Roy and Wanda to Katie's Kafe, when they stopped for lunch. As they were leaving, the two FBI agents stopped Roy as the left Katie's. They pushed their loaded weapons in his face, told him he was under arrest. Then they cuffed him.

"Where are you taking him?" Wanda demanded.

"Don't worry your pretty little head about it, Sweetheart. You won't be seeing him for a while, and there ain't a damn thing you can do about it."

"But why are you arresting him? He didn't do anything."

"He's suspected of bombing a church a couple of days ago."

"That's impossible," Wanda swore. "I've been with him constantly, for several days. He hasn't done anything like that, nor has he been anywhere. Where was this church that was bombed supposed to be?"

"Chicago, Lady. It was in Chicago. Now get the hell out of the way, before I arrest you too."

"Go ahead. That'll be twice the money we can sue you for when this is over."

The FBI man pushed her out of the way, they then forced Roy into the back of their car, and drove away. Wanda called Mack first. After she told him everything she knew, he hung up and called a lawyer. Kalif Anderson was one of the best defense attorneys in the entire upper midwest. He and Mack had worked together on many different projects over the years, and in doing so had become good friends.

Kalif was also honest, hard working, and nearly always willing to help a friend in need. Especially a friend like Mack, a man who like Kalif, had helped a lot of people in his life. So as soon as Mack finished explaining the situation, Kalif dropped everything he was involved in, to do what he could to get Roy freed.

"I'd help no matter what, Mack," he said. "But I've also been forced to deal with those two guys from the FBI in the past. They are damn sure not among my favorite people. I'll do everything I can to get Roy free. And after I do, I'll get together with Roy and Wanda and one of the lawyers in our firm who specializes in this kind of abuse of power. The law suit we file against those two morons, and the FBI, will end up costing them a lot of money."

"You know though, Kalif, none of us care that much about money. We mostly just want to get Roy out of there."

"Hell, I know that, Mack. You don't need it and care even less about it. When we win, you guys can always give it to charity. The environment still needs a lot of help."

"We could, but I think I'll let Roy and Wanda decide that."

"Okay, Mack. I'll let you know how things are going. Just don't expect instant results. It's going to take me doing a lot of maneuvering to get this done."

"I understand. I'll wait for your call."

Lisa and Wanda were waiting for him when he got to the office. Wanda wanted to know all about Kalif and Lisa wanted to tell him about their new client. Mack told Wanda about Kalif. Both what he planned to do to get Roy out, but also his history with Kalif, so she would know that he was more than just another lawyer. Wanda and Lisa had already talked about Donna Slatter, so she left for home when Lisa explained about her to Mack.

"Can I talk to her?" Mack asked when Lisa finished. "I'd like to hear from her, how she got herself into her situation."

"That's probably a good idea, Mack. But first, let's go talk to Sue. She's checking out Donna's husband for us."

Mack was hoping that they would find out that Charles Slater was guilty of at least some sex offenses, but he wasn't. His record was actually pretty clean. He'd only been arrested once. For a bar fight. And that had been years before.

His personal life appeared normal too. He worked a lot of hours, and like so many executives, his main hobby was golf. His second hobby was poker. He played once a week, normally with the same six guys. He had even had a special, seven sided table made for playing. It was kept in his personal man-cave, in the lower level of his home. It was a large room, with its own king size bed. It wasn't normally slept in. It was only used for what he called special occasions.

They were special occasions that his wife, Donna, now dreaded. "It was where," she told Mack, "he makes me perform for other men. In the past, it was me, him, and some other guy. Usually someone different every time. This last time though, I was forced to do it with all six of his poker buddies."

"I know this is hard for you to talk about," Mack said. "But can you explain to me how all of it started with your husband?"

"Is it absolutely necessary. I hate talking about it.'"

"No, it isn't. But the more we know about your problem, the better we can understand it. And that, in turn, should help us to understand your husband. The better we understand him, the better we will know how to handle him if he's there when we go to pick up some of your things."

"What do you mean by handle him?"

"I mean what we'll have to do if he tries to stop you from taking your things. Or even worse, if he tries to keep you there."

"Do you mean you would fight with him if you thought you needed to?"

"That's exactly what I mean. Do you have a problem with that? Because if you do, we can stop all this right now. We have to be sure that you really do want help before we get any more involved. If you are afraid we might hurt him, you don't want our help. You don't want anyone's help. You're just playing some kind of game that we nether want nor need to have anything to do with."

"The thing is, I definitely do want your help. I just never thought it would come to this. Before you plan on hurting him too much, I have to admit that all of this is partly my fault."

Mack wasn't surprised by what she said. He wasn't upset by it either. He'd suspected she probably was partly to blame before he even talked to her. "Okay, Donna, maybe you are somewhat responsible for your problems. Can you tell me anyway, even if you don't want to talk about it, how it all started?"

Donna sighed heavily. She shook her head as if she were trying to get rid of a bad dream. Then she talked. "For along time, Charles was after me to have sex with someone other than him while he watched. I constantly refused. But one night, he invited a young friend of his over for dinner. He was very polite, and extremely handsome. We drank a lot of wine. Charles put some soft, romantic music on. He started it by dancing with me. I was really feeling the effects of the alcohol, which was turning me on. I should have known better, but when he suggested I dance with his friend, I did. To make a long story short, one thing led to another, I ended up having sex with him. Charles loved it. I was ashamed. I vowed never to let it happen again. He thought otherwise. When I tried to refuse to do it the next time he brought someone around, he waited until the man left. Then he beat me. It was all in places that it wouldn't be seen. After that, I went along with his game. I didn't like it, but I thought it could have been worse. Then it did get worse. First it was two men, then three. I knew I had to do something about it, but wasn't strong enough to force myself to do it until he let those six men do it to me, one after the other."

"So now," Mack said, "you think you're ready to leave him and start over? You have to know, that husbands like yours are control freaks. He isn't likely to just let you go. There's no way for us to know how far he'll be willing to go to keep you with him. But if you truly want to be free of him, you have to be willing to fight back. If you're not, then you might as well go back to him and save all of us a lot of trouble."

"It isn't so much, Mack, that I don't want to do this. It's more that I'm scared about the fighting part. My husband is really very strong. I don't want you guys to get hurt if we go there. I know that Lisa said she could kick his ass, but I don't see how that could be possible. Besides, what if he comes home while we're there, with a bunch of his friends?"

"We'll deal with it when the time comes. And as for Lisa, the truth is, my main concern with her when she takes on your husband, is how bad will she hurt him before I can stop her."

Donna opened her mouth, but she didn't manage to get any words out. The best she could do was a drawn out, "Ooooohh!"

Mack let what he'd just told her settle in for a moment. "Along with us going with you to retrieve some of your personal stuff, you're going to have to put together all the information you can about your family finances. Do you know much about them?"

"No, not really. He gives me an allowance for groceries, my personal needs, and other necessities. He takes care of all the major bills as well as any investments we have."

Her situation was beginning to sound familiar. His fiancé, Mandy, was in a similar financial situation when she left her husband. Mandy had struggled hard to learn what her husband did with their money. She actually risked her life to get into his computer to check on him. Mack wasn't about to let Donna do the same thing. They'd get the proper court orders to force her husband to open up their financial records, then they'd hire experts to check the status of them.

Donna's situation reminded him of Mandy anyway. Her husband didn't sexually abuse her, but he did physically abuse her in other ways. He was also doing the same, or at least similar things with their finances. The fact that dealing with Donna was reminding Mack so much of Mandy, was becoming constantly more disturbing to him. He wished he could just walk away from the whole case.

Because it did disturb him, it changed the walking away part from difficult to impossible. If what was happening to Donna was bothering him the way it was, there was no doubt in his mind that it was an important case. Way too important to do anything other than see it through to a satisfactory conclusion.

After talking it over with Donna, they decided to wait a couple of days before picking up her personal things. That gave them the time needed to get ready all of the paper work needed to legally escort her.

Sue proved to be, of the women of Refuge Rescuers, who was closest to her in size. So she furnished Donna with enough clothes to fill her needs until then.

It was Donna's intention then, to stay in a motel until they made the trip to get her things, but Mack and Lisa changed that idea. Donna was going to stay with them. They'd seen too many things go wrong too many times, so they weren't about to let her get very far at all, away from them. They didn't want her anywhere alone either.

They only had one guest room though, and Julie was occupying that for the foreseeable future. So they hoped Donna would be satisfied with sleeping on the couch. Sue saved the day however. When she overheard them talking about it, she invited Julie to stay with her. Julie accepted her offer.

Mack asked them all to get together for a meeting during their evening meal, so they could discuss all the cases the were working on. Everyone's main concern was Roy, and how long it would be before he would be released. Unfortunately, neither Mack nor Wanda knew the answer to that question.

Without going into any details, beyond her being a victim of spousal abuse, they discussed Donna's case then. They didn't get too far into it before Donna interrupted them.

"I find it kind of strange, how most of you are so concerned about my safety. I know we might have some trouble with my husband when we go to get my things, but the idea that someone might somehow come after me otherwise, is stretching it, I think."

"For you," Wanda answered, "it probably is. For us, it isn't. You know what Lisa went through when she was kidnapped. That's enough right there to make all of us very cautious. The thing is, Mack's been through a hell of a lot too." She went on to tell Donna about how his first wife was murdered in connection with the refuge being sold. Then she talked about Mandy, and how she too was murdered.

While she talked, Mack started to acquire a feeling of dread. Something was going to happen. He looked at everyone in the room. He expected to stop looking when his eyes reached Donna. He didn't. It was Wanda that stopped his eyes. Moments of the past flashed through his memory. The first thing that hung in there for a while was when the two of them left for Texas after Mandy died.

"Fuck it," she said when he protested her going with him, "we'll eat when we get to Texas."

His mind drifted again. It shocked him when it stopped on the one time they were ever intimate. They hadn't been in Texas very long. Mack was having a bad night. A nightmare woke him, screaming Mandy's name. Wanda rushed into his room, then climbed on the bed and held him to comfort him. Without thinking, he kissed her. She returned it. That's all it took. They made love then, and while it lasted, it was far better than good. But when it was over, he was riddled with guilt. They never did it again. But a strange thing came over him as he remembered that night. He found himself wishing they had done more.

As he looked at her, all he could do is think about how beautiful she was. It took him a while to get past that feeling. But it did make him feel guilty. She was in one with him then. She wasn't now. Not in the same way anyway. And she was married to Roy. That alone was enough to tell him to knock off any ideas like the one he was having.

She caught his eye then. She held his gaze as a bit of a smile formed on her lips. Finally she mouthed the words, "I know, Mack. I know."

He couldn't help but blush. He looked around to see who had noticed him do it. Only Wanda had. Her smile was still there.

He tried to return it, but was too unsettled to do it. He didn't talk much for the rest of the meeting, and was glad when it was time to go home.

Once there, he tried to settle down, but was restless until they went to bed. Sleep came hard to him when he did, and it was dream filled. They were scattered around, and jumped from things past to things that never happened. Dreams of Lisa took him to dreams of Beth, and how she helped when they searched for Lisa. He dreamed next of Mandy and an early morning walk they took in the refuge. They started at the old school house trail. They were holding hands as they walked, but Mandy's hand turned into Beth's. All the refuge was still there then, and they found a stand of pines to lie down under. They slowly undressed each other as they expressed their love. As the last remnants of her clothing were removed, he pulled her over him. She was ready and wanting him. Just as he was about to slip inside her, his cell phone rang.

Mack sat up suddenly, wondering who could possibly be calling at that time of the night. He didn't realize that he hadn't been asleep all that long, so it really wasn't that late.

"Hello," he said, his voice groggy. "I hope this isn't anything serious."

"I'm sorry for waking you, Mack," said a familiar voice. "But I had to wait to call you when I could do it in private." It was Beth talking to him. "I don't expect you to give me an answer right now. But I want you to meet me the day after tomorrow. In the morning, early. At 5:00 AM, at the start of the old school house trail. I'll wait for you for about a half hour. If you're not there then, I'll assume you're not coming." She hung up.

Lisa turned over then, and asked, "Who was that? It's kind of late for a phone call."

Mack scratched his head, wondering how much he should tell her. It didn't take long to decide. He expected honesty from her, so he knew that no matter what her reaction might be, that he had no choice but to tell her the truth. And because the connection between the dream and the phone call was so strange, he knew he had to tell her about that too.

"It was weird, Lisa. It was really weird. There's been a lot of strange things happening since I talked to Donna. It was Beth on the phone. She wants me to meet her the day after tomorrow early in the morning at the old school house trail in the refuge."

"Why? Did she say?"

"No, she didn't. So I don't have the slightest idea why. Not for sure anyway. But just before she called, I was having a dream. It was the kind of dream I haven't had since I married you. It was about her."

Lisa caught on to the subject of the dream as soon as he told her about it. She felt like she was supposed to be upset about it, but instead found it amusing. She giggled before asking the next question. "Do you have dreams like that about her very often?"

"No, Lisa. That was the first time I've ever had one like that about her. The truth is, I don't have any dreams like that since we've been married. You keep me totally satisfied. But to be honest with you, what happened with Beth was the second really strange thing to happen to me today."

"It wasn't the same kind of strange though, was it?"

"Yes, it was. It wasn't exactly the same, but the same subject."

"Was it with Beth too?" Lisa was no longer seeing any humor in Mack's confessions. Her giggle was gone, replaced with a serious frown.

"No, Lisa, it wasn't Beth. It was Wanda. I told you about the one time we did it, and how I felt so guilty about it. Well, during our meeting tonight, I started to get some real bad vibes about her. They scared me. But then I remembered how she came to me that night after a nightmare. I then remembered every detail of what we did. Before tonight, it's been years since I've thought about it at all. And never the way I did tonight. The thing is, as I was remembering it, Wanda mouthed the words to me, I know, Mack. I know."

"You know, don't you, Mack, that I should be real pissed at you right now. You say I satisfy you, but here you are, having thoughts and dreams about sex with other woman. What happened? Are you tired of me mow?"

"Anything but. In fact, being in bed next to you, is doing a real number on me. Just looking at you does more than a few dozen dreams could ever accomplish."

"I don't know. I think right now, after what you've told me about your lusting after other women, I shouldn't even let you look."

"You're probably right. But then, those thoughts and dreams were nothing more than accidents. Looking at you is on purpose. And wanting you fills a better part of my life. I didn't ask for, nor did I want the thoughts and dreams."

"Mack," she said, "sometimes you talk real nice." She kissed him.

CHAPTER 17

The Steal Men thought they were ready until lights went on in the house at the end of the driveway. They were sure that Mack and Lisa were now in bed. It took Lance a lot of talking to convince the three men with him that it would pay to wait. As slow as he often was, he'd learned enough to know that taking Wanda would be plenty enough to do for one night. A gun fight with Mack and Lisa, along with whatever defense Wanda might put up, was too much. It could even prove lethal.

It took nearly an hour before the lights went off. He decided to give them about thirty minutes to fall asleep before they made their move. He was sure that by then, it would be safe to go after Wanda. What he didn't know, was that Wanda and Mack were having the same problem.

They couldn't sleep. After he and Lisa made love, he held her as he closed his eyes. Instead of relaxing then, as he normally did after loving her, pictures began drifting through his mind. They did the same things to him that dreams of disaster always did. They kept him tossing and turning as sleep completely eluded him.

He didn't want to keep Lisa awake, so he left the bed. It didn't help her any. After hearing about his concerns over his wandering thoughts and wild dreams, she knew why he couldn't sleep. Just as he was concerned about her, she was worried about him. She left the bed and followed him into their living room.

He was putting his shoulder holster on over the plain white tee shirt he wore as a pajama top. He knew he was upsetting her when he saw the frown on her face.

"I'm sorry. I was hoping you'd be able to fall asleep if I quit rolling around on the bed."

"That's what I thought. I just came out here to make sure you're okay. But now you're wearing your gun. You never do that when you're up this time of the night. Why do you have it on now?"

"I still have the feeling that there's something wrong. I know I'm not going to be able to sleep for a while, so I thought I'd go outside and walk around a little."

"Why do you need to carry your gun to walk around the yard in the middle of the night."

"I don't know. But wearing it tonight, just seemed like the prudent thing to do."

"Well, if your feelings are that strong, I'm going to walk with you."

Mack looked at her and grinned. "Okay, but it might be a good idea for you to put a little more on before we go." He let his eyes wander up and down her body. The short nightgown she wore was just sheer enough for him to be actually able to see any part of her body that was touching the material it was made of. "It's a clear night, so there's enough light for your nightgown to be very affective if anyone's watching."

She didn't argue, and slipped on a robe. It covered her, but only just far enough down to cover where here panties would have been, had she been wearing any. Then, just as Mack did, she put on her shoulder holster.

"I know," she said, "it looks goofy with what I'm wearing. But if you're concerned enough because of your dreams and feelings to wear yours, there's no way I'm going out there without mine."

They went out the front door. It was something they rarely did. Almost all of their comings and goings were through the rear door. But since all they planned to do was take a few short walks around their small yard, where they went out seemed irrelevant. And it might have been, if Lisa wouldn't have seen something move out near the road.

She grabbed Mack's arm, put a finger to her lips, then pointed to some bushes growing between Ben and Theresa's house and Wanda and Roy's house.

She whispered, "Something moved there. It might be a deer, it seemed big enough, but I'm not sure."

Mack whispered back. "Stay real quiet. Let's check it out."

He signaled for her to move to her right. He moved a little to his left. They then crept slowly toward Roy and Wanda's house. Lisa was the first to see one of Lance's men. Even in the dim light, she could see that the gun he carried was an AR15. It was a weapon favored by mass murderers, terrorists, and all too many other low-life men with limited mental capacities. She only waited a moment to decide what to do, but in that moment Lance and his men went into action.

Mack and Lisa turned their lights off when they left the house, and Lance had held his men back as long as he could. They were now trying to break down the back door of Roy and Wanda's house. They weren't doing a very good job of it.

What they didn't know, what they had no way of knowing, was that the door frames on their house were steel reenforced. It would take lot more force to get them open than what they were capable of applying. At the same time the Steal Men went into action, so did Mack and Lisa. She made the instant decision to not bother with a warning, and shot the man she was looking at. She didn't want to kill him, if she could avoid it. At the same time, she wanted to take him down and keep him down. So she shot him twice. Once in each leg.

It was Lance who was slamming on the door, frantic now to get to Wanda. She was awake now, and had even taken the time to put a robe on over her pajamas. She yanked open the door, saw that it was Lance, and shot him. Twice. Once in his left leg. Once in his right shoulder.

"You so much as move an inch in any direction, Lance," she snarled at him, "and the next fucking bullet will be between your goddamn eyes." With that, she stepped outside. She could see Mack a short ways away, holding his gun on one of the men.

The problem with that scene was the fact that the third man was behind Mack and was raising his gun to shoot Mack. Wanda didn't hesitate. She used her superior skill with a gun and put a bullet in his head, killing him instantly.

Her shot distracted Mack for a short moment, and his man lunged at him. Wanda didn't like that move either, so she just fired another quick shot. That ended a second life. Lance and his three men once again failed to capture any Refuge Rescuer's women. And Lance lost any chance that he would ever do too Wanda what he wanted to do.

Lisa and Wanda managed to slow Lance's and the other Steal Man's bleeding enough to keep them alive. Mack called Dale, and let him contact all the people who would have to come to investigate the shooting.

Mack then turned to Sue, who was now out there standing next to Ben and Theresa and Julie. They all came out when they heard the shooting, and were wondering what was going on. Mack explained, then asked Sue if she could put together a press release to go to every media source possible on his command.

Of course, she said yes. Mack told her what to put in it, and then asked her to have it ready to go if or when he requested it. She smiled when she saw what it was and said she would have it ready. She left him then to get it ready.

Dale, along with four of his deputies, got there then. Mack didn't wait even a minute to tell Dale what he wanted.

"Call those two FBI agents and tell them to get their useless asses out here now. If they're not here within an hour, I will be doing something that they not only won't like, but they could very well lose their jobs over."

"It's the middle of the night, Mack. Don't you think we could just as well wait for morning."

"That's possible, but we aren't going to. Call them now, or I will hang their sorry asses. And when I do, they'll be pissed at you too. I won't wait. I'm tired of their games."

"Is this about Roy?"

"It is. Whether they like it or not, he's coming home by morning."

"Okay, Mack. But you should talk to his lawyer first."

Mack took Dale's advice and called Kalif. Even though it was a time he didn't normally get calls, Kalif didn't get upset when he heard Mack's voice. When Mack explained all that had happened, Kalif went along with the press release if it was necessary, and said he would be available in the morning if he was needed.

It took the agents over an hour to get there. Mack didn't hesitate to confront them. He immediately got into the lead agents face. "You will make any and all required calls right now, to get my uncle Roy released. If you don't, we will be releasing for the press, *everywhere,* why you arrested him to start with. We will also be releasing the name of your favorite informant. Then, before the day is out, lawsuits against each of you will be filed in both federal and state court. Emails will immediately be sent to all of your superiors, explaining all of the harassment you've been giving Roy and Wanda. Beyond that, I am really more than a lot pissed at you, so I will forever be looking for ways to catch you in mistakes. No matter how big or small."

"You really think you're big time, don't you?" whined the agent.

"Compared to you, I am."

That's when Mack noticed Wanda. She was sitting on the ground, Her head was hanging down, but he could still she that her face had turned ashen. Her hands were shaking, and tears were silently running down her cheeks.

Mack crouched down by her. He gently touched her chin and lifted her head. "What is it? What's wrong?"

"You and me. I doubt that you knew why, but you knew you should be outside tonight. I was awake too. I was thinking about calling you. I had a dream that said we had to be careful. It was right after I had the other one."

"What other one?"

"The one you were having at the meeting. Until you did, I thought you might have forgotten that it happened. Sometimes when I'd think that, I'd get so sad I wanted to cried. I only ever cried about it when I was alone. It was one of the very few things I never shared with Roy. I never shared it with anyone. The only one I ever wanted to share that memory with was you, Mack."

"I've never forgotten it, Wanda. But I aways felt like I took advantage of you. That's what made me feel guilty. Sometimes it still does."

"Don't let it Mack. When it happened, I was so happy. It's always been one of my best memories ever. But that's not the you and me I was talking about. It was the you and me and dreams. If it was only one of us to have the dreams, the feelings we both had, what happened tonight could have ended so different. I know they scare me and you and everyone else, but maybe we should be thankful for them."

"I know, Wanda. What you say is true. And we should be thankful that we have the friendship and the strange connection we have."

"There's something else, Mack. You know that I love Roy to the ends of the earth. But if the day ever comes when we both find ourselves alone. If Roy and Lisa are gone. I want to spend the end of my life with you. Even if we're too old to do anymore than hold hands. I still want to spend it with you."

"Okay, Wanda. You've got a deal. If it ends up just the two of us, we spend it together."

Mack looked around then. The FBI agents were no where to be seen, so he assumed that they left to do what needed to be done to get Roy freed. Dale and all the rest of the law enforcement people were busy doing what they always did at any shooting.

He then noticed Lisa. She was watching them, her gaze intense. He tried to read her expression, but Lisa was holding it neutral. He turned back to Wanda.

"What can I do for you now, Wanda? What do you need?"

"My husband home and safe. And until then, I'd appreciate it if you stay close. Right now, Mack, you are the only one who can get me through this without my going crazy. So ask Lisa to come over here. I need to talk to her."

Her first question when she came over was, "What is it that I can do for you, Wanda?"

"Let me have your husband for the next few hours. I promise that there isn't anything going on that there shouldn't be. I think it's because Roy isn't here, but I'm at loose ends now. You know your husband, so you know how he can make any of us feel safe."

"I do. I also know all the other ways he makes us feel. There's something about him that women seem to trust. Whatever it is, it makes them feel all sorts of other things too. Women just plain like Mack."

"Was that a no?"

"Of course not. I know how you and Mack feel about each other, and I totally approve. So yes, you can borrow him for however long you need him."

"Thank you for that, Lisa. I do appreciate it. And if you ever need Roy for anything, you can borrow him anytime."

"Okay. Now do you want to stay with Mack and me until Roy gets home? Or would you rather Mack stays with you?"

"If it's okay, I'd rather Mack stays with me. When they bring him home, I want to be there the instant he gets there. If I'm at your house, I might not be there for him as quick."

"Okay, whatever works for you."

When everything was done and they were finally alone, Mack and Wanda settled down in a couple overstuffed, comfortable easy chairs in her living room. They were quiet at first, not knowing what to say. They both now felt the discomfort of being alone together for the first time in a very long time.

Wanda changed her sitting position several times, trying to make herself comfortable. She knew though, that it wasn't the way she was sitting that was making herself uncomfortable. It was who they were and being alone together. She finally decided that the way they were reacting was ridiculous, and that it was time to put a stop to it.

She left her chair, moved over to Mack's, and promptly sat in his lap. She wrapped her arms around his neck and kissed him. It wasn't the kind of kiss a sister would give her brother. It was the kind that left the lasting memories.

"If it was a different world, Mack, and I could give you more, I'd do it with never a second thought. But this is the world we have, so for now, that's all I can give you."

She kept her arms around him, laid her head on his shoulder, and fell asleep. She was still there when the FBI agents brought Roy home a couple of hours later.

She was instantly awake when Roy got out of the car with the agents. Wanda flew out to Roy. She would have jumped into his arms, but his hands were still cuffed behind him.

She kissed him first, then turned to the agents. "Get those fucking handcuffs off him this goddamn second."

"You'll do better with us if you watch your language, Lady."

Mack moved close to the agent. "And you'll do a damn sight better with me, if you get the cuffs off him." Mack stepped back.

The agent took off the cuffs. Roy rubbed his wrists. It was obvious from the marks on them that the cuffs were put on tighter than they should have been. The agent holding the cuffs grinned as he watched Roy.

The grin didn't last long. Roy hit him with a straight right hand to his face. The agent went down hard and stayed there.

"What the hell?" The second agent said.

That's all he said. Roy decked him too. then he turned to Mack. "It looks like you were taking care of Wanda. Thank you for that."

He took her hand and led he into the house. He closed the door tight behind them. Mack waited until the two agents recovered enough to get back on their feet.

"You know damn good and well that you both had that coming," Mack told them. "Any kind of retaliation, and I guaranty that I will make you regret it. Ten times over. Now get the hell off my land and the hell out of here. If you so much as come anywhere near any of us again, you won't like the results."

The agents left and Mack went home. Lisa was waiting. He could see the look of concern on her face. "We were real uncomfortable when we first found ourselves alone together. Wanda fixed it by sitting in my lap, kissing me, then falling asleep until Roy got home."

"That's all?"

"No. Roy decked both the agents."

Lisa laughed.

CHAPTER 18

The FBI put a guard on Lance's room. They were determined to monitor his activities by controlling who went into his room. They were no longer so concerned about his safety. Because of his going after Wanda again, and getting two of his own men killed, he'd taken himself from being a big asset to them, to being a big embarrassment.

They knew that arresting Roy was a huge mistake on their part. The law firm that Mack Thomas had working for him, along with Roy and Wanda, were raising hell with them. Lawsuits were already filed by them in federal and state court. Lawsuits that the FBI had a good chance of losing.

Add to that, they had the problem of what to do with the agents who did the arresting. The powers that be in the FBI didn't want to fire them, because they were afraid that it would make it look as if the department was guilty of the things they were being sued for. The final decision for the two was simple. They were sent to southern Mississippi to open a new office in a small town surrounded by swamps and alligators. They were also told that any traveling for them was out of the question.

With them gone, Lance was now without any backup from other FBI agents. The thought terrified him. He'd acted as an informant against more paramilitary militias than the MAGA Fellows. And when he'd infiltrated them, he'd often used them for his own gain.

This time though, what he'd done with the MAGA Fellows was worse. Going after the Refuge Rescuers women was all his idea. It had gotten seven men killed, and counting himself, two wounded. His Steal Men group was certainly done, so there was no backup there. And that meant he didn't have any real backup anywhere. He was on his own, and that was all the fault of Wanda. If she would have just been willing to follow God's commands, none of this would have happened to him. But all of it had happened, and his biggest hope now was that the MAGA Fellows would never learn his former status with the FBI.

They did though, and it didn't mattered how careful the FBI was, someone working in the hospital overheard a FBI conversation about Lance, and the MAGA Fellows now knew the truth about Lance North.

Titus Trump, the leader of the MAGA Fellows was furious. He called a meeting of the toy soldiers. He didn't mince words when he spoke to the men assembled.

"I'm sure that by now you've all heard about the traitor, Lance North. If you haven't, he was working for the FBI. God only knows how much information he gave them. Regardless of how much though, we have to find a way to retaliate. If we don't, we will never gain the respect we need to grow into the power group I know we all hope to become. There's simply too much at stake here to let this slide. Lance is in the hospital now, with an armed guard next to the door to his room. But it's only one guard, so we should be able to eliminate him and grab Lance."

One of the men who wasn't at all sure that it was worth the trouble to go after Lance, spoke up. "I hope you aren't going to try to make getting him out of that hospital seem easy, because it won't be."

"I know that. But it is doable. If we plan it carefully, and don't screw it up when go after him. we can get him."

Another doubter spoke up. "If we do get him, then what?"

"Then we make him pay."

"How, do you plan on killing him?"

"Not right away. I think some video of him suffering will be appropriate. We need to do something, and to have something, to prove that we have the will and the power to contribute to making America great again."

There was some grumbling among the men then, until Titus interrupted them. "Okay," he said, "are you guys with me on this or not?"

More grumbling, until the first man to question Titus about going after Lance stood up. He waved his hands as if to tell everyone to quiet. "I know, the first time I said anything, I doubted as to whether we should go after Lance North. But sitting here with the great bunch of guys you all are, I've change my mind. I think we should go after him, and when we get him, we should put him through hell."

Another man stood. "I agree. The thing is though, if we are really going to get even with him, we've got to make him watch us do in that wife of his he's so nuts over. I say we grab Wanda Thomas first. Make him watch us do her. And do her enough so she bleeds. Then bury them together. While they're both still alive."

The MAGA men started talking to each other, but instead of negative grumbling, it was a chorus of positive sounds. There was nothing like the thought of forced sex to perk them up and make them ready for action.

CHAPTER 19

It had been a while since Mack used an alarm to get up, so the sound of it was a real shock to his system. He rolled over and slapped it off, then forced himself to sit up in the bed. Lisa groaned when she sat up next to him.

"I don't know, Mack," she said. "Getting up this early is a real pain in the ass. I hope your meeting with Beth is worth it."

"I do too, because you're right. Getting up this early is a pain in the ass."

"Do you want me to make coffee while you shower, Mack?"

"You don't have to. Why don't you go back to sleep?"

"There'd be no point in that. I won't be doing any sleeping until you get back home. I'm not going to be much good for anything until I know what this meeting you're having is about."

"You shouldn't worry so much about it, Lisa. Whatever it is, I doubt it's anything that will affect us, or affect our relationship."

Lisa reached up and rubbed the back of her neck. She then turned to him and locked her eyes on his. "After the way women have been acting and reacting around you lately, Mack, I have to wonder about this. Like I told Wanda when she needed you, women are fond of you. They tend to fall in love with you. I know that Beth cares deeply about my dad. She loves all his children and the farm. She knows her life is good, and good for her. But somewhere inside her, there's that spot that still loves you. Sometimes, when she looks at you, there's a longing in her eyes that's so sad that it's hard to look at. So yes, I should worry."

"Even if what you say about her is true, there's nothing for you to worry about. I don't want anymore than what I have now. And that is you."

"Look, Mack, I know that you love me and want me, but I also know that there are others out there who want to at least share you with me. And sometimes that scares me a little."

"Well, I hope that before this day is over I will be able to un-scare you. And I promise, I will work hard today at behaving the way I know you want me to."

"You're not going to promise me that you won't do anything."

"Nope. I want to leave you anticipating a little bit. That way, there's less chance you'll run off with someone else while I'm gone."

"Why would you think something like that?"

"You've said that women like me, and that's kind of a worry for you. The truth is, men love you, and it terrifies me that one of them will steal you away someday."

She shook her head no, kissed him, and went in the kitchen to make coffee while he showered. She had a cup of it in an insulated mug for him when he was ready to leave. "You don't need to worry, Mack. You're the only man who can do it for me, so I'll never leave you. And even if you weren't the only man who could do it, I love you way too much to ever want to lose you."

She kissed Mack one more time and he left. She sat down with a cup of coffee in the living room. She would have loved to have been able to go back to bed and sleep some more. But as she told Mack, she was too worried about what Beth might want from him to be able to sleep now.

So instead, she let her mind fill with memories. Her life with Mack was good, and almost every memory she had of the two of them was good. But now, ever since Kathy told Dale she wanted a divorce, it seemed to her that her marriage was a little off balance.

A lot of that was her fault, she knew. She tried hard, the first day after Kathy made her request, to comfort Dale. She even got the idea that a kind of a date between her and Dale would help. But when Sue and Mack joined them, Mack was visibly upset. She did it wrong. Dale's date for that night should have been Sue. She should have been with Mack.

Several other things had since occurred, and it was beginning to seem to Lisa, that women were more and more often becoming attracted to Mack. And just as bad, he didn't seem to be fighting against that attraction quite as hard as he was before the thing with Kathy started.

When her thoughts were totally tangled up with questions about what was happening with Mack and other women, Donna, who was staying in their spare bedroom, got up.

"I smelled the coffee," she said, "and couldn't go back to sleep. You guys sure got up early today."

"Yes, we did. Mack's meeting someone at the refuge. I got up just to see him off."

"That's a strange place for a meeting. This is a strange time for it too. Do you detectives have many meetings at times and places like that?"

"No. And he's just meeting a friend there today. They're going on one of Mack's famous walks. A lot of people like being out there with him. When it comes to the refuge, Mack's an incredibly good teacher."

"So is the man he's meeting young then?"

"Fairly young. She's close to Mack's age."

"Mack's meeting with a woman at the wildlife refuge? At this hour. Doesn't that worry you? Is she a pretty woman? That husband of yours is one hell of an attractive man. It would be my guess, that there'd constantly be women interested in him. I know, if I were still young and innocent enough, I would be. You are a lucky woman to have a man like him. You are a beautiful woman, but even so, having a man like him has got to be special."

Lisa didn't answer her. Instead, the thought ran through her, "My god, not another one. Is there no end to the women wanting Mack?"

Mack had similar thoughts running through his head. He was out of his truck, looking at Beth. Her shorts only minimally covered her legs, and fit tight to the rest of her. The blouse she wore was white, and made from a silk like material. It wasn't sheer or translucent, but molded to her body. All of her feminine curves were immediately apparent.

Looking at her, Mack shook his head and thought, "Not another one. I wonder what the attraction is? It sure as hell ain't my good looks. Not with those scars on my face."

What he didn't realize. What given who he was, he was highly unlikely to ever realize, was the fact that the scars were part of what made him so attractive to women. To them, the scars seemed to fit perfectly with his kind and gentle eyes, along with the obvious strength he had. A strength that women instinctively knew was there to love and protect them.

Beth let him look at her. She liked that his eyes roamed up and down her body. When the roaming stopped, and his eyes met her her's, she moved up to him. Her arms went around his neck and she pulled him close. The kiss they shared was filled with passion, and left no doubt about why she wanted to meet him on this day.

"Wow," Mack said. It was the first word either of them spoke since they got there.

"I've waited a long time to do that, Mack."

"I have to admit, it was nice. But I also have to tell you, that has got to be it. I still have some pretty strong feelings for you, Beth, but I can't act on them. Not now. Lisa's too important."

"I was afraid you would react that way. You being who you are. I had to try anyway."

"Does Bob know you're here?"

"Yes. We've talked about me doing this several times. He's uneasy about it, but he understands all the reasons. He also knew before we finally decided I should do this, that it was unlikely that anything would happen."

"If you were so sure I wouldn't do this, why did you set this up?"

"Because making love with you is only part of the reason for it. We are here now, and hopefully you have some time. I would like to walk in this refuge with you. Just being close to you for a while will mean a lot. Maybe you'll even let me hold your hand. And before our time is over today, I'd like it if you kissed me again."

She had tears in her eyes that slowly trickled down her cheeks. He used his tongue to remove her tears, then kissed her. She returned it with the passion still controlling her. Her hips rolled against him, and his hand moved over her breast. She wasn't wearing a bra, and the fibers of her blouse made it feel as if she wasn't wearing anything.

Mack pulled away, took her hand, and they started down the hiking trail. His emotions were already mixed, but as they walked close together and he felt the constant touch of her hand, he found himself torn between what he was feeling now, and how he knew he would feel if he went home to face Lisa if he let what he was feeling at that moment control him.

As they walked, Beth slowly began to feel better about the way things were going between them. As she thought about it, she more and more wanted them to become friends. The kind that could come to this place Mack loved so much. To walk with him and listened while he talked about what it was, what it stood for.

She loved the way he explained about how it was recovering, and how, even though it burned nearly everything, the fire wasn't near as bad as for the refuge as it would have been if it were destroyed by chainsaws. After the fire the soil was still intact. That wasn't true after the chainsaws cut everything down and the heavy equipment hauled it away.

She loved the closeness of him. His warmth, and the way he focused on her. He made her feel almost as if there were no one else anywhere that mattered. Only her.

But he also reminded her that as much as she loved the life she had now, she lost something too, when she walked away from Mack for that life. It was too late to ever get what she had with him back, but she would sure have liked to get the one thing back she was hoping for when she decided to meet him in that place that morning.

Mack was thinking much the same thing. He found the time they were spending together satisfying, and hoped they would have more days like this in the future.

They stopped at a grassy knoll. As Mack knew she would, Beth sat close to him as they rested. She was obvious what she wanted when she rested her hand high on his leg. He thought about moving it away, but it was such a pleasant sensation that he left it there.

Beth smiled when he didn't do or say anything about her hand. She moved up a little. When he didn't do anything to stop her, she asked, "Do you like that, Mack?"

"How could I not like it? There's not a man alive who wouldn't love to feel your hand on their leg. You're a beautiful, sexy woman, Beth."

She sighed. "It would be nice though, if you would give me a stronger response." Before Mack could answer, his cell phone started to ring. He checked to see who was calling. "It's Lisa. I suppose I should answer it."

"It would be a good idea,"

Beth got up and walked away from Mack. She called Bob. She talked softly, so he couldn't make out what she said. And that was fine with him. He had no desire to listen in on Beth's private conversation.

He answered his phone. "I'm surprised that you called. What's going on?"

Lisa sounder rather chipper when she answered Mack's question about what she was doing. "Things are going good," she said. "But I have something I needed to tell you. I'm going to have lunch with Dale. Donna will be with Sue and Julie while I'm gone. Other than that, everything just fine."

"That doesn't sound serious enough for you to call me. But it's always nice to talk to you. Where are you guys going to go eat."

Lisa chuckled. "This is why it's serious. As you know, Kathy's gone until Sunday for her concert, so we're having lunch at their house. And if you get home before me, it's because I'm once again trying to totally resolve the issue I have about who and what I am.

I hope my doing that isn't going to upset you. Especially when you consider what you're probably doing today."

"I'm jealous as hell, Lisa, but it's okay for you to try one more time to to take care of that issue. And I'm glad you told me. It might have upset me if you didn't. But it's a no on what I'm doing. So far it's just two old friends taking a walk in the refuge. Something you know I love to do."

"That sounds okay. But you do have some issues that need settling with her too. I don't want you to use me as the reason for not taking care of those issues."

Beth was done talking, so Mack said, "I don't know how long we will be here, but if it's going to be much later, I'll call you."

"Okay, Mack, I'll talk to you later."

Beth sat down next to him again. Her look had gone from a light, teasing one, to something a lot more serious.

As soon and Mack saw it, he asked, 'Is it time to leave now?"

"No, there's no hurry."

"What did Bob have to say?"

"I'm not so sure I should tell you. It was something I never thought he would say to me."

"Was it that bad?"

"It wasn't at all bad. It was just different, and unexpected. It changed for me, what this day is about."

"He convinced you that I'm right. It's better that we don't let things get out of hand. That we keep the boundaries between us where they are."

"No, Mack," she shook her head, "that's not at all what he said. He said to tell you that he understands what there still is between us. That he's known it all along. And that it will be best for all of us if you take advantage of the situation you're in. There will never be any hard feelings on his part."

"What did he say about Lisa?"

"He said that Lisa, more than anyone, will understand. She knows how much I still love you."

"You've really got me in an odd position, Beth."

She rested her hand high on his leg again. Squeezing it she said, "We'll take our time. I want to make it last as close to forever as we can. I want our second time to last even longer."

"I should say no, it's better if we don't do this. But then I remember that there are times that walking away doesn't really make the kind of sense it's supposed to."

When they started, Mack had memories flash through his head like lightening during a strong summer storm. Gradually though, the building passion overwhelmed all other thoughts and feelings. It was only the two of them and what they shared, what they gave, and what they traded. For a way to short, bright shining time, they lived together what they once were.

She quickly rose as high as she'd ever been, and Mack held her tight as she rode over the crest. He held back, and the instant she was settled back, close to the earth, he took her to new heights. It was her fourth time rolling over that wave that he joined her.

"I've been remembering, all this time, how good it always was for us. But this…this went way beyond the memories. I hope you have it in you to take me there again before we have to leave this little part of heaven. But even if you don't, I will never forget today, Mack. No matter what, I won't forget."

"I won't either, Beth. I won't either." He wondered as he said it, why this part of life seemed to be either on or off, alive or dead? Why couldn't it be what it was, enough love for everyone to be shared.

They held each other, slowly falling asleep. When they woke up, they made love again. Then it was time to face the real life they were going back to. They kissed goodby in the parking lot. She was crying when she got in her car. He just felt the empty spot she created inside him when she left him the first time.

But this time he told her, "It isn't goodby this time, Beth. This is going back to life as it is. But we can never stay apart again. You know that."

"I know it, Mack. I'm counting on it." She smiled as she drove away. Her tears continued.

Lisa was home when he got there. She greeted him with a kiss filled with the kind of love only she could give him. "I know," she said, "from the look on your face, that you and Beth managed to take care of what needed taking care of. Dale and I managed to get past that final hurdle too. It has already helped me to fight back all those things haunting me. And it was okay. He was good to me."

She dropped her head, clenched her fists, then shook them hard in front of her. "But damnit, Mack. It wasn't you. All the time, I kept thinking that it just wasn't you. My body might have taken pleasure from it, but it wasn't complete. So you have to know, more than ever, I am your woman. You don't own me and probably can't control me, but I goddamn well am yours. And that's all I want to talk about what today was, for the rest of today. Maybe even until next week sometime."

Mack didn't answer her. He felt the same as she did. He was her man. No matter how full of distractions like Beth and Dale their world offered, they belonged to each other. He knew they would never lose or throw away Beth or Dale, but no matter what, it would still always first be Lisa and him."

He took her hand and led her into the bedroom. She let him undress her, then waited on the bed for him to join her. There was no talking when he did. As he moved over her, she took him in hand and guided him. As he slipped inside her, something clicked between them. They both felt it, and both knew it was unlikely that either one of them would ever *need* a day like this one had been again. If anything ever did happen in the future, it would be for other reasons, and for other needs.

Quickly, Lisa cried out, "Mack, Mack, Mack. You're my only love, Mack. No one else. Only you." Then she softly moaned as she climbed over her mountain.

When it was over and they rested, holding each other, they were both glad that what happened to them that day could happen. And still leave them who they were. And better than that even. Who they wanted to be.

CHAPTER 20

Lisa stayed as close to Mack as she could for the rest of the day. During their evening time outside on the deck, she spent most of it on his lap. That night, she stayed in his arms until morning. They didn't make love then, but it was only because Donna was up already.

She woke up almost two hours before Mack and Lisa. It was the day they were going to pick up her personal things, and she was sure that if her husband was home, they'd have some serious trouble with him. So she was extremely nervous, and dreading what they were facing.

It was different for Mack and Lisa. It was as if a veil that had been hanging between them was lifted, and they could see each other clearly again. Somehow, all the feelings that started building with Lisa's date with Dale after Kathy left him, that were clouding their feelings for each other, evaporated. They were again the couple they were in the beginning. The things they'd done with others were now in their proper place. They together, were still who they wanted to be.

Mack loved having the old, now new, feelings back. The fog of doubt was gone, and he again felt confident that he and Lisa were indeed one in their love for each other. But he also knew that they had a job to do today, and they couldn't let their new found euphoria interfere with their judgement. They would be moving into dangerous territory, and they needed to have their wits about them.

As they grew close to the time to leave, Donna became more and more agitated. She was scared. So scared that she was close to backing out of the plan. With the fear ruling her, she was talking herself into giving up and going back to the man who treated her like a captive prostitute, as if her life had zero value. It was Lisa who convinced her to continue with their plan.

"If you go back to him, Donna, the first thing he's going to do is beat the hell out of you. Then, likely as not, instead of six men, there will be twelve next time. After that, he will use whatever force he needs to use, to keep you in sexual slavery for the rest of your life. Is that what you want?"

"Of course not. But I don't want anything to happen to you either, Lisa. Not you or Mack. I'm afraid of what my husband will do if he catches you there. I know what he'll do to me. But that doesn't matter so much. He's done it to me before. I can survive him doing it again."

"The thing is, Donna, you don't have to. If you're that scared, we can wait and go another time. But you can't go back to him. If you do, he will eventually kill you. If not directly, it will be what he forces you to do that will kill you."

"You sure do know how to make it hard for a person, don't you, Lisa?"

"We are trying to help you make your life better, not harder. I know that it's the decision you have to make today that's hard, not what I'm doing to you."

"Either way, I'm still afraid of what he will do if he catches us there."

"I know you are, but we aren't. We've dealt with people a lot worse than your husband."

Donna ran out of arguments. The only thing that would stop them from getting the job done today would be her fear. So she took a deep breath and decided to go ahead with the plan. They would go and get her personal things. She hoped though, that they would do it without her husband knowing anything about it until long after they'd been there and gone.

What they hadn't told her was that they were bringing backup. Roy and Wanda would be following them to Beth's. They didn't tell Donna about them, because they didn't want to take her without her showing at least some confidence in what they were trying to do.

As soon as she did, Mack and Lisa didn't waste any time getting things ready. Lisa chose to sit in the back seat of Mack's pickup on the way. She didn't want anything to give Donna negative thoughts on the way to her house. Not even uncomfortable rear seats that the quad cab of his truck provided. Also, with her sitting up front with Mack, Lisa thought he might prove to be a distraction from what they were doing. At least it seemed to her, that he was one too damn near every other woman he'd been around lately.

That thought didn't bother her though. She and Mack had what they had, regardless of what someone else might think of their relationship. Those thoughts filled her head until they got too Donna's.

There wasn't any sign of anyone around, so Mack and Lisa took her inside. Roy and Wanda waited outside in Roy's pickup while Donna quickly packed. Lisa helped with it as Donna took things out of closets and drawers. Together, they managed to do an efficient job of it. They were nearly finished, and Mack was loading the last of Donna's suitcases and boxes when her husband, Charles Slater, arrived. Two cars parked in the driveway behind him. There was one man with him, three in the car behind his, and two more in the last car.

Charles charged out of his car and hurried into the house. The moment he saw her, he rushed to Donna. He grabbed her arm and spun her around to face him.

"And what the fuck is it that you think you're doing, bitch?" He yelled. He moved his hand back like he was going to hit her.

Lisa then grabbed his arm, and using all her strength and the right movement of her body, she managed to put it into a hammerlock. She jammed it high on his back, until he moaned from the pain.

"If you so much as try to touch her," Lisa threatened, "you damn well will regret it."

"You've got your head up your ass, Lady." He looked around at his friends, now watching him with their mouths open. "Okay, Guys, kick some asses," he told them.

They hesitated before they went after Mack and Lisa. Watching Lisa take control of Charles as quickly and easily as she did, shocked them into a state of uncertainty. By the time they made their move toward Mack and Lisa, Roy and Wanda were in the house. With little difficulty, they dispatched the first two men who moved to go after Mack and Lisa.

Lisa jammed Charles's arm to the breaking point as she pushed him away from her. Now that she was finally close to him, she couldn't think of him any other way than him contentedly watching a bunch of men as they raped Donna. She took the thought of that personal. So personal that it dredged up memories of being sixteen and being defenseless against what felt like an endless stream of rapists.

As Charles turned to face her, she cleared her throat and spit in his face. The splatter covered a good part of his face when it landed right on target. His eyes popped open wide as soon as what she did to him registered. He wiped off his face with his shirt sleeve and charged her, Which was exactly what she wanted him to do.

She swiftly and effortlessly stepped out of his way. As he went by her, the instant his right leg touched the floor, she slammed her foot into the side of his knee. He fell to the floor, screaming in pain.

Two more of his friends moved to rescue him from Lisa. She met one of them with her elbow, which smashed into his nose. He didn't fall, but he did lean against a wall as he tried desperately to stop the bleeding. All Mack had to do to stop the other one was look at him.

Then Mack said, "It's like this. We have papers making it legal for us to chaperone Donna while she gets her personal things. We intend to do that very thing. Now, you can all get the hell out of here, or we can continue to kick your asses. Frankly, I don't care which. But either way, you won't be raping Donna today."

One of the undamaged men spoke up. "We haven't ever done anything with Donna that she didn't want us to do. The more of us that did it with her, the better she liked it. And if Charles like watching it, so what. That was between them two."

"You can try to hand me whatever kind of excuse you want to, but there still won't be any of that kind of thing today."

The man turned to Donna. "Tell him, Bitch. Tell this goddamn fool the truth. You wanted us to do you the way we did."

Donna, now aware of just how capable Mack, Lisa, Wanda, and Roy were, snarled her answer. "I never wanted any of what you and the rest of Charles's friends did to me. I didn't fight with you, because I didn't want to get beaten after you finished."

Charles was on his feet again. He looked around at his friends, "Let's kick some ass now. These people just got lucky. Ain't but two of them men, and they look like a couple of wimps. When we're done with them, we'll have two more women for our fun."

Lisa stepped in front of him. "There'll be no fun for you today, you rapist son of a bitch. All you're going to get today is a lot more pain. From me. I hate you. And I am definitely looking forward to showing you how much a person can be hated. One final thing. When I finish with you this time, along with the pain you'll be feeling, your manhood will be gone too. Sex for you will just be a bad memory."

Charles looked around again. None of his friends seemed at all anxious to start anything. He desperately wanted to get at Lisa first. Then he wanted to help his friends beat the hell out of the other three people who came with Donna. And finally, he wanted to once more watch his friends with Donna. One at a time. The way he always liked watching them do her. He wouldn't join them, but his hand would do it for him.

Finally, after a rather lengthy silence, Wanda spoke up. "I can see," she told them, "that you brave boys are more than a little bit hesitant about what to do next. That's as it should be. Because if any of you so much as make a move toward any of us, you are doomed. As far as Charles here, our biggest concern is how much damage Lisa will do to him before we can force her to stop working him over. Once she gets started on him, she isn't going to want to stop. The last man she hated as much as she hates Charles, is still in the hospital. Before we could get her off him, he was neutered."

The friends didn't move. They didn't know what to do. They were sure though, that if they did try to help Charles, it would cost them. They were wondering now, if the free sex they'd been getting from Donna was worth it. She gave them their answer.

She moved next to one of the men who was with the group of six who recently raped her. The look on Donna's face told him not to respond. He was particularly rough, and loved to twist and pinch her nipples. She grabbed his manhood and squeezed. He was wearing lightweight slacks, so she managed to get a good hold on him. He doubled over, and as he did she let go. But she grabbed his nose this time, and twisted until she felt something that was stationary, move. She wiped the blood on her fingers onto his shirt.

"It's time for all of you goddamn bastards to leave now. And if I ever see any of you again, anywhere, I will probably kill you. You've all raped me for the last time." She actually smiled at them. "And just so you know, these two men here are teaching me how to shoot. I'm getting pretty good at it." They believed what she said.

The three men who were hurt by Lisa, Wanda, and Roy, were already planning to leave. That would leave the friends of Charles out numbered, so they all decided to go. That left Charles there alone. He was so angry that his words came out with a sputter. He had to repeat himself three times before they could understand what he said.

"Donna's my wife," he said, with a large whine in his voice. "And none of you have the right to keep her from me. I demand that you leave my home. You have to let her stay with me when you go."

"Donna will decide her future from now on. Not you."

"She doesn't have the right to do that. If any of you read your bible, you would know that."

"Donna," Mack said, "you didn't tell us he was one of those. How could you forget to do that?"

"What do you mean, Mack? Once of what?"

"He's one of those religious nutcases. No wonder he's done the things he's done to you. There's nothing like religion to screw up a person's head. His kind of religion is the same as greed and lust for power, when you talk about a source of pure evil. A man with his beliefs has less worth than even a single HIV or covid virus. "

"But I'm religious too, Mack."

"As long as you keep it to yourself, I won't hold it against you."

"Why would you hold my religion against me? My faith is what carried me through what Charles's been doing to me."

"Do you have the same religion he does?"

"Well, sure. Most married couples have the same religion."

"And you go to the same church?"

"Of course we do."

"Even after he uses that religion as an excuse for what he'd done to you?" She just shook her head in answer this time. Mack shook his too, as he tried to rid himself of the disgust he felt toward her beliefs. "Why would you buy into that bullshit after what he's done to you? Your religion says that you, being a woman, have no purpose but to serve him."

"I know that, but there's good things too."

"Really? Like what?"

"Well, like how Jesus loves us, and how he's always there to protect us."

"Like he did with you?"

"But I wasn't worthy. I allowed it to happen once. That first time. So the other times I was paying for my sin."

"And how much longer were you supposed to pay? When was it, exactly, that Jesus was going to come and save you. Maybe, because your religion says that men are far more important than women, he was going to continue to let them have at it with you?"

"Yes, but…"

Mack knew the discussion was hopeless. No matter what he said, no matter what arguments he used, he would never change her mind. He doubted that she would ever take a close look at what she was so sure was true. The real truth was, she was brain washed.

"Like I said to start with, Donna, if you keep it to yourself, I won't hold it against you."

After listening to their short discussion, Charles was feeling more emboldened. He was sure he could convince Donna to do what he wanted, if he could use his religious beliefs on her. So he spoke up, "Donna, you have no choice but to follow your faith. If you go against God's teachings, by going against me, you will surely rot in hell."

Donna cringed from his words. She looked at Wanda, who was the one closest to her now, for some kind of reassurance. Instead of trying to convince Donna that he was wrong, she turned to Charles.

"I'll tell you what, Asshole. Since that god of yours is so almighty powerful, and so much on your side in what you do, I'm going to let you prove it. Right here, and right now, I'm going to let Lisa tear into you. If your God in so great, he'll lend a hand in your victory. In which case, we'll leave Donna with you. If, however, God doesn't come to your aid, this time when Lisa gets to working you over, we aren't going to stop her. Not until you are on the edge of dying. And by then, you will probably have lost the ability to walk. you will be blind, and best of all, your manhood will be gone."

Charles's initial reaction was a thrill to have the opportunity to kick the hell out of the little bitch who tried to break his arm. And then to regain custody of Donna on top of it. But before he started on Lisa, he looked around. He noticed Mack first. Charles knew, just from looking at him, that he loved his wife. So why was his expression one of no concern for her welfare. Given the difference in his size compared to Lisa's, should alone give him concern.

He continued looking, stopping for a moment on each face. None of them showed even the slightest sign of worry. Roy was the exception. He not only didn't look worried, he had a smirk filling his face. And the sparkle in his eyes said that he was looking forward to watching the fight. A fight that he knew would end with the result he wanted to see.

Charles dropped his head. He couldn't look at any of them again. He had no idea how good Lisa's abilities were, or what her power was, but he could suddenly feel the pain in his arm when she had it pushed up behind his back. He was convinced now, that she was what they said she was. He couldn't beat her, and she did hate him. He was beaten and she hadn't laid a hand on him.

Mack knew that all the fight was out of him, so he told him to go sit in the corner. He did. They finished loading up Donna's things, and even though they hadn't planned it, they waited while she got into his stash of cash that he always kept in a box in a bedroom closet. She took out half of it, and showed it to Charles.

"I'm taking it," she said, "because you owe me this much a million times over."

Before they left, Mack told him, "Be smart now, and don't come looking for her. If anything happens to her, if she disappears, we'll know you were behind it. Then we will come hunting you. And it would be a good idea for you to remember, where we live, we have thousands of places to hide the body. Yours wouldn't be the first."

Charles just cringed when he heard Mack's words. Admitting to defeat in a fight with a woman before the fight even started, had diminished his ego considerably. He didn't pray either. He'd always just used his brand of religion as an excuse for doing things like forcing his wife to have sex with his friends. He knew that praying wasn't something that actually worked. So it was a seriously diminished man who was left behind, sitting in a corner.

Lisa sat up front with Mack on the way home. Donna got into the backseat without comment. She didn't complain either. Not after what they just did for her. She couldn't be anything but thankful after, within a few short hours, they'd freed her of years of torture and terror.

They didn't get far into their ride home before a chuckle escaped Lisa. She tried to stop it, but couldn't help herself. Finally, Mack asked her, "Okay, Lisa, what's so funny?"

"You, Mack. Sometimes the things you come up with."

"I don't think I know what you're talking about."

"Your last comment to the idiot. We have thousands of places to hide the body. Yours wouldn't be the first. That sure did a number on him."

Thinking about it now, Mack had to agree with her. The question was though. Would the warning hold, or would Charles come after her anyway.

CHAPTER 21

Kathy spent three weekends in a row in concert. It was something she tried to avoid, but all of them were within driving distance from home, so they didn't take up near as much of her time. She was able to do the rehearsals at home, and they managed the trip there and back in her tour bus.

But they were over now, and she'd spent as much of the time between them with Dale as she could. During that time, Dale told her about what he and Lisa did while she was at one of her concerts. Somewhere in her head there was something, she was sure, that would tell her to be upset and jealous about it. The trouble was, she couldn't find that somewhere. It did give her the opportunity though, to tell Dale how she felt about what had happened so far between him and Lisa and her and Mack. Dale wasn't surprised by what she said. He actually agreed with it. Then they decided what to do about it.

What she wanted right after that, was the chance to talk to Mack about it. So she called him and they set a date for the following Saturday. It was time for their monthly walk in the refuge anyway.

When Donna, who'd been with them for nearly two weeks now, learned that Mack was taking Kathy hiking in the refuge without Lisa, she asked Lisa about it.

"So now Mack's going on another hike in the refuge with another woman. And that woman is Kathy Magee, the singer? She's beautiful. Why is he taking her? My God, Lisa, if I were you, I'd be a lot more than just jealous. I'd be damn scared."

"No, Donna. I'm not scared. She's married to Mack's best friend. All four of us are friends."

"I suppose, but two people like that…I don't know. It just seems natural, once they get out there, they'll be doing it."

"They go on their hike together once a month. Most of the time when they do, I spend the day with Dale, her husband. We are real good friends too."

"Really. Is he anywhere as good looking as your Mack is?"

"He is, but in a different sort of way. He's the kind of man who can make a woman want to undress him."

"Well, have you undressed him yet?"

"What would you like to do today, Donna? Dale and Kathy live just across the meadow behind our house. We could walk over there so you could meet him if you want?"

"I want," Donna answered.

I want was something Kathy was saying to Mack at about the same time. Specifically, she was saying, "If you don't mind, I want you to tell me about the adventure you had that led to Lisa and Dale finally actually having sex? He said that she initiated it, and that she decided to finally do it because of you finally getting something settled with some woman."

"I know what she did, but it was as much because she needed to get past the things haunting her since she was raped. The rest of her reason for doing it was because it was Dale she was doing it with. Given how bad her experience when she was kidnapped was, I'm surprised at how well she's been able to handle it."

"And you know that I already know all that. What I want to know, is what it was that you were up to that day. Dale said that whatever it was that you were doing, it and what he and Lisa did, has seemed to change you guys. There's been kind of a quiet tension between the two of you. It's gone now. I can't explain exactly how, but it's like you're back to who you used to be. So what the hell were you doing that changed both of you?"

"Are you sure you want to know?"

"Yes, because who you and I are to each other won't last unless we are as honest with each other as you are with Lisa and I am with Dale. Like any and all good relationships, we don't own each other. But I still want to know."

"Okay, I'll tell you. I was with Beth."

"Beth? Bob Anderson's wife? What the hell for? You and her split a long time ago."

"That's true. Trouble was, she felt like we'd left something undone. She still feels guilty about breaking up with me the way she did. It was her idea that we meet and spend the day together. At first, I was determined to keep it completely platonic, but then Lisa called to tell me what she had planned for the day. That's when it changed."

"With the exception of one question, that's all I need to know."

"What's the question?"

"Are you planning more walks with her?"

"No, but the way things have been since you asked Dale for a divorce, I damn sure don't have the slightest idea of what's going to happen next."

"You might not have, but I do. It's time to stop the charade. I don't know for sure what you think about it all, nor do I know for sure what Lisa thinks. But Dale and I agreed last night that it's time we quit pretending. So we decided that things between us should no longer be taboo. When they happen, they happen. None of us want to change partners, nor do we want to make this a regular part of our lives. But there's no sense in running from who we really are any longer."

Mack looked at her, his expression blank. "See, Kathy, I told you I didn't know what was going to happen next."

"But you know part of it now?"

"That I certainly do.

"Good. Let's find that grassy hill we were on before."

While they were on their grassy hill, testing the softness of the grass, Lisa and Donna were visiting Dale. He knew Donna was still staying with Lisa and Mack, so he wasn't surprised to see them.

"We came over," Lisa said, "mostly because Donna wanted to meet you." Lisa introduced them. "She thought it was strange that Mack and Kathy were going to be hiking out in the refuge together. So I told her about us, how we're all friends. She then wanted to meet you, so here we are."

"Well," Dale said, "here I am, Donna. Just an ordinary guy whose had the incredible luck to be married the most beautiful and wonderful woman a man could hope to find."

Donna, being the naturally nosey person she was, just had to ask. "But don't you worry when your wife goes off with another man, the way she's doing now?"

"Not at all. Mack's my best friend. He wouldn't do anything with Kathy, any different than I would with Lisa."

Donna giggled. "You guys sure are a trusting bunch. Kind of refreshing, actually. You all somehow make me believe that if anything ever did happen between any of you, it would be mostly love, not just sex. That's what it was with my husband. Just sex." She moved her head around, as if she was trying to decide if she should say anymore. She had a gleam in her eye when she decided to continue to talk. "I hated everything with my husband. I was determined, all the time he had control over me, that if I ever escaped, I would have to be in love before I could have sex again. I know now that it could never happen. But after getting to know Mack and Lisa, and now meeting you, Dale, I have to tell you, I wouldn't turn you down if you ever wanted it." She turned to Lisa. "Mack either." She looked at the floor then, blushing slightly.

Lisa took her hand and gave it a light squeeze. "It's okay, Donna. I can't blame you for that at all. These two men that Kathy and I have, have tendency to do that to women. But don't get your hopes up. They are extremely loyal. To us as well as each other."

Dale took them out on his deck. They sat down and he went into the kitchen and made a large pitcher of ice cold lemonade. They talked then about how lucky the four of them were. Living next to a beautiful meadow, filled with wildlife they could watch, was a big part of their luck.

Donna seemed to thrive from feeling free while they talked and watched what was unknown to her. The meadow was a much different world from what she was used to seeing. Lisa and Dale watched her relax, while at the same time her entire body seemed to soften. As it did, the harsh lines etched into her face gradually melted away. Before Lisa or Dale realized it, she transformed from the somewhat haggard person, into a very pretty woman. Dale was the first to notice.

"You must like it here?" he asked.

She wasn't sure she understood what he asked. "I'm sorry, what did you say?"

"I asked you if you liked it here. You look different now, than you did when you got here."

She didn't know how to answer him. Too often in the past, any answer when her husband asked a question, was the wrong answer. She decided though, that here an honest answer would probably be best. "Yes, I do like it here. It's so peaceful. Someday, I'd like to have something like you guys have."

"You'd probably want a bigger house though. Most people wonder why we don't have a bigger one."

"I think what you have is perfect. More than I'd need."

Lisa, who'd been listening to them, got an idea. "I don't know for sure if we can do it. It will depend on Mack. But we have the cottage." She looked at Donna to see if she had any interest in what she just said. Donna was now on the edge of her chair, her eyes boring a hole through Lisa. That was enough for Lisa to continue.

"It's only a one bedroom, manufactured home. Mack lived in it before we were married. It's the little house out closer to the road. But it has everything a person needs. A full bath, dishwasher, full size electric cook stove, and decent size refrigerator. All the furniture is still in there, so you wouldn't need to replace any of that right away."

Donna looked at her with complete disbelief. "Are you talking about me living in it?"

"I was, but if you don't think it would be suitable for you, it's okay. I'm sure we will be able to find somewhere else for you to live when the time comes."

"I think you took me wrong, Lisa. It's not that it isn't good enough for me. It's that it is way more than I could have hoped for. Living here, close to you guys, not to mention, this beautiful meadow. There's no place else I'd rather live. The only thing I can say is, if Mack says it's okay and I can stay here, I'm not sure I'm worthy enough to accept the offer. You guys are so special, I don't think I'm quite good enough for you."

"Nonsense, you're good enough for anyone." Lisa gave Donna a hug.

When Mack got home, his answer when asked was, "Damn right she can." He gave her a hug too.

"I think," Lisa said then, "tomorrow we will have a family cleaning party. It'll be our way of going to church and giving thanks, by making a home for our new friend, Donna."

CHAPTER 22

It was decided at breakfast. They would shut the Refuge Rescuers office down for the day. It was Sunday, so it wasn't part of their normal working hours anyway. Only Theresa would be doing something else for a few hours. she would be at the community garden she managed.

Weekends were the day when most people were able to visit their garden plots, so she like to spend part of both days there, to help and answer questions.

There were a lot of other questions being asked that day too. Mostly it was Mack answering them. Once they started digging through the cottage, they found a lot more stuff than they'd expected to find when they started. A lot of what was in there was long forgotten. It all belonged to Mack, so he had to decide where things should go. It didn't take him long to decide to send nearly all of it to the local thrift store. It was a charity that helped women with all types of problems. It was Lisa's favorite, so Mack let his stuff go there, rather than an environmental charity.

When they stopped for lunch, Kathy sang a few songs for them. She sang a hymn for Donna because it was Sunday. Then a few love songs. At the end, she sang one to Dale, then one to Mack. Lisa laughed when she did the last one. Mack blushed.

Donna was particularly impressed with her performance. She'd always liked Kathy's music, but never realized how good she really was, until she heard her sing in person.

The day went well, and by late in the afternoon, they had all of Mack's personal things out of it. A few things they'd moved to his and Lisa's house, but the bulk went to the thrift store. By dark, they had cleaned the whole thing, and Donna moved in that night.

She would have been somewhat uncomfortable staying alone, but a special alarm system for all the houses was already installed. If anyone tried to break into any of the houses, including the cottage, an alarm went off in all the houses. And the alarm was different, depending which house was broken into. That helped give her confidence in her safety. Even so, she offered to let either Mack or Dale spend the night with her. Kathy and Lisa nixed that idea.

It was getting late by then, so they all called it a day and went home.

When Mack and Lisa got into bed that night, Lisa told him, "I don't totally agree with what Kathy said yesterday about our relationships. I don't think we should be open about what we've done, or might do. Having the world know, doesn't make us anymore free. And I think I'd like it if you don't do it with anyone else for a while. Sharing you occasionally with Kathy is one thing. Sharing you with anyone else isn't something I'll be willing to do anytime soon. Especially given how much sharing you've been doing lately."

"If that's what you want, I won't object. Keeping you happy is more important to me than anything else I do"

"You aren't going to get mad at me for being so demanding then?"

"No, I'm not going to get mad at you. I just want you to be happy and satisfied."

"Really. Happy and *satisfied?* You haven't told me though, what I could or couldn't do to be satisfied."

"You're full grown now, Lisa. I trust you to use good judgment when it comes to that. You know that my only request is that you are always honest with me. As for the rest, I don't own you, and I don't want to."

"Do you think I'm trying to own you, Mack?"

He moved his hand to her shoulder and gently pulled her closer to him. "Maybe, a little bit. But it's okay. I kind of like it. It means that you need me some. That's not always a bad thing when you love someone."

"No, I guess not. You need to keep it in mind though, that there are several women around here, who in one way or the other seem to need, or at least want, something from you. I prefer that you pay closer attention to my needs from now on. Because I won't like it much if you try to fulfill those needs or wants that they have."

Mack sighed, but managed a smile to go with it. "As long as you don't stop keeping me as satisfied as you have since even before we got married, I'll be more than willing to follow that rule."

"That was my next plan, if you're up to it?"

"When have I not been?" She slid as close to him as she could, and kissed him. That's when the house alarm went off. It originated at Roy and Wanda's.

Mack and Lisa leaped from the bed, threw on barely enough clothes to cover themselves, picked up their guns, and raced out the door. They didn't get far before they realized the problem. About twenty men were milling around Roy and Wanda's house. Rather than spreading out and finding strategic positions, they remained bunched up. Most of them carried blank expressions, similar to a severely retarded child. The rest of them just looked confused.

They were yelling for Wanda to come out, and they couldn't understand why she didn't. As far as they were concerned, she should have done what she was told to do immediately. That's what terrified people do. And she should be terrified now. They were all wearing their military garb, and dressed that way they should be scaring everyone silly.

The MAGA Fellows were there to retrieve Wanda, so they could use her to put her former husband, Lance North, through hell while they forced him to watch them torture her.

There were some flaws in their plans though. The number one flaw was the fact that even though they out numbered the Thomas's and their friends, they hadn't practiced the raid they were staging, so none of them knew for sure what to do.

The MAGAs also had superior weapons for killing people. Nearly all of them carried AR15s. Their problem with that was the fact that only a few of them knew how to use them effectively. They hadn't been trained at all. They didn't have any decent leadership. Titus Trump, the leader of the MAGA Fellows, decided that his bone spurs in his feet were acting up too much for him to participate with his men on this raid.

Their biggest mistake, however, was their failure to learn anything about Wanda or anyone around her. All they knew about her was the fact that she was married to Lance, or possibly divorced from him. There were also rumors that she knew how to shoot a gun.

When Mack and Lisa got close to Roy and Wanda's, they heard Wanda warn them that they better leave. The MAGAs answered with a few gunshots into the house near Wanda. That was enough for Wanda, so she decided to teach them a lesson.

Since they were completely exposed where they were, she gave them serious lessons on shooting. She started with the men who did the shooting. For the first one, she took off a serious piece of his right ear. The second one, she shot in the thigh, about an inch away from his manhood. The third lost part of his left ear. The fourth man got it in the other thigh.

"Okay, you clowns," she yelled at the men still standing in the same place as they were before she started shooting. She did it so fast they didn't have time to react. "it's like this," she continued, "either you load up and get the hell out of here, or I start shooting foreheads instead of ears and thighs. And just so you know, I frankly don't give a good goddamn which it is."

All the MAGAs stood frozen in place except one. He lifted his AR15, intending to shoot in Wanda's direction. She fired first, hitting him in the hand reaching for the trigger. He dropped the rifle.

Mack decided then that he'd had enough. He moved in close to the rather feeble gunmen. "Okay, idiots," he told them, "It's time to put down the guns, then lay down on the ground until the police get here. I am just not in the mood for anymore of this kind of shit today."

A big man close to Mack decided he could take him. He lunged at Mack, who wasn't about to let him. He simply smashed the butt end of his gun into the man's face, breaking his nose and knocking him out.

By then Roy, Wanda, Sue, Ben, Theresa, Dale, Kathy, and of course Mack and Lisa, had encircled all the MAGA Fellows. The only exception was Donna, who stood in the background and watched.

Dale had hastily put on his uniform shirt, so he was officially in charge. He signaled Mack to follow him, and they walked into the confused group of men, disarming them as they did. As they took each man's weapon, they emptied them, then threw them out of the way of the group, and into the dirt."

Dale also took the time to call for backup. A lot of sirens were wailing in the background. Shortly after several deputies got there, a big old school bus arrived. It was transportation for the twenty plus men who were now under arrest. Mack, Roy and Wanda agreed to ride in the bus on the way to the sheriff's office.

On the way there, when ever any of the prisoners got restless, all Wanda needed to do was point her gun their way. That quickly settled them down.

The jail wasn't built to accommodate all the men, but Dale decided to stuff them into the cells anyway. Also, because of the late hour, they didn't have the staff to get the paperwork done in any kind of hurry. That meant the prisoners had to wait to make their first calls. Then, when they did call someone, it was most often a friend or relative. Only a few thought to call a lawyer.

Among the first of the attorneys to arrive was a man Mack hated. Ralph Saxton was a man who consistently found fault with Mack. Even though Mack always proved him wrong. This time, he managed to get three of the MAGAs to sign on as his clients.

"This time," he threatened Mack, "the lawsuit I'm going to file against you will cost you millions."

Mack laughed at him. "What kind of nonsense are you going to file in court this time, Asshole? Do you think it'll amount to near as much as the one I will be counter filing against you? Also, don't forget, my lawyers are way smarter than your's are." Ralph always served as his own attorney.

Dale stepped in then. He told Ralph, "You'll have to find somewhere else to do your paperwork, Ralph. As you can see, with this many people here, there just isn't any room for you."

"This is a public place," Ralph countered, "and I have just as much right as anyone else."

"Okay, but you are damn sure going to wait until some space frees up. There isn't any now."

"But there is. Your office isn't being used right now. I'll do my paper work in there."

"No, you certainly will not. That's my private office. It's not open to the public." Dale turned his back and walked away.

CHAPTER 23

Titus Trump was having a fit. His would-be soldier men failed again. He sent twenty men to do a job four or five should have been able to accomplish, and they all landed in jail. He knew they weren't very well trained, but that wasn't his fault. The primary fault was with them. They didn't like to train. Dressing up like soldiers was one thing. Training like one was something entirely different.

They believed that the outfits they wore, along with the AR15s they carried, should be enough intimidation to allow them to handle any situation. Someone shooting off parts of their ears wasn't something any of them signed up for when they joined the MAGA Fellows militia. So the thirty or so men who hadn't quit the group and weren't in jail, didn't appreciate it when Titus tried to lecture them.

One of them stood up when Titus took a break from his incessant lecturing. "Before you keep on with anymore of your hammering on us because those guys in jail did a lousy job, you should remember one thing. None of us was there. Neither was you. So how about you back off some, and we all try to figure out what went wrong?"

"Well damnit," Titus complained, "I was getting to that. We got to somehow get to that Wanda Thomas bitch when she's alone."

"I got a better idea. Let's forget about that Wanda bitch. We can come up with enough ways to torture Lance North even if we don't have her to make him sick and sorry."

Titus didn't like this idea, and it showed. "The thing is, if we forget about her now, it means that they won. Do we really want to let liberal trash like them win? At anything? We all know that we are superior in strength and brains. So we should be able to take her. All we need to do is figure out how."

A second man from the bunch stood up. "I think we should go to the hospital and get Lance. A couple of us can dress like some of them hospital people and wheel him out. If we do it real early in the morning, they won't notice so much. Then we can haul him over to where them Thomas people are, and make him scream until that Wanda bitch gives her self up to us."

For the first time in a long time, Titus smiled. He looked at the man who came up with the idea. "I'm sorry," Titus said, "but I don't think I know your name."

"That's okay. I just joined last week." He looked at his leader with confidence in his eyes. "My name is Kegan, Sir. Kegan Kayson."

Titus smiled again, and patted Kegan on the shoulder. "Well, Son, I have to say that I am real happy to have you in our militia. You are the kind of men we so desperately need if we are going to stop those vile, evil liberals from taking over our country. A country God meant to be white. Not filled with the riffraff and rabble of them other, colored type races."

"You are right there," Kegan agreed. "We gots to do our most best to keep them guys the hell away from us. We got to send them black ones back to Africa, them yellow ones to China, them Mexicans back to Mexico, and them red Indians back to wherever they came from. Russia or someplace like that."

Titus was becoming increasingly pleased with this young man. As they talked, he grew more confident in his intelligence. Especially about the races. He was sure Kegan would be a continuous supply of good ideas. So he made a quick, but positive decision about him.

"It's like this, Kegan," Titus told him. "With only me in charge, without a second in command, we've been short on leadership. But now that you've shown me that you're brighter than most, with that good idea of yours about Wanda, how would you like to be my second in command?"

"Well, gosh, I really didn't expect anything like that," He lied, feeling as he did that he could run the group better than Titus, "but I sure will do my most best for you."

"Good. What we've got to do now, is plan our grab of Lance North and how we're going to force that Wanda bitch to surrender herself to us."

The plan they came up with was as simple as Kegan presented it in the first place. They also were lucky in their timing. A head-on crash on the four lane, that involved six drunk teenage boys and a semi load of roofing, made the hospital extraordinarily busy at a time of the day when they were the shortest of staff. Trying to save the lives of the seriously injured boys took priority over a couple of orderlies wheeling a cart around.

Lance was still in pain from his wounds, so he'd been given pain killers and a sleep aid the night before. It was enough so that he was too groggy to react when he was wheeled out of the hospital and loaded into a van.

They took him directly to the Thomas ranch and parked in the driveway that led to Roy and Wanda's. Kegan blew out a living room window with a twelve gauge.

"You, in the house." Kegan yelled. "We want Wanda out here now. She doesn't come out here, and we torture her boyfriend Lance until she does. Or until he dies."

Roy and Wanda were sound asleep, so they didn't have an instant answer fo Kegan. It only took Roy a couple of minutes though, for him to decide that there was no way Wanda was going out there.

Then Lance screamed. The agony it was filled with was horrifying to listen too. "We can't let this happen, Roy," Wanda said. "I don't have so much as a shred of caring for Lance, but we can't just let him be tortured the way they're doing it."

"I know, but we'll have to think of something other than you going out there."

Mack and Lisa joined them then. As Roy explained the problem, Lisa started thinking about ways to stop the torturing other than another shoot out. This time the MAGA Fellows were deployed so they could actually defend themselves. Even with Wanda's excellent marksmanship, there would be loss life if they tried any conventional ways to stop the torture. Lisa wasn't terribly concerned about any MAGA Fellows getting wounded or killed, but she definitely didn't want anyone in her family shot. Deadly or wounded.

She thought about all the ways she'd been kidnapped, and the ways she'd escaped. After the third time she ran every incident through her mind, she remembered the black skirt and the switchblade knives. Lance screamed again.

She grabbed Mack's arm to get his attention. "I've got an idea on how to stop this without getting an of us shot or killed," she said, "but I have to run home for a minute. Don't do anything radical until I get back."

As soon as she was inside her house, she shed the pants she was wearing. She put on a black skirt with a special pocket she'd sewn into the back of the waist band. It held a special switchblade knife. The knife's blade popped straight out the front, rather than swing out like a normal switch blade. Lisa had also made sure it was surgically sharp. She also grabbed two more of the same knives before she rushed out of her house and back to Wanda's.

When she got there, she explained to them what she wanted to do. Mack and Roy immediately decided it would be too dangerous. Lance screamed some more.

"I know it's dangerous for Wanda and me. But so is anything else we might try. And this is better than a gunfight. It will be nice if we can stop this before we have thousands of dollars more in house repairs to do."

Wanda considered all their options while they talked. "I think," she said, "that Lisa's right. Her idea gives us the best chance of ending this without a hell of a lot of shooting."

"I still don't feel right about this," Roy complained. "It shouldn't be you two who's going out there."

"That's probably true," Wanda agreed. "But right now, it's the only option we have. So we're going."

Lisa's the one who responded to the militia leader, who for the first time on one of their attempts at accomplishing some kind of criminal activity or another, was with his men. Titus Trump answered her, "What do you mean, you are going to go with Wanda when she surrenders to us."

"I mean just that. Either you take me, or Wanda doesn't go."

"Why the hell do you want to go with her?"

"She's like my sister. I don't want anything to happen to her."

Titus Laughed. "You can come, but you can forget about protecting her." His voice was filled with confidence, which told Lisa that her plan had an excellent chance of working.

Just before walking out to the militia, she opened the top buttons of her shirt. She wasn't wearing a bra, so doing it provided an excellent distraction. Wanda quickly did the same thing. None of the macho MAGAs picked up on the real reason for the position of the buttons. They were instead, a single minded bunch. Their heads were filled with nothing other than thoughts of what they are going to do to these two beautiful women.

Because they knew the MAGA Fellows were so confident, Lisa and Wanda carried their knives in their left hand. Lisa had a backup in the waistband of her skirt. Wanda had her backup knife in a back pocket.

A smiling Titus, dressed in his full uniform with all his soldier stuff hanging from it, waved them over to him. Watching them walk to him, he decided that he would let Kegan have Wanda first. He would take Lisa. He knew he was going to very much enjoy doing all the things to her that only a real man like him could do. And he would keep his uniform on. He deemed it appropriate that he should wear it while taking what he wanted from an enemy woman.

At the same time, Kegan was growing ever more excited about what he was going to do to Wanda. So excited that he when she got real close to him, he decided to show her what he was going to do to her. He grabbed the top of her blouse and tried to rip it open. The buttons were sown down solid though, so he only managed one of them. It was perfect for Wanda. With a quick nod to Lisa, she made her move to get behind him as he struggled with her next button. She snapped open her knife, swiped it across Kegan's cheek just deep enough to draw a lot of blood, and used that distraction to get behind him. She moved her knife to her right hand, grabbed his hair and yanked his head back with her left hand, and held then lightly slid her knife across his throat. It was just deep enough to draw some blood, but not enough to cut his artery.

"You know now how sharp it is," she said, cutting his more of his skin just enough to hurt, "so you'd best tell them all to back off."

While Wanda was doing her thing with Kegan, Lisa sliced a shallow cut about six inches long across a confused Titus's belly. Just as Wanda did to Kegan, she got behind him. It was a bit of a reach, but she held on tightly to his hair as she pulled his head back and rested her knife against his throat. She cut him there just enough to tell him he was in serious trouble.

"If you so much as make any kind of move I don't like," Lisa told the MAGAs who were now just as confused as their leaders. "I will cut his throat.

They didn't move until they heard the sirens in the distance. Then it was suddenly a scramble for their vehicles and a mad dash to get away. Wanda and Lisa continued to hold on to their captives. Everyone in the house watched the MAGAs run, but didn't shoot. They knew that now they had reason enough to have them arrested. So they avoided the chance of anyone getting shot this time.

In their rush to get away, the MAGAs forgot to take Lance with them. He was awake by then, and called out to Wanda. She ignored him. And after she turned over her prisoner to Dale and the sheriff's deputies, she stayed as far away from him as she could. That didn't help her situation with him any. For now he was sure she loved him. Why else would she have risked her life so save him?

Kegan Kayson didn't have any of those illusions about Wanda. She told him, just before the police got there, that if the paperwork for killing someone wasn't such a hassle, she'd gladly cut his throat, just to watch him bleed.

He didn't answer her. From then on, he avoided any kind eye contact with anyone there. He was too embarrassed to look at anyone, given how wet his pants were.

Titus was determined to stand up and be brave and belligerent with anyone who had any kind of authority. He might have pulled it off, at least partially. But when they stripped his custom made uniform of every vestige of his cherished military equipment, it was way too much for him. He cried.

CHAPTER 24

A thunderstorm rumbled through in the morning, with rain coming down in torrents. There was enough wind to bend the trees, and the lightening and thunder was constant. It was a large summer storm and lasted for over an hour.

When it was finally over, the ground was littered with leaves and small branches. Out in the woods, a few long dead branches broke away from their trees and fell to the ground. Some of them were large enough to eventually hollow out and make homes for any number of small creatures.

The storm also left behind clean, fresh air that only exists after a good hard rain filled with the effects of lightening. Mack sucked in deep breaths of it as he wiped the rain off his favorite chair.

The sun was now out, and its light sparkled as it shined through the droplets of water hanging on to the tree leaves. Something that sparkled even brighter, for Mack, then the dripping water, was his wife, Lisa.

She too, wiped off a chair close to his and sat down. He watched her move as she did the chair, then just looked at her for a while. It took her a few moments to notice what he was doing. When she did, she gave him a curious look and said, "What?"

"Nothing in particular. Just you."

"Okay, Mack, what does that mean? Just me. You're not making sense."

"I meant that it was just you I was looking at. First I looked at out meadow, and the water dripping off the trees. I was thinking how beautiful, they were, and how everything out here is. Especially after a really refreshing rain storm. I was kind of wondering how anything could possibly be anymore beautiful than what all that out there is. Then you came out here and I remembered. You are. You're the most beautiful thing in my life Lisa. You make me wonder everyday, how I can be so lucky to have you as my wife."

Lisa smiled, yet tears lightly rolled down her cheeks. Mack had told her the same and similar things many times since they were married, and they always meant a lot. But sometimes like now, when they'd just spent a fair amount of time in bed making love, and he had no reason to say those things, they meant something extra. He said them now, only because he meant them.

She left her chair and sat in his lap. He put an arm around her and let his open hand rest on her blouse. He moved his other hand to her leg, caressing it softly. She lay her head on his chest, and enjoyed his touch. It wasn't something he was doing because he wanted something. He was doing it simply because he loved her. Even so, she was reacting to his touch. She adjusted her position on his lap, purposely to make him feel her against him in just the right places. It worked. He definitely felt her. He responded by squeezing her breast lightly. She wasn't wearing a bra, so he could feel her nipple stiffen under her lightweight t-shirt.

She kissed him, pushing her tongue in his mouth. He moved his hand up her leg, then between her legs. She opened them. He reached for the button on her shorts.

"Should we go back to bed?" he asked her.

"No, not this time."

She stood, then pulled him up on to his feet. She unbuttoned and unzipped her shorts. They were tight, so it took a bit of twisting, but she shook until they dropped down on the deck. She stepped out of them. She wasn't wearing panties. Mack did the same with his shorts and underwear. He sat down again and she moved onto his lap, straddling his legs and facing him.

She slowly moved her body, sliding herself back and forth over his hardness. "I don't want to hurry," she said. "I want to remember this time forever. I love you, Mack Thomas, and I want you to know. You are for me, the most beautiful thing I've ever known. I wish, most of the time, that I had more to give you."

"You give me more than I deserve, Lisa. And what you're giving me right now is the most awesome thing any man could ever want."

"I'm glad you think so. I want you to know too, that you're the only man who's ever gotten what you get from me. No matter who or what or how, you are the only one."

She made a couple more moves before she suddenly stiffened, then cried out as she climaxed. She slid back and forth rapidly on his lap, drenching Mack. She continued to slowly ride over him as her strong reaction to their love eased up. She then reached down taking a firm hold on him, she guided him to the fight spot.

As she settled down on his lap, his hips rolled to meet hers. They continued their slow motion loving until they heard voices not too far away. "Oh shit!" Lisa bitched. "Why visit us now."

They barely managed to dress, and were just pulling their t-shirts on when Dale and Kathy joined them. Kathy chuckled when she saw them. "Oh oh," she said, "did we come at the wrong time?"

Lisa answered her, "You could say that. But come one up on the deck. You're here now, and there's no real harm done. I'll make it up to Mack later."

"I'm sure you will," Kathy agreed. "I'm sure you will."

Dale, who was easily embarrass by incidents like this, pretended he wasn't noticing what they were talking about. Mack just smiled, He didn't much care one way or the other what they thought. As far as he was concerned, he and Lisa were married. If the wanted to do it outside, so what. They lived in the country, and normally the deck they were on was private.

He didn't get to ignore it long. Kathy sat on his lap, put her arms around his neck, and kissed him. "Sorry about that," she said to Lisa, "but my kissing Mack is getting to be a tradition at times like this."

"It's okay," Lisa said. "I know you don't mean to do any harm."

"You are right about that. I don't. I just don't want to live anymore, in a world where we can't show affection to each other when it's there. I look back on all those years when I was too shy to show much emotion of any kind. It seemed then, that the only place I dared show any was when I was on stage singing. I like this better. Especially with Mack."

"You don't mean Mack better than Dale do you?"

"Of course not. But it's always been okay to show affection too Dale. And I try hard to show him how much I love him. With Mack though, I don't see him all that often, so I do very much enjoy sitting on his lap and kissing him. If it bothers you though, Lisa, I will move."

"No. It's okay. I just don't ever want any of us to forget who belongs to who."

"I don't think it's possible to do that. At the same time, I don't think it's all bad to share a little bit, the love we all have for each other. Like, it wouldn't be a bad thing if you sat in Dale's lap right now."

"No, Kathy, it wouldn't. It won't be a bad thing either, if I don't. So I'm not going to." Lisa looked over at Dale. "You know how I feel about you," she explained, "so you know that my not sitting on your lap has nothing to do with you. It's just that this afternoon, I'm not up to sharing any part of myself with anyone but my husband."

"Maybe we should go," Dale said.

"No," Mack finally spoke. "Instead of you leaving, let's have a small party today." He turned to Lisa. "What do you think? Should we make some calls and get everyone over here for a party?"

"As long as I don't have to dress up for it, it sounds good to me."

Kathy and Dale agreed to the idea, so they made the calls. Roy and Wanda volunteered to go to town to pick up the beverages. Ben and Theresa put together a couple of trays of vegetables and dip for snacks. Sue fried up hamburger which she seasoned for tacos, and chopped up the toppings to go in them. Donna was so surprised by the invitation that in never occurred to her to volunteer to do or bring anything.

Mack brought out a CD player for background music, but about two hours into the party, Kathy decided to sing for them. It was the one thing she could do for them, that no one else could. Near the end of her impromptu concert, she did what was beginning to feel like a tradition at this type of gathering.

She sang two love songs. The first one was directly to Mack. This time, she held him close, her face close to his as she sang. Dale danced with Lisa while she sang it. She kissed him at the end of the song.

The second love song she sang to Dale, holding him as close as she held Mack. The kiss at the end was full of passion, and left Dale with a broad smile. Lisa and Mack danced as she sang, and enjoyed a passionate kiss of their own at the end.

Sue danced with Dale then, and to his surprise, Donna asked Mack to dance. It was a slow song, and when she moved in close, Mack finally realized how good she looked. She was wearing a light cotton dress that wasn't particularly tight, but did flow over her body in a way that did show off her figure. And it was a figure worth showing off.

She made the most of it too, as she danced with Mack. She knew how to show him that she was wearing little to nothing under it, without broadcasting that fact to anyone else. Other than Lisa, that is.

Her first thoughts were a serious irritation, but quickly got past them. She realized that it was taking a lot for Donna to flirt with Mack. After what her husband had done to her, if she wasn't as strong as she was, she could easily be hating all men. Instead, she was having fun teasing Mack.

All in all, it was a nice party. As always, the drinking was moderate by everyone, so all the conversation was friendly, if occasionally loud when they talked about the environment or the latest Republican created disaster.

They all sensed too, that it would be a could idea to end it before it got too late. Theresa and Donna did the cleanup before they left, so there was nothing for Mack and Lisa to do when everyone was gone but relax. Lisa however, had other ideas. Shortly after everyone was gone, she left Mack on the deck and went inside the house.

She showered and washed her hair. Then after drying off, she put on Mack's favorite nightgown. Her hair was in a pony tail and her face completely free of makeup when she joined him on the deck.

"I think," she said, "it's your turn in the bathroom."

He stopped his head shaking that started the instant he saw her come back on the deck. "You're right. I won't be long."

When he rejoined her, all he was wearing was lightweight shorts and a t-shirt. As soon as he sat down on his favorite chair she was straddling his lap, this time facing him. She pulled her nightgown up to her waist. Her hips rolled against him until she felt him grow beneath her.

She left his lap, pulled the nightgown over her head and off. She slid his shorts down and he stepped out of them. His t-shirt was next. Once again, she moved over him, guiding him as she did so.

"If anyone comes here now, they'll just have to watch."

And so they did. Far back in the trees, she watched with a full smile on her face. Watching like this was a first for her, but she found herself liking it. It was a strange thing she knew, to take pleasure from watching someone you love make love to someone else. It was also something she knew she wouldn't forget.

CHAPTER 25

Charles Slater wallowed in the defeat he suffered from the Refuge Rescuers, until he knew he couldn't just let it go. He had to get even with those people who took Donna away from him.

It wasn't just the principle of the thing that drove him. The thought of once again watching his wife being ravaged but a group of his friends was an even stronger drive. It was for him, the only sexual stimulus that really did it for him. Everything else was a let down. So he needed to get her back.

The problem he faced was how? He could no longer count on his friends. To a man, they were just plain afraid of going up against any of the people who were part of Refuge Rescuers.

He looked up a few companies that provided bodyguards, but none of them offered the kind of service he wanted. He was becoming discouraged by then, but continued to search the internet for some kind of person or group who, for the right price, would assist him in his quest.

After a lot of searching, he found a group that claimed they could provide any number of services to people who had been abused by the system. All anyone who wanted those services needed to do to hire them, is prove they were worthy of them. Which actually meant, prove they weren't the police.

Charles gave them a two hundred dollar deposit before they would schedule a meeting with him. Then they did a background check on him, and were sure he wasn't a cop before they had a second meeting.

The man doing the interview said, after questioning him, "So all you really want is to get your wife back? No revenge for what those people did to you?"

"Well, I guess I would kind of like it if I could get some."

"What would you like best? Do it yourself, or have someone do it for you?"

"Do it myself, if it's possible. If not, the other way will work."

"I think we'll be able to help you out. We've recently hired two men familiar with that Refuge Rescuers bunch. They hate them, actually. They were in the hospital, after being put there by them Refuge people. They were under armed guard. But one of them cops fell asleep. That left one of the guys the chance to escape. He did one better, and took out both cops. He took the other prisoner with him when he left the hospital."

He waved at an armed man watching the meeting. "Bring those new guys in. I want them to meet their new employer."

The new guys soon joined them. "Charles," the man holding the meeting said, "I want you to meet Jelly Norton and Lance North."

At the same time this meeting was happening, Mack was talking to Dale on his cell phone. "They both escaped? There was a cop guarding each of them, and they still escaped? How did they manage that?"

"One of the cops fell asleep. He was on his third shift in a row. He shouldn't have been there, but they were short of help. You know how the chief of police is. Whatever is easiest for him. To him, it's no big deal that they escaped. It doesn't even seem to be bothering him much, that two of his officers are in the hospital with head wounds."

"And now those two are our problem again."

"It sure looks like it, Mack. We'll be on the lookout for them too, and we will be responding to any and all calls you guys might make."

"I appreciate that," Mack said. "It's just too damn bad that the town cops won't be reacting the same way."

As soon as he ended his conversation with Dale, Mack notified everyone else connected with Refuge Rescuers. Lisa was his first call. Their conversation was short, because Mack was anxious to notify everyone else about the two men being free now.

Lisa was in Kingsburg, shopping with Donna. They were at the local hardware store so Donna could buy a few things she needed for her new life in the cottage.

A man neither one of them had ever seen came up to Donna and said, "I have a gun in my pocket." He took her by the arm and tried to lead her away. She refused to follow him. "I'm going to shoot you if you don't come with me."

"And if you don't let her go," Lisa told him, "you are going to wish you did."

He laughed. "There ain't nothing you can do to stop me. You ain't much more than a little girl."

Donna managed to shake herself free of him, then kicked him in the shin. All that did was aggravate him, so he tried to grab her again. She managed to step away from him. Lisa moved in on him. He tried to push her out of the way, but she was ready for him, and before he knew what happened, she had his arm securely locked behind him.

"Call 911," she told Donna.

She did, and because Dale put out an alert out for incidents like this, after Jelly Norton and Lance North escaped custody, a deputy was there in a couple of minutes. He smiled when he saw Lisa, holding a much larger man with what looked like not much effort.

"What'd this one try to do?" the deputy asked, as he put the handcuffs on him.

"He tried to force Donna to go with him. He said he had a gun."

The deputy searched him then. He was carrying.

Lisa and Donna followed the deputy to the sheriff's office to sign the papers, charging him with attempted kidnapping. When questioned, he said that he'd met three men in a bar, and they offered him five hundred dollars to go into the hardware store and bring her out. The didn't tell him what he was up against.

When he described the men who made the offer, it verified to Lisa that Lance North and Jelly Norton were two of the men. She was also sure, from the description of the third man, that it was Charles Slater. Something that surprised her. She was sure that he didn't know Lance or Jelly. So how did they meet, and why were they working together now?

Even more curious, why did they spend five hundred dollars to send someone, who they knew had no chance to succeed, after Donna? For the moment, it made no sense. Experience taught Lisa though, that all too often it was the things that made the least sense, were the most dangerous. It was the top of their list of things to discuss at the meeting she called for that evening.

Lisa was the first to comment on what happened. "It not only could have been dangerous for us, but Donna especially, it was really damn annoying."

"Maybe that's the point," Roy said. "Just keep annoying you until you get so frustrated, you make some kind of mistake."

"That could definitely could be at least part of what they're trying to do," Mack said. "At the same time though, five hundred dollars is still a lot of money just to annoy someone."

Lisa wondered then, if it really was much money at all for Charles to spend. She and Mack were in his house when Donna got her personal things. It was worth close to half of a million dollars, so he had to have a fair amount of cash available.

She asked Donna, "Can Charles afford to spend money on something like that?"

"Sure. He's got enough money to do something like that for a long time. He's really cheap most of the time, but he could spend a lot of money that way if he wanted to."

Paul, who had so far been quiet, said, "That's a real damn shame, that he's going to be able to keep on doing shit like that. When people like him have money though, they can all too often get away with all kinds of crap."

"Not always," Sue said. "Sometimes it's possible to take that privilege away from them. Tell me, Donna, do you know anything at all about his finances?"

"I'm not sure I know what you mean about me knowing about his finances," Donna answered. "I don't really know much at all about investing or any of theses kind of things."

"That's okay. What I need to know from you are things like where he banks, what kind of credit cards does he have, and does he have a regular savings account?"

"I know some of that. I don't think I know all of it. What good would it do if I knew all of it anyway?"

Sue stood up. "You guys can fill me in on what all you decide later. It's time we go to work, Donna. You and I are going to help good old Charles out with his money. Mack has told me about a lot of environmental charities that can use some of it."

Sue and Donna went to her office then. With Donna's help, Sue went to work on Charles's Slater's money. It started to disappear rather quickly, along with several credit cards.

While she was doing that, the rest of them continued their discussion about the trio of men determined to do them as much harm as three men could ever manage to do.

"It's weird that those three have connected," Lisa said. "Even more, we've got to wonder now, who else are they going to connect with, and what kind of gang will they end up being."

"That's for sure," Mack agreed. "Titus Trump and his latest little Trumpy, Kegan Kayson, have been released on bail. There isn't anyone other than us to do anything about it."

"How likely are they to put together a cohesive group?" Roy asked. "They know Lance was an informant for the FBI. Charles never was part of their militia. At least two of them want to take over for Titus. So what do they have to hold them together?"

"There are a few things I can think of," Mack explained. "Number one is the fact that they all hate us. Then you have that pathetic religious nut, Lance, who insists that Wanda is still his wife. Jelly Norton hates Lisa after she made him look like a fool in front of the other men. I don't even have to tell you about the most recent of the useless creatures on the list. Charles is obsessed with the idea of watching his wife being gang raped. And last, there is all those used to be MAGA Fellows without a place to play soldier. They are all stupid enough to follow any of the three, or maybe even Titus or that Kegan, almost anywhere. Anything so they can dress up and play soldier."

"The biggest thing we have to do now," Paul said, "is to be on constant alert. If we let out guard down at all, one or more of us will pay for it."

"I think," Lisa said, "that we have to do more than that. We don't have any choice, actually. I for one have been on guard too damn long already. If that's all we do, they'll beat us just by wearing us down."

Wanda agreed with Lisa. "I think that we need to find out where they are. Whether they're together or scattered around. Then we should do to them what they're doing to us."

"But," Paul argued, "if we push them too hard we could easily cross the line and do something we shouldn't."

"That's entirely possible," Lisa agreed. "If we were still cops, crossing some lines would matter. However, given the fact that we are no longer cops and aren't held to such rigid standards, some over the top hassling of all of those puppet-boys might be a good thing."

Mack's face carried a half smile now. "I agree with Lisa and Wanda. It's time to go on the offense. First thing tomorrow, let's start hunting all of them. Once we locate at least some of them, it will be time for our harassment of them to start."

"Just so you know that I'm with all of the rest of you one hundred percent," Paul said, "I want to be part of the search and the harassment."

"No one has ever doubted your loyalty, Paul." Mack said. "There's not really any of us who wouldn't trust you with our life. We all know that you being who you are, that you have to warn us when we talk about pushing the legal boundaries. But we also know that when push comes to shove, you are always with us."

"That's good to hear, because I always am."

CHAPTER 26

Julie greeted the couple with her usual smile when they came in the office. They returned her smile by taking out their guns and pointing them at her. Julie backed away, after she pushed the silent alert button inside the counter she was standing behind.

"We need to see Wanda," the woman with the gun demanded.

"She's not here," Julie answered her.

"Yes she is. Our resources said she was here, so she has to be."

"Well, I'm sorry to disappoint you, but your resources are wrong. She's out on a case, and she won't be back until late this afternoon."

"I don't believe you. Where is she hiding?"

Mack, who was working with Sue, joined them at the desk. "We've been expecting you," he explained, "so we put Wanda to work someplace else today. You might as well put your guns away." He lifted his arm, and using his thumb, he pointed out the four people behind him. Each of them had a gun pointed at the couple. "If you insist on keeping them in your hands, we'll be forced to shoot and kill you."

The woman dropped her hands to her sides. Her shoulders slumped, and she shook her head in disbelief. "Those bastards told us that you guys didn't carry guns. They said you were a bunch of liberals, so you wouldn't know how to use them anyway."

"And you believed them." Mack chuckled. "It would be my guess, you also don't realize how stupid you are. Where did you meet those guys?"

She named the bar. It was in the next county north. "We were sitting in a booth, drinking a pitcher of beer when they sat down with us. They started talking, and bought the beer the whole time they were with us."

" Did your resources pay you with a check?"

The woman looked surprised that Mack would know that. She nodded her head. "They did. They gave us a bonus for taking a check instead of cash."

"Good for them. Your problem now is the fact that the check they gave you is no good. The reason they gave it to you, is because they don't have any money. We took it all away from them. And yes to the other question you have. Of course they knew we would be well armed. They lied about that."

The man with the woman tried hard to puff himself up and look like mister macho man. He didn't quite make it, but told Mack what he thought anyway. "I think you're the one lying. If you took all their money, how could they buy us the expensive meal like they did last night?"

"More than likely, because they have some cash left. Not so long ago, one of the men who hired you had a lot of money. He doesn't now. We have ways to do some near magic stuff when we want to. Things like turning him from rich to broke in just a couple of hours."

"Even if you do, you can't do anything to us. We haven't done anything to you. Besides, those guys will get you if you try to do anything to us. You can't even have us arrested. They guarantied us that the sheriff in this county, and all the judges, were paid off."

Mack laughed this time. "The sheriff is my best friend, and at least half the judges are completely honest. But we aren't going to have you arrested. We aren't even going to shoot you. What we are going to do is take your guns, and then any ID, blank checks, credit cards, or anything else you might have with you. Then we are going to let you go."

"We can't let you have our IDs or anything else that you want. You might do something with that stuff you shouldn't."

"Actually," Mack said, "that's exactly our plan. When you are gone the hell out of here, we will be using everything we take from you to totally screw up your lives. It's going to take you a very long time to get your lives back together again."

"What the hell are we supposed to do to live in the meantime? We've got to eat and pay the rent, the same as everyone else."

"I hope you don't think that I, or anyone here cares one damn whether you eat or sleep on a park bench or any other damn thing. Because we sure as hell don't. You came here thinking you could make an easy buck. You were wrong. Decent people don't do things like that. If you need help, you're going to have to get it from the three guys who hired you to come here to stick guns in our faces. Now hand over what we want, then get the hell out of here."

With a great deal of reluctance, the couple gave Mack everything he wanted. Their faces told the story of how dejected they felt as they left. Mack couldn't feel any remorse about what they were about to go through.

Sue was given all the material they left behind. When she finished with it, the couple were no longer officially part of society. The only thing she couldn't get at was their church membership. They were evangelicals, and their church believed that doing anything with electronics or online was a mortal sin, and would send a person directly to hell. So there was no way Sue could get at that information.

"They were two people," Sue told Mack, "who had no idea that they would have gotten off easier if we would have had them arrested, then what we did to them."

"That's fine. The payback we gave them for coming here thinking they could do whatever they wanted to do, wasn't at all too harsh. With some luck too, what they'll be going through will be seen by more people like them. Maybe it'll teach them something. And who knows, maybe they'll catch up with those three useless, evil ones, and get a little vengeance of their own.

Regardless though, what we did today should at least go a little ways toward frustrating them.

"It should," Sue agreed. "We were once again ahead of them, and their little frustration game went nowhere with us."

Mack was wrong. It actually went a long way toward frustrating them. They had all agreed that they would be able to cause the Refuge Rescuers an endless amount of frustration and anxiety with their tactics. It was such a good plan. It was so simple to talk people into doing what they wanted done, even if they normally wouldn't do them, by telling them lies and giving them what the people considered a lot of money. It seemed almost fool proof, and should have been. Instead, it cost them their ability to purchase anything they wanted or needed. Charles was the only one of the three who had money to start with, and now he couldn't access any of it. The people from Refuge Rescuers were proving to be a lot more difficult to defeat than any of the three could have imagined.

Almost as bad, the people they hired to cause the Rescuers frustration were now bitter enemies. That left as their last hope, the remnants of the MAGA Fellows. Men who wouldn't give any rational person a whole lot of hope. With the exception of three or four of them, they were a very long way from a fighting force.

They loved their dress up like soldiers time, but many of them carried equipment they bought at surplus stores that they didn't know how to use. It's difficult to use something when you don't even know what it's for.

Of the three men hell bent on revenge against Wanda, Lisa, and Donna, Jelly Norton was the only one who had even an inkling of what they were facing. Had he enough sense to use his knowledge, he would have been gone from Minnesota while he could still go. But like most men who lived how he lived and did what he did, he was too stupid to quit while he was ahead. But even if he was smart enough to back off, the depth of his hatred for Lisa was enough to keep him wanting to punish her.

Lance and Charles were equally abscessed. For Lance, it was the idea that Wanda was still his wife. He was so completely indoctrinated by the dogma of his most recent evangelical church, that he now actually believed that she belonged to him. He was so possessed by it, that he found it impossible to pull himself away from it.

Charles was also locked into a fantasy of Donna that he couldn't get rid of. No amount of any kind of sex could replace the excitement he felt when he watched a group of men attack and rape his wife, Donna. He didn't know why it turned him on the way it did, nor did he care. He only knew that he needed to get her back. He needed it so bad that he was now willing to commit any atrocity to do it.

CHAPTER 27

It was a relief for Mack and Lisa when Saturday rolled around. It was once again the one day of the month that Mack and Kathy went on their walk in the refuge. Normally it was also the day Dale and Lisa did something together.

This day was going to be different. Dale and Lisa wanted to go with Mack and Kathy. They could have gone on their own, but thought it would be more fun this way. Being able to listen to Mack as he talked about the refuge, and the changes constantly happening since the fire that burned almost all of it, was an added treat.

Donna surprised them then, when she asked if she could go along too. They agreed to her coming along, even though they were somewhat hesitant about it. They wondered how she would react to the way they related to each other.

Whenever Kathy and Mack walked in the refuge, Kathy held Mack's hand. It didn't matter whether it was only the two of them or all four of them. Kathy held his hand. She kissed him occasionally too. As it was with the holding hands, it didn't matter if it was two or four on the walk.

Dale and Lisa weren't nearly as insistent on doing those things as Kathy was, but they did hold hands occasionally along the way, and did kiss each other when they took a notion to do it.

So Donna's eyes widened and her mouth opened some when Kathy took Mack's hand and walked with him rather than Dale as soon as the hike started. Lisa walked near Dale, but not quite so obviously friendly as Kathy was with Mack.

Not sure what to do, Donna walked on the other side of Dale from Lisa. The three of them let Kathy and Mack take the lead. As they got deeper into the refuge and the trail narrowed, Kathy took the lead, followed by Mack. Donna and Dale constantly switched positions, with Lisa bringing up the rear.

They frequently stopped to examine something that Mack pointed out. When they did, if there was enough room, Kathy always stood next to him, either with an arm around him or holding his hand. When Kathy did that, Donna switched from watching them, too checking Lisa's reaction. It didn't take her long to wonder why Lisa didn't react at all.

Lisa was at the same time watching Donna. At first she considered trying to explaining to Donna why the relationship Mack had with Kathy didn't bother her. Instead, she decided that it all was too personal for anyone else to understand. On top of that, she knew that Dale wouldn't be at all interested in trying to explain to anyone why he wasn't upset or concerned about Mack and Kathy.

When they stopped to rest, Donna sat down at a spot a few feet away from the rest of them. There were a few uncomfortable moments until Dale caught Mack's eye. He nodded toward Donna. They both got up and then sat down next to her.

Dale put an arm around her shoulders. "I think we're probably making you uncomfortable with the way we've paired up. We do it because we are all good friends and trust each other. But I think that even if we weren't paired up in a way that a lot of people might not approve of, our being paired up at all would make you somewhat uncomfortable. So for the rest of the walk, how about you and I pairing up? We won't do any more than hold hands and kiss a little."

"Believe it or not," Donna said, "you're not making me uncomfortable because you're pairing up. It's not even so much who you are pairing up with. What's surprised me is how you treat each other. You all seem to care about each other so much. I don't know, nor do I care, if you ever let things go further than a little kissing and holding hands. It's the love that seems so strange to me. I haven't ever had anything close to what you guys have. Not with a man anyway."

"As much as Dale and I wish we could," Mack said, "we can't give you that kind of love. But there's no good reason you can't stay around here and be our friend. A little hand holding and a kiss now and then won't hurt anything either."

Donna finally smiled. "That's one offer too good to refuse." She turned to Dale and kissed him. It was one of those kind which burned itself permanently into his memory. Mack was next. She stood up with him before kissing him. His memory of what she gave him was something that would float in the background of his mind, as long as there was a mind to hold it.

They resumed the walk then, with Donna sometimes holding Dales had, and sometimes Mack's. Kathy and Lisa relented then, and occasionally held each others hands.

They were near the end of the walk when Dale's cell phone went off for the first time that day. Almost immediately after he answered it, his back went chalk white. "When?" he asked. A moments silence, "How many?"

He turned his back on them and slowly walked away. When he came back to them he looked sick. His skin was pale and his face was covered with a cold sweat. He was slowly shaking his head.

Lisa took his hand and held it tight. "What is It, Dale? What's wrong?"

"It's unbelievable. Three men just shot up a wedding. They killed the bride and groom, the maid of honor, and the best man. They said, before they escaped, that if we don't turn you three over to them by noon tomorrow, the next time they will kill a lot more than four. I have to get to town. Want to come along Mack?"

Mack looked at Lisa. "Okay?"

"Yes, go. Maybe you'll catch the bastards this time."

Mack rode with Dale in the sheriff's car. They made good time going int Kingsburg. But they weren't in any kind of time to do anything about the three men who did the shooting. Charles, Lance, and Jelly were long gone.

By the time Dale and Mack were parked at the scene of the murders, the murderers were parked among some trees. As close as they could get to the three women they wanted. They were sure now, that with Dale and Mack busy in town, the women would be relatively easy. They were, after all, just women. And best of all, Dale and Mack wouldn't be expecting them to attack until tomorrow.

They were being careful anyway. Jelly Norton was quietly moving the eighteen MAGA Fellows they brought with them, into spots he thought would be the most affective during their planned attack. They were all determined that this time, they would kill each and every one of the Refuge Rescuers group.

Lisa didn't know they were so close, and wasn't consciously thinking about any of them being a threat to her when they got home. But shortly after they got there, she got an uneasy felling in her gut. It quickly turned into a sharp pain. She grabbed Donna's arm to hold herself up. She knew then, they were in some kind of trouble.

Wanda and Roy came out of their house. "I don't know what it is," Wanda said. "But something's serious wrong. Where's Mack. I think it happened to him too. Maybe we can figure out what it is."

Lisa was near doubled over now. "He's in town. He went with Dale. There was a shooting at a wedding. I think the trouble will be here."

"Me too. Let's get everyone into Ben's house. It's the best place to protect ourselves. We better call Mack."

Lisa called him while Wanda and Roy gathered everyone together and into Ben's. Guns were passed around, along with extra ammunition. It took a few rings before Mack answered his cell phone. When he did, he said, "yes, Lisa, I know something's wrong there. I got the image before we even got here. Dale can't leave. This crime scene is just too serious. I'm looking for a ride now. I'll be there as quick as I can."

Lisa looked around at everyone in the room. She was sure there would be more than the three men who wanted them so desperately outside. She was also sure that if they all stayed in the house to defend themselves, some of them would be wounded or killed, even if they won the battle. She didn't want that. She knew their best chance overall was to attack, rather than just defend themselves.

She pulled Wanda and Roy aside to discuss the situation with them. They knew that the men getting ready to attack were spreading out, all around the house. That meant that getting outside and into a position where they could do some significant damage, was going to be extremely difficult. They had one thing though, that the men outside weren't likely to anticipate. And that was Wanda.

"I think," Lisa told her, "that if you watch closely, sooner or later one of those guys hiding behind a tree out there, is going to expose one part or another of his body. You are the only one who's a good enough shot to hit that spot, even if it is small."

"The problem with that," Wanda argued, "is that likely as not I'll only wound him. Probably not so serious either."

"I know. But if you hit two or three of them, only wounded or not, it will make them somewhat gun shy. That's all I'll need to get out there and under cover somewhere behind them. When I get behind them, I should be able to finish what you started. That'll give you and Roy the chance to get out there too. After that, the hell we can raise with them will be endless."

"The thing I don't like about your idea, Lisa," Wanda continued to argue, "is the simple fact that we won't know how bad any of those guys are hit when you go out there. It will leave you in too much danger."

"Not a hell of a lot more than we will all be in if I stay in here, and we let them attack. We do that, and it won't matter if we win. There will be more than one of us down. It could even be most of us. Which means, the odds are much better if I go. We could send Roy, but I move faster than he does, and you are going to be too damn busy to go."

"Well, let's see how good the shots I make before we decide that you should go."

"Good enough." Lisa paused and stared into Wanda's eyes. "Just as long as you do your best shooting. And don't forget, I know how good you are. Don't pull back because you think you need to keep me safe."

Wanda knew Lisa well enough to not try to fake it and miss a shot. Lisa was determined to do everything she could to keep everyone else safe, so she might go even if Wanda made a bad shot.

Wanda also knew that she wasn't likely to have much time with any shot, so rather than trying to watch for movement from the four trees behind the house, she concentrated on one of them. She chose the largest tree of the four, because she figured the man behind it would be the most confident, since his tree offered the most cover. The confidence he had might lead to carelessness.

Which was exactly what happened. It was just in a very unexpected way. The man drank several beers earlier, as he anxiously waited for them to make their move. He didn't finish the last one until just a few minutes before he was stationed behind his tree. So it wasn't long before the inevitable happened, and he desperately needed to relieve himself. So he started to do that very thing. His problem was, that in his haste to keep from wetting himself, he didn't pay any attention to where he was standing. That left a target for Wanda.

She was surprised when she saw the first steam come out from the side of the tree. She couldn't believe it when the tip of man's penis appeared next to the tree too. She only felt an instant of guilt before she shot the tip off, and the spray of clear fluid turned red.

The man attached to her target screamed. Then yelled, "They shot my cock off."

The other three men behind those trees heard his words. There's nothing Wanda could have done to make them angrier than what they were now. They were incensed. How could anyone do that to a man? Nothing they ever did to a woman was as bad as what was done to their friend. They all stuck their heads out from behind their assigned tree, hell bent on shooting and killing whoever it was who shot their friend.

There was one very big problem with their plan. When it came to the contest between Wanda's and their shooting, there was no contest. She instantly picked a target and fired. The first man was the most cautious. He only stuck his head out far enough to try to see what was going on. Al that left for Wanda to shoot at was his forehead. So that's where she shot him. The second man started to move back behind his tree. Her only target by them was the right side of his chest. She was sure when she fired that it was unlikely that she killed him. The last man was the quickest, and her only shot was his left shoulder.

All four of her shots were good, as far as Lisa was concerned. She was outside just before Wanda fired her last two shots, and behind the tree men before they realized she was there. Her plan worked better than she could have hoped it would, so she decided to take advantage of it.

She told the men, "Drop your weapons and lie face down or die. You've about a minute to decide. And while you're doing that, I don't care what your decision is. I would as soon kill you as not."

The man with the bullet in his forehead was dead, so he didn't respond. The one with the chest wound was in a lot of pain and bleeding, so he dropped his AR15. The man with the lost sex life was still bleeding, but was also crying hard over his loss, so he too gave it up. The man with the shoulder wound stepped out in the open and aimed his AR15 in Lisa's direction. Wanda shot him between his shoulder blades, killing him.

She and Roy quickly moved outside then. They zip tied the hands and feet of the two men still alive. Then the three of them split up and the hunting started. As they moved around, they maneuvered themselves behind the men who had been sure the battle would be over by now. When they called the men out, about half of them surrendered. The others thought they could shoot their way out. Often as not, when they made that move, they exposed themselves to someone in the house, looking out a window. They, in turn, would tell the man to surrender. This turned out to be another fifty fifty deal. That meant only half of them needed to be zip-tied.

As Lisa, Wanda, and Roy, along with some help from the people in the house, whittled down the eighteen former MAGA Fellows, the three primary criminals stayed together. It took them a while, but they were finally beginning to realize they were in big trouble.

"I think," Charles said, "it might be a good idea for us to get the hell out of here."

"As much as I hate leaving my wife here," Lance said, "I think you're right. There'll be another day for me to go after Wanda."

"Not me," Jelly said. "I'm going to get Lisa to follow me out into the woods. When I do, I'm going to kill her. If I can, I'll do her first. Either way, I will kill her."

"Come to think of it, I think I'll try to grab Donna too," Charles claimed.

"I guess, I should go after Wanda too, if that's what you guys are going to do." Lance said, but with less conviction than the first two.

Lance was the first of the three to think he had his woman baited. The problem he ran into was the fact Wanda was actually the one to bait him. When he grabbed her from behind, there was no doubt in his mind that he had her this time. She couldn't get away from him now. Except she was in far better condition than he was, and because of that, she was stronger. When he wrapped his arms around her, she grabbed his thumbs. Before he could even think about it she had them in her hands. Just as quickly, she bent one of the far enough to break it. She held the other one at the point of maximum pain without breaking it.

Wanda twisted around until she was facing Lance. She reached up with both hands and dug her finger nails deep into his skin, high on his face. As soon as he screamed from the pain, she pulled her deeply imbedded nails down his face, leaving four deep gouges on each side of his face. As he reached for his his new wounds, she pounded his now exposed stomach with both hands. A couple of minutes of that and she stepped back away from him. She didn't want to be near him while he lost the contents of his stomach. She was tired of him by then, so as soon as it was convenient, she hit him once, knocking him out.

Donna wasn't anything like Wanda or Lisa when it came to fighting, but she had quick hands and had a pent up wish for revenge. She also had a secret weapon. She was carrying one of Lisa's pop-out switch blade knives. When Charles came after her, she didn't try to do anything clever or sophisticated.

She simply took out her knife and slashed him across the chest. When the blood flowing from his wounds got his attention, she picked up a good size rock from the ground and hit him on the head with it. She wasn't particularly strong, but she was strong enough to knock him out. On impulse, she kicked him in his pride and joy parts while he was down.

Lisa knew exactly what Jelly Norton was trying to do as he moved back in the woods. His plan was to lure her as far back as he could, so he would have enough time to rape her before he killed her.

What he never would have figured out was the fact that getting him back in the woods was exactly what she wanted. This time, she didn't want anyone around until she was finished with him. This time, when she was finished with him, he will have committed his last rape. In fact, this time it was her intention to leave him in the kind of condition that he would have committed his last rape, or almost every kind of crime he could ever do. He was laughing when she finally decided he'd gone far and caught up with him.

He was sure he had her now. She didn't have a chance against him this time. She thought otherwise, and had thought through the fight she was about to have. She already knew, step by step, how she was going to take him. And there was a good reason she was so confident in what she was going to do. She had no intention at all of making this any kind of fair fight. Instead, she simply planned beating the living hell out of him.

As she expected he would, he tried to get ahold of her. He thought he could control her after he did. She was ready for his move, and as she planned, she ducked under his arms. He moved his upper body so hard trying to get his hands on her that he threw himself slightly off balance. She moved up fast, and before he knew what happened, she gouged his eyes. One of them popped out of its socket and the other received a deep scratch right down the middle of it. He was now effectively blind. She next went after the part of his body she most wanted to damage. She kicked him in the groin. Once. Then again. When he bent over as he grabbed himself, she kneed him in the face while she held his head in place, thereby making the blow much harder. She broke his nose doing it. Before he could respond to her, she dropped her two hands together into a single fist and brought it down on the back of his head.

He fell on his face and lay still on the ground, moaning. He was thoroughly defeated. She was tempted anyway, to turn him on his side and kick his face in, but decided it wasn't worth the effort. Prison already wasn't going to be any fun for him.

She knew there was no way he could escape now, but she zip-tied his hands and legs anyway. As she walked away from him, she knew she was supposed to feel guilty about hurting him more that what she needed to. She couldn't make herself do it. Of all the men who raped her all those years ago, he was as cruel as the worst of them. As far as she was concerned, what she just did to him was only a start of what he had coming. Not only for what he did to her, but for what he did to countless women and girls over the years.

When she was interrogated after all the various police arrived on the scene, she simply said that he'd attempted to attack and rape her. All she did was defend herself. No one disagreed with her. They all knew who and what Jelly Norton was.

Given that there were so many MAGA Fellows there to attack the Refuge Rescuers, even the most skeptical of the police had to accept that they'd only defended themselves. So this time there are no macho lawmen to insist they arrest someone from Refuge Rescuers. Something that in the past had all too often happened to Lisa.

That left only one person upset about the whole thing. Mack. He felt like he should have been there. But more than that, he was upset with Lisa. Twice she'd gone out of her way to risk her life. First, when she went outside when there was still a good chance she could be shot doing it. The second time was when she met Jelly Norton in the woods. If she would have made a mistake, he could have killed her.

"But none of that happened, Mack," she said. "The truth is, you don't have any right to be upset with me. When I did what I did, I took the playbook directly from Mack Thomas. So if you want to sleep in the guest room for the next month to two, keep it up. Otherwise, shut the hell up. You damn well know that I did the right thing. Expecting me to let other people get hurt, or maybe even killed, just to keep myself safe? I damn well don't think so."

"It's just that I love…"

"That doesn't cut it. I love you too. But we are who we are, so sometimes we have to do things someone else wouldn't do. I've put up with you doing the same thing, and I've never liked the fact that you do it. When I do things like that, it's no different than when you do it. And don't ever give me any of that, but you're a woman crap. Take a look at the useless pile of garbage in the woods over there that the medics are working on. Then if you think that, *but you're just woman,* crap is justified. come back here and explain it to me."

As much as he hated it, Mack knew she was right. She had once more been able to show him that his attitude toward her was wrong. As far as her job and the sometimes need to be concerned for someone else more than she thought about herself, she was right.

Knowing that any further discussion with her right then would only make things worse, he walked away. He stayed around home until he was sure that everyone was okay, and that no one was going to go after Lisa for what she did to Jelly Norton. Then he got into his pickup and drove away. He drove around the county for a while, but nothing helped him eliminate the feelings of being out of balance. Something just didn't feel right to him, and even though he couldn't pinpoint it, he was sure it was between him and Lisa. It was a feeling he definitely did not like. It was a reminder of the women in his life who were murdered because he didn't follow his own instincts. The very instincts that drove Lisa crazy."

He knew that the best place to return at least some of his balance was the refuge, so that's where he went. Since he had no interest in going home and fighting with Lisa, he decided to take the longest hike he could. He figured that if he got off the beaten path often enough, and walked slow enough, he could make the hike last until well into the evening. Hopefully, she would be asleep when he got home. And then, when he did, he could sleep in the guest bedroom. He was sure it would be a good idea to let her calm down for a good long time before he got too close to her. If getting close to her again was ever going to be possible.

But this time he was reading her wrong. Most of the anger Lisa showed toward him was far more an extreme frustration with the world around her than any animosity she felt toward him. She was more than tired of a world where too many men thought of women, and treated women, as if they were mere objects for them to use. So she'd taken that frustration out on Mack. And she'd done it primarily because he'd shown a little too much concern about her safety.

But was he wrong to do that? Not really. She knew that one of the major things wrong with life and the way most people dealt with each other was the lack of enough concern. So she vowed to make it up to him as soon as he got home.

She took an early shower that evening. Then dressed in Mack's favorite nightgown. She put on a lightweight robe over it, then sat down with a novel she was reading to wait for him. The book was interesting enough to keep her from watching the time, so it was a bit of a surprised when she looked up from her book to find most of the house dark.

It was now much later than she thought it should be. It wasn't like Mack to be out this late without calling her and telling her where he was. Worry was now her closest companion. Another two hours went by before her cell phone rang. It was Mack.

"I'm at the refuge," he said. "It's really peaceful here, so I think I'll hang around for a while longer. Feel free to go to bed whenever. I'll sleep in the guest room when I get home. That way I won't wake you up."

"What the hell are you talking about, Mack? Why the hell do you want to sleep in the guest room when you can sleep next to me?"

"I just don't want to bug you anymore than what I already have, Lisa. I know you hate it when I get protective and concerned about you. I'm sorry I screwed up and did it again today. I kind of feel like I should kind of stay away from you for a while, and give you the space away from me that you seem to want so bad."

"What do you mean by stay away from me?"

"Move out for a while. Maybe back off from the agency."

"Don't be crazy, Mack"

"I'm not being crazy. I'm trying not to do what I've been doing. The trouble is, I'm having a hard time changing who I am. I know I'm often over protective of you. Sometimes other people in the agency too. But that's who I am. I have a problem with facing the time when someone else gets buried that I could have saved. But if I'm not around, I won't be driving you crazy."

"But that's exactly what you're doing now, Mack. I'm sorry I jumped on you so hard today. I was out of line. The problem is, I'm so goddamn frustrated with the constant harassment from men who think that they can do whatever they want to do with women, only because we are women. When you bawled me out for taking too many chances, it came across as just another way of a man trying to show his ownership of a woman."

"Well, Lisa, if I wasn't convinced I should stay away, at least for a while, what you just said convinced me. If my loving you so much I'm always worried about you and afraid I might lose you, makes you feel like I'm trying to own you, then I'd best get the hell out of your way."

"Oh god, Mack, I'm sorry again. I didn't mean it that way. And I don't think you were really that much out of line. Like I said, I'm just frustrated. And the truth is, Mack, I'm kind of haunted. What they did to me way back then seems to keep popping up in my face. I've done things I know I shouldn't do because of it."

"Aside from the piece of shit whose ass you so thoroughly kicked today, what have you done that you think you shouldn't have?"

"Dale. I shouldn't have done with Dale what I did with him."

"You didn't do anything that was really bad. You needed to get past what was bothering you, and that was the best way to do it. If I'm not upset, why should you be?"

"You don't really want to know."

"Actually, yes I do. So if you ever want me to come home again, you'd best tell me what you think I don't want to know."

"Are you sure you want to hear this, Mack?"

"Remember what I've said so many times. Honesty matters. If we can't be honest. nothing is going to work for us. So tell me."

"Well okay. I just hope you won't hate me for saying this. Sometimes when I'm alone with Dale, I feel like it would be nice to do it with him again. I keep telling myself that now that I've proven to myself that getting raped like I did hasn't turned me into a freak, I should never want to do it with anyone but you."

"We've been through that already, Lisa. No one person can satisfy any other person's every need. Sometimes that includes love. Because of what life's done to all of us, and because of a lot of the things you've gone through with Dale, you and he have a very special kind of friendship. If you occasionally have the desire to take those feelings into that place, I won't fault you for it. Not as long as you're honest about it anyway. So you can now officially stop feeing guilty about those feelings. And I think that for now, you will feel freer to take advantage of them, if I'm not around."

"Are you just looking for a reason to get rid of me, Mack? 'Cause it sure is starting to sound like it."

"That's the last thing I ever want to do. But I don't think I can change my feelings about you. If I'm with you, I'll always want to protect you from the world. You and I have talked about my history enough for you to know that. So what you said to me today tells me that I'm making you very unhappy, being who I am. Given who you and I are, the only way I'm going to stop making you so damn unhappy is to get the hell out of your way. You deserve the chance to be whoever it is you want to be."

As hard as she tried, Lisa couldn't control her feelings any longer. She started to cry. Her tears continued for several minutes before she could talk again. "Please, Mack," she finally said. "Don't do this. The last thing on this earth I want is for you to leave. You're not holding me back. You are the one who is holding me together. Please come home now. I need you right now more than I'v ever needed anything in my entire life."

"Are you really sure you want me to. Because if you're not, I still think it would be better for you if I go."

"I couldn't be more sure of anything, Mack. Come home. I need you, and I want to feel your arms around me."

"Okay, Lisa, I'll come. I want to hold you again too. More than you can know. But I don't want to make you unhappy. So if I do, I want you to tell me so I can stop doing it. Even if it means my leaving you."

"I will, Mack. But for now, please just come home."

Mack moved away from the tree he was sitting next to and leaning on and got up. He knew the trail well enough to walk it safely with the small amount of moonlight there was. He got about halfway to the parking lot his truck was in when he heard the moans.

It took him a few minutes to find the source of them. It was an old man, lying on his back. His backpack and sleeping bag were lying along side of him.

He looked up at Mack. "I'm not in as bad a shape as I look. Let me rest here for a while, and then I'll be moving on.'

"Do you want some help to sit up?" Mack asked him.

"Not just yet. Let me rest these weary bones first."

"Well, I can't let you lay here like this. I'm going to call for some help."

"Can you do me a favor though? And please don't call no cops. Cops don't never like us homeless types. Give me a little time, and I'll get to moving on."

"I'll give you some time, but you aren't going anywhere until I get you something to eat."

"You don't have to do that."

"Actually, yes I do." Mack took out his phone and called Lisa. When she answered, he told her, "It's me, and I'm about to screw up your life again."

"What's wrong now?"

"On my way out of here I found someone who needs help. I thought I'd let you know first. I'm going to call Roy now. I'm going to have him come and give me a hand with this guy. I'm going to bring him home so we can feed him a decent meal."

"Well, I was just going to call and tell you I was about to do to you, what you just said I was going to do to you. Dale and Kathy just came over. We can come and help you with whoever it is you're helping. That is, if it's okay with you."

"Of course it is." He told Lisa where he was and sat back to wait. The man on the ground next to him watched silently.

CHAPTER 28

A s they waited for help, Mack asked the man on the ground, "Do you have a name? Or would you rather not tell me?"

"Jasper," the man answered, his voice just above a whisper. "Jasper Klug. I'm nobody, so I've got nothing to hide. And I'm really not important enough for you to be fusing over."

"You are a living human, aren't you?"

He snickered at Mack's comment. "At my age, only more or less. It's been a few years since I've felt much like a whole one."

"I don't imagine it took too long to feel that way, once you became homeless."

"It hasn't been the homeless living that's done it to me so much as it was a lifetime of hard work. The idea that hard work never hurt anyone is pretty much bullshit. Enough of it over time, and it kills your body. But I can't complain. I worked that way because I wanted to."

"Is that why you're homeless now? Because your body is shot.?"

"Not so much. It's mostly because I don't want to be any kind of a burden to anybody. Including you. So when your help gets here, I'd appreciate it if you'd all just go and leave me be. I'll get through this. Or not. Either way, I'd much prefer to do it on my own and not burden you."

They heard voices then, as Lisa, Dale, and Kathy walked up the trail. Lisa ignored Mack and immediately moved over to

Jasper. She knelt down next to him and asked, "Is there anything I can do for you? Are you thirsty?"

"A drink of water would be good, if you have one."

"I've only got the bottle I've been drinking out of. If you don't mind my germs too much, you can have the rest of it."

He gave her a bit of a smile. "Drinking from the same bottle a person as pretty as you've been drinking out of, is nothing short of an honor ma'am."

Lisa held the back of his head as he sat up to drink. He was surprised that she would do that, given his condition. It had been several days since he'd had the chance to take any kind of bath. When he finished drinking, she again held his head as he lay back down again. She turned to Mack then.

"What are we going to do? We damn sure can't leave him here."

"I think we should take him home with us. Give him a chance to get cleaned up. He's not that far from my size, so he can wear something of mine while his clothes are being washed. After that, we should feed him."

"Then what? Take him to a homeless shelter? Or does he have relatives we can take him too?"

"We are not going to dump him off at any homeless shelter. They're pretty much only good for over night. And all too often not that much good for that. I don't know about his relatives. I think for tonight, he can stay in the guest bedroom. Tomorrow we'll see what we can figure out."

It never occurred to Lisa to disagree with Mack. Jasper was a person who needed help, and they were two people who could give him that help. Dale and Kathy were, to some degree, unsure about their decision. Even so, they went along with it.

Mack walked out to the parking lot and drove his pickup up the trail to where Jasper was still laying. He voiced a mild protest against what they were doing for him, but wasn't strong enough to do anything to stop them.

When they got him home, the first thing they wanted to do was get him in the shower. They found a stool for him to sit on while he was getting washed, but they still had a problem. He couldn't do it himself. Mack and Dale, being typical males in that department, didn't want to do the washing. Lisa then volunteered. Kathy helped her undress him.

"You know," he said, trying unsuccessfully to complain, "I'm kind of embarrassed about this." But even if he was, he did nothing to interfere with what they were doing.

When he was sitting on his stool, Lisa turned the water on and tried washing him by reaching into the shower area while standing outside the shower. It didn't work very well. When her frustration reached too high a level, she decided that enough was enough. She stripped down to her bra and panties and climbed into the tub with him.

It was a vast improvement over what she started doing, but because she still had to help hold him up, it was clumsy. It only took a couple of minutes of watching Lisa struggle, for Kathy to realize she should help. It only took a couple of minutes for her to join Lisa and Jasper in the tub.

They were just starting to get Jasper properly washed when Dale came into the bathroom to see how they were doing. At first he was shocked by what he saw. Quickly though, his shock turned to laughter as he saw the humor in what was happening. He also knew it was something that needed to be shared, so he called Mack.

When he joined them in the bathroom he just smiled. What they were doing could have been thought of in many different ways. For Mack, it only looked like a simple act of human kindness. Even when Lisa showed the courage to use a washcloth to clean his most private places.

When they finished with the shower and had Jasper dressed in some of Mack's sweats, they moved him to the mast comfortable chair in their living room. Lisa and Kathy, still in their wet underwear, went into the master bedroom to dress.

Mack asked him what he wanted to eat. "A fried egg sandwich would be good," he answered, "if you've got any eggs."

"We do. We have our own chickens. I've got some fresh from the garden sliced tomatoes and lettuce to add to it if you want some?"

"That would be great."

When he got the sandwich, Jasper took small bites and chewed slowly, but managed to handle it without any help.

Lisa and Kathy joined Mack and Dale then. They were wearing two of Lisa's nightgowns, with light robes over them. Kathy didn't sit in Mack's lap, the way she usually did. Lisa did, and she made sure she was comfortable when she did, with a considerable amount of wiggling before she settled down on him. She followed that by putting her arms around him. A long, passionate kiss followed, along with letting her robe flop open enough to let Mack see how sheer her nightgown was.

"Are you feeling any better yet?" she asked him.

"Some. Are you mad at me for screwing up your night, the way I do everything else?"

"Don't do that now, Mack. Please. You don't screw everything up. Not ever. I don't know anyone who does as much right as you do."

"Not even Dale. At least he doesn't piss everyone off by being so damn over protective as me."

Kathy spoke up. "Are you kidding me, Mack? If anything, he's worse than you are about that. He spends most of his life worrying about other people. He hates it when I go to my concerts. If he could, he'd be at all of them. And he's almost as bad with Lisa. Now, he won't so much as kiss her, unless she starts it. He's afraid, after all that's happened, he might hurt her if he did. And I think, most of all, he worries about the two of you. The way you keep getting in situations that could literally get you killed. And you always seem to do it to save someone else. Like Lisa did today."

"Speaking of today," Dale said. "What you did, Lisa, was something else. It was incredibly brave, to go out there when there was such a good chance for you to get shot. I have no doubt that you probably saved some lives. But it still bothers me when you put yourself at risk like that. You're lucky that Mack isn't super upset with you."

Lisa sighed heavily. "Actually, he was. We even got to the point today that he considered leaving me. He thinks he's in my way, that I'm not living the life I want to because of him."

Kathy stared at her, a frown on her face. "Well, Lisa, is he? Is he keeping you from living the life you want to live?"

"No! Of course not. It's just that after we finished with all those men today I was feeling really frustrated. When Mack bawled me out for taking too many chances, I jumped all over him. Way more that what I had any right to do. We had a fight and he left. That's why he was in the refuge."

"Don't forget the other reason, Lisa," Mack said. "If you're going to tell them about me being controlling, and the fact that I was, that I am, thinking about getting out of your way."

Lisa looked at her lap. She felt guilty about what she'd said to Mack about her feelings for Dale. It was true that she sometimes wanted to take the love she had for him all the way. But it wasn't only her consideration for Mack that she didn't. She was still held back because she was raped. Any man, even Dale, still left a mark on her emotions when she went beyond holding hands or kissing. Only Mack could take it as far as it could be taken, and still not leave a mark. With him, the mark was the glow of love.

Lisa lifted her head and looked at Dale. "We talked about you and me, Dale," she said. "He said that if I wasn't doing with you what I wanted to do with you, because of him, it was proof he was in my way."

"Mack," Dale pleaded, "if I'm in any way hurting your marriage because of my relationship with her, I will damn well back off. I think Lisa will agree with me. The last thing either one of us wants to do, is to do something that might split you guys up."

"It's not what you've done or what you might do. It's the fact that Lisa thinks I'm trying to own her that's the problem. I love her and I'm always concerned about her. I know I'm probably too protective. but you all know why that is. To ask me to change is asking too much. That alone is enough reason to get out of her way. As far as what you and her do, I only worry about that in how it might affect her psychologically. I don't abject though, because so far, it seems to have helped her cope with what bothers her about it all. Not to mention the fact that doing or not doing that with someone other than you partner is blown way out of proportion most of the time. If you think it through, there actually isn't anything wrong with it. It's our perception of it that's the problem. Not the act itself."

"I told you, Mack," Lisa pleaded, "I don't think you're trying to own me. I was wrong to say any of those things I said to you. You can be over protective. But that's who you are. All too often I have a hot temper, I say things I shouldn't. Things that are wrong. But that's who I am, just like you are who you are."

Jasper cleared his throat. They were surprised to hear anything from him, after he'd been so quiet so long. "Is it okay for me to say something?" he asked.

He got the same yes answer from all four of them.

He spoke directly to Mack first. "I've lived a long time, Mack. I'm more than eighty years old and pretty much shot to hell. I've been out here, on my own for more than five years. Before that, I was married sixty-one years. It's never more than a couple of hours that go by before I think of her. It wasn't a perfect marriage, but I sure do miss her. The thing I most regret is that I could have spent more time with her than I did. I've been watching you and Lisa, Mack. And listening. You've got to get your head out of your ass. You love each other. More than most it seems, from what I've seen. It doesn't matter if you disagree on some things. It doesn't matter if you fight. You can't leave her. You are two people who want to be independent. You want to do most things on your own. At the same time, you depend on each other more than most. You need each other more than most. Your biggest problem is the fact that you are so much alike. That means those things are going to be a forever a voice of contention between you. You can't let them control your life. What you really can't do is spend too much time with her. You can't in any way spend enough time with her. You get old like me, and if she's gone before you, you are going to regret every damn minute you didn't spend together that you could have. Now, for me, what I miss the most about my wife are the things she did that aggravated me the most. So don't ever again think about leaving her, even if you do come between her and her lover over there. Even if she does continue to do brave, heroic things that risk her life. You got to stay with her and love her. And you've got to make love to her every chance you get. You can't wait, either, for the chances to come along. Make the chances. Believe me, she is damn well worth it. And walking away from her would make you the biggest goddamn loser who-ever was. Not to mention, really really stupid."

He dropped his head and struggled to breath. His talk exhausted him. They let him rest for a while before speaking to him. Lisa was the first one to do so.

"Would you like to go to bed now, Jasper. We'll help you in there if that's what you want to do?"

"If you don't mind, I'd just as soon stay up for a while yet. I've still got a couple of questions I think I'd like to ask."

"I've got a big one for you, Jasper," Dale said, "if you're up to it?"

"Ask away."

"Why are you homeless? You come across was the kind of man who didn't live a life that would leave you without anything."

"It didn't. I had what I needed to live what you might call a normal life in retirement. I walked away from it. My kids meant well it guess. But they said they couldn't stand for me to be alone. I even sold my house and tried living with them for a while. It might have worked if it would have been just me and them. But they had kids, and those youngsters hated having me with them. Said I was an embarrassment when they brought their friends around. It made for a lot of family fighting. By the time I knew I had to get away from them, I'd already given them most of the money I'd set aside for retirement. So there was no way I could pay for a place to stay. Not with what I get from social security. I left anyway. I haven't looked back. And I don't intend to. My only goal, for the rest of my life, is to not be a burden for anyone. That includes you guys."

"You're not any kind of burden on us," Mack said.

"Not today maybe. But given a little time, I will be." He took a couple of deep breaths, then turned to Kathy. He knew all their names now, from listening to them talk. "Kathy, you've been the quiet one so far. Is it because you don't like what we've been talking about?"

"No. It's mostly because I don't have as much to say about it as everyone else. I'm gone a lot, so I don't get the chance to do as much with these guys as they do with each other."

"How about the fact that your husband is having some kind of thing going with his friend's wife?"

Kathy gave him an unexpected smile. "I like it. No. Actually, I love it. It's good for both of them. Lisa always feels better about herself after. It does even more for Dale. All this started because of a really stupid mistake I made. Dale used to be kind of stiff. He couldn't let loose of himself. Since my mistake, which was asking him for a divorce, a lot in our life has changed. Mostly for the better."

"And you consider his having sex with Lisa for the better?"

"Very much. It's changed him in a lot of positive ways. Dale's always been close to the kindest, most considerate man I've ever known. He's always cared deeply about what really matters. But he was also too uptight."

"Aren't you kind of jealous though?"

"Not at all. Because while everything else was going on, I fell in love with Mack. Mostly, about once a month, I spend a day with him in his wildlife refuge. He's teaching me about it. When we're there I get to hold his hand and kiss him if I want to. A few times, the best times of all, we've made love. So why would I get jealous? I live with a man that I'm deeply in love with, but I get to spend some time with a man who somehow makes me feel free from all the demands of life that aren't near as important as they're supposed to be. More than that, he makes me feel young. With Mack, even when we make love, it's still okay to play. Mack and I would never try to trade Lisa and Dale for a life together. We'll never be partners. But we can damn well be playmates."

"What about you, Lisa. How do you feel about all this?"

"Like I wish that I could finally convince Mack that no matter what I say or do, he matters more to me than life itself. Like Kathy, I'm glad they have what they have. Those Saturdays they have together are great for them. When they come home after a day in that refuge, they're almost like children. They always have a new spirit. She's right. They make great playmates."

"Don't you worry though, about how it might affect your relationship with Mack?"

"I don't know if I should answer any more of your questions, Jasper," Lisa said, wondering now why she answered the questions she did. "None of us know you. And here we are, answering personal questions we'd normally never consider answering."

"It doesn't seem to make any sense I guess. But you folks have been so kind to me, I thought I'd try to give something back. I could tell earlier, that you all wanted to talk. That you needed to talk to settle some issues. I thought that If I asked some of the right questions, it might help you talk. But if I'm getting too personal, I'll quit. If you'll give me a couple of more hours to rest here, I'll be on my way tonight. I know what a burden us old men can be, just by being around."

"You'll not be going anywhere tonight," Lisa told him. "Other than on the queen size bed in the guest room. And as far as me worrying about how the relationship Mack and Kathy have, of course it worries me. The same way my connection with Dale worries Mack. But we can't let those kind of worries stop us from living. We do what we do, only because all four of us are over flowing with love for each other."

"That's a good answer, Lisa. It makes sense of the fact that you four have a lot of genuine love for each other."

"That's right," Kathy said. "And no matter what it might show, I need some lap time with my sometimes lover, Mack."

Lisa got up and sat down on Dale's now vacant lap. She kissed him long and hard, their tongues wresting as they did. Kathy and

Mack were in an embrace every bit as passionate. The biggest difference in what they were doing, was when Kathy took Mack's hand and laid it on her breast. She then pushed her robe out of the way, so his hand was closer to her skin.

"I think," Jasper said, "it's time for me to go to bed now." He laughed, enjoying the fact that his presence suddenly embarrassed them. "I might be an old man, but watching you four is causing a definite reaction where there hasn't been one for a long time."

"Is that a bad thing or a good one?" Lisa asked.

"It's good, in that it can still happen. Bad because I can't do anything about it."

Lisa looked at Mack, a twinkle in her eye now. "That's kind of sad, isn't it, Mack."

"It is," he agreed, wondering from her look, how far she was going to push it this time. "Are you going to help Jasper to bed now." Her look was intentionally telling him she had something in mind.

"I sure am. Will you give me a hand, Kathy?"

"Yeah, right." She too knew that Lisa was up to something. But after all their talking, she was in the mood to assist her with it, no matter what her mischief might be.

They helped Jasper into the bedroom. It was near thirty minutes later when they came out. They both carried the smiles of someone pleased with something that happened when they did.

"It's time to go home now, Dale," Kathy told him. "I think I'm going to need a lot more of your loving than I normally do."

"And that's exactly what you're going to get."

"Good. And you, Mack? Are you going to stay now?"

"Yes, Kathy. It seems different now. There's something about that old man that helped change how everything feels. The things he said about his wife. About how he never spent enough time with her. I don't ever want to feel that way about Lisa. I think maybe, sometime not too far away, we are going on vacation."

"That sounds like a good idea," Dale said, "but right now, I want to take my bride home and to bed."

"That's good," Kathy said, "but don't count on a lot of sleep."

As soon as they were gone, Mack and Lisa showered together. She didn't bother with her nightgown when they went to bed. She was ready for him, and very much wanted him right away. He was too curious about something to take care of her until she told him what he wanted to know.

"You have to tell me, Lisa, what it is you and Kathy did too or for Jasper when you put him to bed."

"That's another are you really sure you want to know question."

"I'm sure. It'll drive me pure crazy if I don't know."

"Well, we actually did a lot. All of it stuff we weren't supposed to ever do. Especially to a stranger. The first thing was us taking our robes off. As you know, our nightgowns were sheer. Then Kathy leaned over him so he could feel her breast. He actually groaned when he touched her. He said that he hadn't felt anything that good since long before his wife died. He started to move his hand over himself as he looked at us. He had an erection. Pretty big too, for such and old guy. I don't know what made me do it, but I touched him then. He pushed his hips against my hand. I just left it there, not moving it or anything for a while. But he was getting into what was happening, so I kind of wrapped my hand around him. You know what happened then. Kathy wanted to be the one to clean him up."

Lisa stopped there, waiting for some kind of reaction from Mack. After the volatile day they'd already had, she was sure there had to be one.

"So," Mack grinned when he asked, "did he say thank you?"

"Not until," Lisa said, pleased with his reaction, "Kathy kissed him. She really made him feel it when she did, too."

"I think that was an extremely kind thing to do for him. I'm proud of you Lisa."

"That's good, Mack. Because it felt like the right thing to do at the time."

"How about now? How does it feel now?"

"Like it was the right thing to do."

"How about me. Do you still want me around? Or have you had enough of me and my trying to own you?"

"Please, Mack, no more of that. I don't think that. I have never thought that. We have so much you know. We should never fight the way we did today. What I want more than anything else, is to do what Jasper said we should do. Spend as much time together as we can. As short as life is, it's the only sane thing for you and I to do. We know how unlikely it is that we'll ever change the way we do things. So our lives could be shorter than most. Let's not ever waste whatever time we have."

"I agree. But what do you think then, about my idea of you and I taking a vacation?"

"I think that's a fine idea. But it's something we can talk about some other time. What I want now is you. I want to share with you as much of what two people can share as we can manage in one night. After we do that, then I want to do it again. I want to hold on to you forever. And I don't ever want to hear again that you're thinking about leaving me, Mack. Not while we're alive or even after we're dead. You have to promise me that you won't ever do that again. It nearly killed me this time. Next time it might."

"I promise," he said, then moved over her.

He fulfilled her wish, and stayed with her until she told him it was okay to go to sleep. He was still inside her when they did.

Morning came too early, even though it was already after eight. Jasper was gone when they went to check up on him. Every trace of him went with him. It was as if he'd never been there. Mack was disappointed to find him gone.

"I think," he told Lisa, "that it would have been good to know him better. I would liked to have him around a lot more. If not for the rest of his life, at least long enough to get to make him a friend. I'm pretty sure that he had a lot to teach us about living. Me especially."

"One thing though, Mack. I'm glad Kathy and I gave him the treat that we gave him."

"Sometimes, Lisa, doing what most might consider a bad thing, turns out to be about the best thing you can do."

"Yes, and sometimes there's a reason for everything. Like all that happened yesterday. As bad as some of it was, it did in the end lead us to him. And all those questions he asked did go a long way to fixing you and me. And for me, as selfish as it is, having you and me fixed is the best thing I could ever have. We have problems again, I think we should always try to remember that lonely old man."

"Yes, and maybe all the lonely old men out there whose families have forgotten them."

"Yes, and the old women too."

"We are lucky, Lisa. We still have each other. I think we should always take advantage of that, for as long as we can."

"I agree. Like right now."

She took his hand and led him back to bed.

EPILOGUE

In the next news cycle, the latest gunfight involving Refuge Rescuers and the Thomas family was the feature story. Lisa's heroic gamble that should have been featured in the story was only briefly mentioned. Instead, it was Wanda, and Wanda's shooting that caught the medias attention. They did a whole segment about her and her shooting ability. A couple of channels even did some research on her, and talked about other gun battles she'd been in.

Their far and away favorite incident though, was the shooting of the man behind the tree. They made it a point to emphasize how small the target was, and how close to impossible her shot was. They especially talked about what the target was.

They followed that with a short segment about rebuilding a penis. They had no choice though, but to admit the damage Wanda caused wasn't repairable.

Wanda got her first call to sponsor a gun manufacturer less than an hour after the broadcast. After that, she got offers, along with a lot of guns, to promote all kinds of outdoor products. The one she choked on though, was the one for condoms.

She turned them all down, but they were all so persistent she bought a new cell phone and got rid of the old one. The last thing she wanted to do was make money because she was forced to shoot someone. Especially that kind of shooting.

✶✶✶✶✶

The three morons who were so sure they could capture and dominate Wanda, Donna and Lisa, were all convicted of enough crimes to draw relatively long prison sentences. They didn't do too well in that environment.

Jelly Norton, the rapist/murderer was now blind. He never made it to his final destination. While he was still in the hospital, word got out about his capture and where he was now.

He was under armed guard in a hospital in Minneapolis. Late one night, a male nurse went into to his room to give him some medication. He was treated instead, with a knife. One not quite sharp enough to do a proper job on his throat.

So when the nurse, who was the father of one of his rape victims, left him, he was bleeding. Just not near as fast as someone with their throat cut normally would. So he got to lie there for a while, knowing he was going to die, but unable to do anything about it.

Lance made it to prison, but he was quickly singled out by a large group of prisoners who thought he was cute, even if he was as big as he was. About a dozen of them decided to make him their wife. They kept him constantly busy. Busy enough so that when he sat down on the toilet to relieve himself, it was always painful and there was always a large supply of blood left behind.

Charles Slater was big and strong too, but he was still considered to be pretty boy type handsome. A lot of prisoners were attracted to him, but he was too much for most of them to handle.

So they got together in groups, and manhandled him until he was forced to submit to their demands. Frequently, he found himself with several men jammed into various openings in his body. Always, when that was happening to him, there were several men watching the show. All of them obviously enjoying it.

*****

Donna fell in love with her cottage home, and grew equally fond of the people she was around. With Charles in prison, she liquidated all her belongings. She ended up with enough money to get by for a long time, but wanted to have something productive to do.

She talked to Mack about some kind of job. He brought it up in a meeting, and everyone agree that they should hire her. They gave her Julie's receptionist job. She loved it, and was exceptionally good at it.

Julie was then put to work with Sue. She was already good with computers, and seemed to have at least some of Sue's talents for research. She was also put into private detective training.

*****

Kathy was the first to notice it in them. Mack and Lisa had always treated each other with love and respect, even when they disagreed. Now though, they always seemed to cherish the time they were together. Lisa especially, seemed to want to keep Mack as close as she could. She could still be as feisty and independent minded as ever, but even when they disagreed and argued, she kept him close. When Kathy asked her about it, her answer was simple.

"I have too. He's the one who holds it all in place. I think if I get too far away from him, I'll get lost."

"He does that. And for you, I don't think there's much of anything he wouldn't do. Anything, that is, but *not* trying to always protect you."

As much as she loved Mack, Kathy was delighted in the positive changes she was seeing in her friends. It was especially good for Lisa. It was good for Mack too, but didn't have as strong an effect on him.

When Kathy mentioned it to him, he agreed that things were better, and that the best thing that had happened was Lisa's realization that she was normal, and that it wasn't such a terrible thing that men found her so attractive.

"What about you, Mack?" Kathy asked him. "Do you realize how attractive you are to women. They get to know you at all, and they fall in love with you."

"I don't think so. How could I be attractive to women. Especially with the scars on my face."

"They are part of what does it. That and who you are. Mack, I'm probably stupid for telling you this, as much as I want you all to myself, but you're like a magnet to women. They all just plain love you."

He laughed. "Well, I hope you're wrong. You and Lisa are already more that I can handle. Not that I'm complaining. That old man, Jasper, was right. Time together is what's most important."

"Yes, and for you and I, it is important. But for you and Lisa, it's essential."

*****

Given the conservative nature of the Republican appointed judges, most of the MAGA Fellows involved in the attacks on the Refuge Rescuers, were given relatively light sentences. Mack, Dale, and Paul managed to visit all them after they were locked up.

They did it in the hope that they could convince at least some of them that what they'd been doing was a gigantic waste of time. They only managed to convince a few of them. The bulk of them had too much faith in their current messiah, Donald Trump, to listen to any thing reasonable.

*****

Bob Anderson, along with his wife Beth, was more than a little worried when they went into the doctor's office. He had been having some difficulty doing his normal day to day work. It was enough to interfere with everything connected to running a hundred milking cow dairy farm. One of the worst symptoms was a shortness of breath. Along with that were frequent, rather severe, chest pains.

After the doctor listened to his chest for a while, he shook his head, then told Bob, "I hate to have to tell you this, but the problem is your heart. It's my guess that it's the same thing as your dad had. Yours is worse than his was though. As tough as this might be for you, the best thing you can do right away is to quit farming. If you don't, likely as not, it will kill you."

Bob looked at Beth, his expression showing her how sorry he was about this happening. She loved the farm and the way of life it gave them. It was the catalyst that pushed her into the decision to break up with Mack when she did. As much as she loved him, she loved the farm and what she had with Bob even more.

It would all be gone soon. Even so, she was still going to stay with Bob, and be the best wife to him she could. It would be hard, she knew, to tell the family about all the changes that would take place. But even harder than that, would be every time she thought of Mack, and what she'd lost by giving him up. She was now among the rare group of people who managed to learn. When you have to make important, even critical decisions, there is rarely a perfect one.

*****

Mack was surprised by the phone call. It was Sandy Dennis, the man who first came to Refuge Rescuers with concerns about what the MAGA Fellows were hoping to do. He and Mack did not hit it off very well, when Sandy admitted to being a confirmed Republican. They got past their differences, but Mack was left feeling somewhat disappointed in him.

So what Sandy called to tell him came as a very pleasant surprise to Mack. "I just had to tell you, Mack," Sandy explained. "I just voted in the special election to the county board. I voted for the Democrat. The first time in my life to do that. From all that I've learned since my first meeting with you, it won't be my last time to do it." He laughed. "Just thought you'd get a kick out of it." He hung up.

Mack smiled as he nodded his head yes.

*****

It was an old time country road. Barely wide enough for two cars to pass each other. It was lined on both sides with a mixture of woods and open pasture. Here and there small herds of dairy cows grazed contentedly on lush, green grass.

Jasper Klug moved slow on this day. Even though the sun was shining and the temperature was in the perfect mid-seventies, his body was telling him that it would like to rest some. It definitely wanted some relief from the hip pain he constantly suffered from.

It was a giant old weeping willow that caught his attention. Its heavy branches flowed smoothly to the ground, creating a place inside them next to the trunk of the tree that felt like a room. It looked like a safe place for an old man to rest.

He crawled inside it. The ground was soft, so he sat down with his back to the tree. One more time, he felt for the envelope in his pocket. It was still safely there. He'd have to mail it soon. He felt a peace flow through him. It was something he'd only felt once in many years. As he remembered that recent time, he thought about Lisa and Kathy. They did something for him that he thought would never be done for him again. He loved the memory of how they looked and how they touched him. And that brought a few tears of thanks. It was good to know there was still that kind of kindness, that kind of generosity in this world that was now so harsh.

He was tired, so he closed his eyes. Even with tears in them, he smiled over the memory. It was a good one to have. Slowly then, sleep came for him. As it did, his breathing got ever more shallow, until it stopped.

✦✦✦✦✦

It was Mack's birthday, and Lisa insisted on having a party for him. He agreed to it, but insisted on one thing. No presents. If anyone wanted to do anything for him, he requested that they donate to an environmental organization. A second choice would be to any that helped female victims of abuse.

The party turned out to be a good time for all, with the food being especially good. As was normally the case, Ben and Theresa did the cooking. After everyone ate their fill, Kathy sang for them. To no one's surprise, she did an especially large amount of flirting with Mack while she did.

Even so, Lisa managed to capture him for several dances. In between, she danced some with Dale. They purposely kept them as platonic as possible. They didn't want to do anything that might take away from the feeling it was Mack's special day.

For the last hour or so, Lisa sat on his lap. She held on to him in such a way that there was no doubt how she felt about him. Even more, it showed how much she really needed him.

Shortly before people started to leave, Kathy handed Mack a package. It was wrapped in a light, colored tissue like paper. "I know," she said. "No gifts. But this one is kind of for both of you."

Mack reluctantly took the package and slowly opened it. It was something he rarely wore. A t-shirt. He held it up for everyone to see. Almost as one person, they nodded their heads yes as they looked at the front of it. Mack looked at the back of it first. It said:

Yes He Is

He turned the shirt around so he and Lisa could see it. It said:

Lisa's Refuge

Like everyone else, Lisa nodded her head yes. She put her arms around Mack and kissed him. "I love you Mack Thomas," she said. Then she cried.